Praise for Nikki Everts

Evidence of Uncertain Origin is a wonderful historical mystery, cunning and political, but most of all: surprising and intriguing. Skeptical Kit and her imaginative and emotional younger sister Sondra make delightful sleuths, exploring Montréal during the FLQ crisis of the late 1960s. I enjoyed this novel very much.

      Sandra Gulland, author of the *Josephine B. Trilogy*

Evidence of Uncertain Origin is a tale of sisterly love, human failings, misplaced loyalty, betrayal, forgiveness, danger and intrigue, delivered with a historically interesting twist. It is an engaging and suspenseful read.

      Sue Williams, author of *Ready to Come About*

A gripping novel of family loyalty and intrigue set in the midst of Québec's FLQ crisis of 1969. Everts' fast-moving prose has the reader eager to keep pace with sisters, Kit and Sondra, as they seek to determine the truth behind their beloved grandfather's death.

      Kate Anderson-Bernier, author of *A Gap in the Fence*

Evidence Of Uncertain Origin

Nikki Everts

Arboretum Press

Arboretum Press
Guelph, ON, Canada
www.arboretumpress.com

Copyright © 2019 Nikki Everts

ALL RIGHTS RESERVED

This book contains material protected under International and Federal Copyright Laws and Treaties. Any unauthorized reprint or use of this material is prohibited. No part of this book may be reproduced or transmitted in any form or by any means, electronic or mechanical, including photocopying, recording, or by any information storage and retrieval system without express written permission from the author.

3rd Edition (2020)

ISBN (paperback): 978-1-7771783-1-4
ISBN (e-book): 978-1-7771783-2-1

This book is a work of fiction. Names, characters, places and incidents either are the product of the author's imagination or are used in their historical and geographical setting.

Cover design: Anthony O'Brien

For

Peggy Jeanine Bloom, whose paperback mystery novels, sequestered in the drawer of her bedside table, furtively purloined and read, initiated me into this genre

Arthur Hammond, who introduced me to Senneville Veterans Lodge and from whom I borrowed many of the personality traits that drive this story

Montréal 1969

1. Avenue-du-parc
2. Avenues-des-pins
3. Baie-d'Urfe
4. Botanical Garden
5. Île Sainte-Hélène
6. Lac Sainte-Thérèse
7. Notre-Dame des Neiges Cemetery
8. Rue Saint-Denis
9. Sainte-Anne-de-Bellevue
10. Senneville Veterans Lodge
11. St. Anne's Hospital
12. Westmount

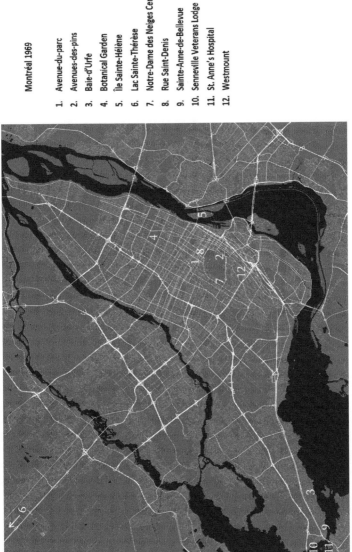

Introduction

This work of fiction is set in the Montréal, Québec of 1969. During this time a militant group, the *Front de libération du Québec* (the FLQ or *les felquistes*), was ramping up their efforts to create a sovereign French Québec, separate from predominately English Canada. Their activities had become increasingly violent, shifting from the destruction of property to the killing of people.

The damage promulgated by the FLQ alluded to in this novel is based on actual events. I have added a few fictional incidents to move the plot along, but have modelled them on their historical counterparts to the best of my ability.

Most locations are as close to their true form as I could render them except for the police interview room and lac-Sainte-Thérèse which are figments of my imagination. The main characters are my own inventions as are the situations they face.

Prologue

Iris psuedacorus
Fleur-de-lis

Montréal
Tuesday, March 4, 1969

*S*irens burned through the chill air. The two watchers stepped back into the trees across the street from a block of flats where six Sûreté du Québec police cars and a white van screeched to a halt. Car doors opened and slammed shut; officers pounded up the wrought iron stairs and disappeared into Pierre-Paul Geoffroy's home.

He was not there, of course. The watchers knew he was sitting in a jail cell, or, more likely, being subjected to the brutal interrogation members of the Front de libération du Québec expected from the police.

The shorter of the two men cursed under his breath.

Evidence of Uncertain Origin

"Regarde," he muttered, nodding toward the growing crowd of onlookers across the street. "The fools; don't they realize we are revolutionaries, not common criminals! They should be throwing rocks at those dirty pigs, not standing there like so many stupid sheep." He spat on the ground.

The taller man put his hand on his companion's shoulder. "I expect there are many in the crowd too fearful to do anything except watch. Once we strike the match, they will ignite."

Pulling their collars up against the damp cold of the late winter afternoon, the watchers strolled across the street to blend in with the unsuspecting gawkers, two of many pressing against the police cordon for a closer look. Officers were emptying Geoffroy's flat. They carefully carried box after box down the winding stairs and loaded them into the van.

Mostly papers, but some dynamite, the watchers noted. About 200 sticks of it they guessed and possibly a bomb or two.

The watchers broke off from the crowd and sauntered away. Several blocks later, they settled themselves on a bench in a small park on rue Saint-Louis. A few curious passers-by glanced at the two men and shook their heads. The lowering clouds and ensuing darkness hurried them homeward to dinner and families.

The shorter conspirator grabbed the newspaper they'd been reading, wadded it up and threw it towards the nearest garbage can. He missed. "Merde!"

His comrade laughed, a dry sound like leaves in a fire, then shook out two cigarettes; the other man grabbed one, glowering.

After a long drag, the taller man asked, "'Suspected FLQ cell'? 'Cooperating with police'? What do you make of it?"

"'Cooperating' with a little encouragement, tabernak!" The stockier man hit his hand with a fist then sat up straight. "Maybe he's turned informer."

"No, Pierrot would never betray his country; whatever he told them, he's figured an angle on it. Besides, he must've known they were after him."

Annoyed, the other man spat into the dirty snow. "How can you be so sure?"

"Because, my fine friend, he gave me 100 sticks of dynamite two days ago."

The shorter one's wolfish eyes glinted.

Stretching, the tall man stubbed out his cigarette on the side of the bench, flicking it into the snow bank behind him. "Anyone could see it was only a matter of time: fifteen bombings including the Montréal Stock Exchange and the Liberal Party's Reform Club, 27 people injured. Of course such grand success by 'les felquistes' would draw unwanted attention." He smiled at the litany of their combined accomplishments. The street lamps blinked on and it began to snow.

His companion grunted, "He damn well should've left us with some money while he was at it."

Standing up and stomping his feet, the tall man smirked. "I've been working the plan. And my clever little scheme has already funded your clever little bombs. No reason why the money won't keep flowing."

"It had better!" the short man shook himself like a bear, dislodging the snow that had already collected on his coat.

"It will, it will." The tall man clapped his comrade on the shoulder. "To quote our good friend Charles de Gaulle, 'Vive le Québec libre!'"

"Ha! What a hornet's nest de Gaulle stirred up. I was there in '67 in Montréal, you know, when he gave us our rallying cry, right there on the City Hall steps with Québec's flag, the blue fleurs-de-lis, waving proudly behind him: 'Vive le Québec libre!'" The shorter man was grinning by the time they parted.

Large, wet snowflakes glistened in the muted glow of street lights, covering the two men's footprints.

Evidence of Uncertain Origin

Senneville, Québec
Friday, July 25, 1969

Henri Lalonde was thinking about the shopping list his wife had given him that morning before work. Just off his shift at Ste. Anne's Veterans Hospital, Henri was sweaty and his back hurt. No matter, he still had to pick up the groceries and beer before he could collapse into his easy chair at home.

The hospital was snugged in at the western tip of the island of Montréal so Henri would have to take the scenic route home along Senneville Road. It always put him in a foul mood. He couldn't enjoy driving under the cool canopy of trees; they reminded him of the stifling July heat waiting for him in his own small flat, twenty kilometres to the northeast in Pierrefonds. Even though it would be well after dark before he got home, his brick building held the day's heat like an oven.

The road twisted along following a lake front that he couldn't see because it was blocked by those *maudit* mansions the damned English millionaires had built. Henri rolled down the window and unbuttoned the top of his orderly's uniform. At least he and 'Tonette would be heading up north for the weekend, his big Buick pulling the little camping trailer he'd built with his brother-in-law.

Henri had passed the entrance on the right to the Senneville Veterans Lodge. Many of the patients he lifted, shifted, pushed and pulled had lived there before sickness forced them to make the move to the hospital up the road in Sainte-Anne-de Bellevue.

Just past the clipped lawns of the Veterans Lodge property was a few metres of bush. The trees and brush hid a driveway beyond them. A movement there caught Henri's eye as he came even with the tree line. A man in a wheelchair hurtled out in front of his car. Henri braked, but not before impact. He heard his tires screech and felt a grinding thump. The man flew up in the air, bounced off his windshield and landed with a sickening thud on the road in front of his car.

"*Merde!*"

PART I
Proletarian

Apis mellifera
Honey Bee

Hamilton, Ontario
Friday, September 19, 1969

G roaning, Kit rolled over and tried to end the persistent jangling noise by switching off her alarm, to no avail. It must be the phone. She threw off the covers, grabbed her ratty terry cloth bathrobe and staggered out to the kitchen, yanking the receiver from its perch on the wall beside the fridge.

"Who the hell is this?" Her response was whispered despite the annoyance. She didn't want to wake up Paul.

"She woke up screaming again, Kit," the voice of her brother-in-law was tremulous and low.

"Good God, Jean-Pierre, what's going on?" Kit held the

phone against her ear, while she shrugged into her bathrobe, suddenly alert. Dread knotted her stomach. God, she wished she hadn't quit smoking. "Do you think she's headed for another nervous breakdown?"

"I don't know, Kit, that's the problem; I just don't know."

"Well, it can't be post-partum depression again; Max is three and a half now, and she's been fine for two years." Vivid guilt assailed Kit along with the image of Sondra's sad, disheveled face watching them abandon her to the psychiatrists at the Douglas Mental Hospital. Sondra returned home three months later, subdued, not her usual vivacious self, but not in black despair either. Like nasty tasting medicine, or shots, or going to the dentist, Sondra absolved them, knowing it had been necessary, but informed them with sudden fierceness that she never, ever wanted to go back. Sondra, her Sondra, hadn't re-emerged for another year.

"I know. So, she's your sister, I thought, like, maybe she'd called you or something, or written you a letter, or—"

"Or what, 'psychically communicated' with me?" Kit snapped. Sondra's belief in such things had always frustrated Kit. "Sorry, J-P, I don't do well with all this."

Another intake of breath. "You and me both, Kit."

Silence over took them, and Kit stared out the small kitchen window, a brick wall the only view; ambient light from the street diluted the darkness and silhouetted the drooping geranium on the sill. I should water the poor thing, thought Kit.

She sighed; focusing on the concrete reality of her surroundings did nothing to quell her growing anxiety and confusion.

"Do you think it might have to do with your grandfather's death, Kit? I mean it was almost two months ago . . ."

"Probably," Kit shivered, then said, "That must be it." She struggled to keep the lump out of her throat.

Evidence of Uncertain Origin

"You OK, Kit?"

"I'll be fine."

The line between them fell silent again, Kit glanced at the bedroom door and thought of Paul's tousled blond head on the pillow. She had to hand it to Jean-Pierre, he did try. She wondered if Paul would notice if she started acting peculiar or would he keep plugging away at medical school, as oblivious to her as he had been for the last few years of his studies. She wondered if he'd even noticed when she'd quit smoking.

"So? What do you think, Kit?"

Somehow she must have missed J-P's last remark. "Ah, about what?"

"I mean about coming for a visit."

"A visit? That might be difficult J-P. My job: the bank might fall apart without me, besides the bills paid, the student fed, the wolf kept from the door. *Apis mellifora*, J-P, *Apis mellifora*."

"What are you talking about, Kit?"

"You know, J-P, the honey bee; I'm the only worker bee in this hive, eh?" Kit said, picking at the chipped, faded grey countertop.

"Yes, but I thought you said at the funeral that you still had a couple of weeks of vacation; I mean, I'd even pay for your train ticket—both ways."

Kit shifted in her seat, crossed her legs and started swinging her foot back and forth, wishing even harder for that cigarette.

"Come on, Kit, don't you miss your old hometown? You've always said there's nothing like Schwartz's smoked meat, and no one makes bagels like they do here in Montréal."

Kit listened, considering.

" . . . you've always been close, and maybe you could, well, figure out what's bothering her. Besides, if it is this grief business, I'm sure having you around would help."

"OK, OK, J-P, I'll come."

"*Merci*, Kit!" Relief was evident in his voice. J-P paused then cleared his throat. "Just don't tell her I called you."

"What?"

"I mean, I've thought this all out, Kit, if she finds out I called you, she'll think I'll be pumping you for information about her, and she'll clam up on you too, afraid I'll commit her to the Douglas Mental Hospital again."

"I see your point. I guess I could call her and invite myself down for a week or so around Thanksgiving."

"Perfect! Thanks, Kit. You've always been there for your little sister, haven't you?"

Always, thought Kit. "*Toujours*," she said to J-P as she hung up the phone.

Evidence of Uncertain Origin

Montréal
Thursday, September 25, 1969

Sondra sat at the old oak kitchen table with her head in her hands. The steady drip, drip of the faucet reminded her that a pile of dirty dishes waited for her in the sink. The quiet of the flat without the children and Jean-Pierre echoed inside her head, bouncing off the walls of the deep pit she could not get out of. Down there in the dark her nightmare replayed itself over and over again. It had haunted her nights for weeks and now it had invaded her waking hours whenever she was alone.

The dream always started the same way:

She is seated in the backyard, where she and her sister Kit had lived in Pointe-Saint-Charles with Grannie Win and Gramps. The sun is shining; there isn't much growing, just a lot of very green grass and a lot of light is getting through, like it does in Montréal during early spring before all the leaves unfurl and get in the way.

She is seated at the old card table, and she is expecting someone. She looks up and sees him. It's Gramps and he's walking towards her, no wheelchair, no cane, no crutches. And he looks different than she remembered him; he isn't all grey and wrinkled. Instead he looks to be about thirty-five or forty maybe, mature. She'd never seen him that young in person. He was already more than fifty when she'd been born, but she would recognize him anywhere. She stands. She is so glad to see him.

He gazes at her, as though he is both happy to see her and sad at the same time. He stops across the table from her, and just looks at her. She feels his love and acceptance and approval of her. Then a different expression comes into his eyes, urgent and apologetic.

He fades back into his old self, and sinks into a wheelchair, as though he can no longer bear his own weight. For the first time she notices that he is holding a bunch of papers, and he is shoving them across the table towards her. He wants her to take them. As she reaches out for them a shadowy form comes from behind Gramps. She is looking at the papers, and only sees what happens next out of the corner of her eye. In a rapid movement two hands with long tapered fingers grasp Gramps' head from behind and twist it to the left. There's an awful sound like a branch snapping. And Gramps is dead, drooping like a rag doll in his chair.

She would wake up screaming and sweating, unable to sleep again for hours. "It's just a bad dream," she'd say when J-P reached over to comfort her. It was a lie because she didn't believe for a moment that it was "just a bad dream." It was a message from beyond the grave: Gramps had been murdered.

The golden light of an early autumn afternoon had shifted so that it now poured from the window over Sondra, casting her shadow on the table's uneven, scarred surface. The sun still carried enough heat to be uncomfortable so she sighed and shifted.

Why hadn't she gone to see Gramps in that last week before he'd died? What had been so god-awful important that she'd ignored the urgency in his voice when he had called her? He never had asked her to visit him before. In fact, he'd always discouraged her visits, telling her, "Don't you worry; I'm as fine as I'll ever be, and the sound of your voice is good enough for me. Besides, you've got enough on your hands, Sondra."

True; she had had a lot on her hands those last weeks before he died. Summer was hectic with both children home:

endless trips to the park, scrambling to get them to swimming lessons and play dates. She'd been planning to call Gramps to arrange a visit the day it happened. The day he died. Now it was too late.

    Her own busyness did not excuse her. If she had visited him, he'd still be alive. She was sure of it; she was guilty of neglect, and that neglect had killed Gramps. What would Grannie Win have called it? A sin of omission? Yes, she was to blame and his death was on her head. No matter what anyone said she knew this to be true. She deserved to die.

Nikki Everts

Hamilton to Montréal
Friday, October 10, 1969

Kit had shaken her sour mood from the night before and was, well, almost content. The painful fact that Paul, consumed by his studies, had forgotten about her trip retreated under the pleasurable anticipation of travel, of seeing Sondra and her family, of being back in Montréal.

She caught the train with no trouble in Hamilton and the transfer in Toronto went well. She'd even had time to buy a coffee and Toronto's *Globe and Mail* before boarding the 9:30 Canadian National to Montréal. Her fingers tingled; she missed the cigarette that until six weeks ago had always accompanied her coffee. She sighed, opened the newspaper and settled back in to her seat.

The headlines were disconcerting: 'Letter Bomb in Montréal Injures Three.' The article revealed that the *Front de libération du Québec* was morphing into a deadlier organization than they had been. Just last month the *felquistes* had bombed the mayor of Montréal's home. No one had been injured, but that was dumb luck. Up until now they had targeted buildings not people, but a few days ago two FLQ members had been wounded and an undercover policeman killed in a shoot-out at the Murray Hill Taxi Company. Kit read on; the article quoted from the FLQ's newsletter, *Victoire*: "During 1968 we tried to make people understand, in 1969 we will kill those who have not understood." It looked very much as if the *felquistes* were trying to make good on their threat. Kit looked up from the newspaper. Feeling exiled, she had romanticized her hometown, forgetting until now the seething political emotions that roiled beneath the glamour and sophistication of Montréal.

So much had changed in the two short years since Expo '67 placed Montréal on the world map with its exciting international exhibits on Île Sainte-Hélène and the gaudy fun of La Ronde's amusement park rides. They'd even built a shiny new subway system to ferry people under the St. Lawrence River to the two islands where the World's Fair and the fun park were located.

Now that Montréal workers had no more big projects, Kit figured the FLQ's Marxist nationalism would have even more of an appeal to the proletarian masses. She'd read about the massive layoffs when the Vickers shipyard in Montréal closed this year; the workers had all been fired with only two hours' notice. Of course, the usual left wing groups backed the FLQ's socialist agenda. Even the English students at McGill University had marched with those from l'Université de Montréal and with the labour unions in support of the FLQ last summer. If she'd still been a student at McGill, Kit thought, she'd probably have joined them.

She folded up the paper as they pulled out of the Kingston, Ontario station. The coffee was long gone and Kit relaxed into a pleasurable melancholy as she watched the autumn scenery clickety-clacking by. The rushing red and gold autumn leaves against the somber grey sky glimpsed through the train window made her think of endings: the end of summer's beauty, the end of childhood, the end of love, the end of life. All losses swirled together and coalesced into the memory of Gramps' funeral.

Tears welled up, and she had to choke back a sob. Gramps was only seventy-four when he'd died this summer in a freak accident, so unexpected and awful. No wonder Sondra was having a hard time coping.

Anxiety clenched her gut—Sondra. Kit had always been

Sondra's protector and comforter: during their mother's descent into the bottle, the divorce, her father's absenteeism and even after their grandparents had taken them in. On the street, in the school yard, Kit, bigger even than the older kids, had fought off the bullies. At night, she'd comforted Sondra who cried for their mother, and later for their father. And here she was, dashing off to save her little sister once again. Well, at least I have one purpose in life, Kit thought. At least I'm important to someone.

Kit had been feeling unremarkable and insignificant before Gramps' death. Its shocking suddenness drilled into her consciousness the truth that life was precarious and therefore precious. Kit shifted in her seat, uncomfortable. What the hell am I doing with my life, she wondered.

Kit had studied biology, dreaming of the day she would discover and name a new species she'd found in some remote corner of the world. Then she met Paul and had fallen hard for him. Her dreams could wait while she supported his. Four years later and she was waking up to the drab reality of her life as *Apis mellifera*. Not the queen, Kit lamented, but the little worker bee. While she didn't forage for pollen, nectar or propilis, her job at the bank, stuck in one of many identical cubicles, reminded her of a hive. And like the little female workers, she too slaved away, "carrying out the many tasks necessary for colony development and survival" so Paul, her resident drone, could complete his medical studies. He was hardly ever home and then only to sleep, study or eat. He had no time for her, and she wondered what all her efforts would amount to. Would a queen bee arise to lure him away from her?

Even their love-making had tanked. Paul's busyness wasn't the only problem; Kit felt as weakly sexed these days as a worker bee. The disengagement with her own life had been so gradual that she didn't recognize it until Gramps' funeral: the sweltering August heat at his gravesite, the still dead air, the unbearable loss knotting her heart, the words of the fat priest sweating in his surplice, "Ashes to ashes, dust to dust . . . " Her hopes, her dreams, her marriage and her life seemed as empty as the sound of the dirt's dull thud on Gramps' coffin. They might as well be buried with her grandfather.

Kit emerged from her dire thoughts, took a deep breath and glanced out the window, surprised to see that they were already approaching the bridge to the Island of Montréal. Soon they would pass through the quaint little town of Sainte-Anne-de-Bellevue at the western-most tip of the island. She craned her neck to gaze out at the dull grey waters of baie de Vaudreuil on her left. As the train rattled over the bridge, she caught a glimpse of the shoreline boundary of Gramps' last home, the Veterans Lodge in Senneville, one town further north along the coast from Sainte-Anne-de-Bellevue.

We're almost there, she thought, collecting her things. Soon they'd be arriving at the Bonaventure train station, the Gare Centrale in Montréal.

Sondra stood at the stove in the kitchen mindlessly stirring a pot of minestrone soup while the Canadian Broadcasting Company's six o'clock news anchor regaled her with the standard police reassurances about the most recent mailbox bombings. It worried her as much as anything could these days. She glanced at the stove's clock; why was it taking Kit so long to get here from the train station? Had another bomb gone off to harm her or delay her arrival? Her anxious thoughts swirled around her mind like eddies in the soup she was stirring.

J-P was in the living room reading aloud to Deirdre and Max. She could hear his soothing baritone reciting the familiar words from Maurice Sendak's *Where the Wild Things Are*, Max's current favourite book. It helped that Max was the main character's name. If she weren't so tired she'd abandon the soup and go watch her son's little face brighten at the first mention of his name. She knew that he was seeing things he did not yet have the words or skill to describe. But he would one day, and sticking around to help him was one of the few things that kept her tethered to this life.

Sondra flinched at the clang of the bell on the downstairs door. She heard the children shout a welcome as their little feet pounded down the stairs to see who could be the first to hurl themselves at Kit.

J-P stuck his head around the door. "Kit's here, *chèrie*," then turned to follow the children.

Sondra could see them in her mind's eye: Max, fearless and determined, usually won, dodging around his more cautious older sister; his baby fat legs deceptively sure footed on the stairs.

She was glad that the children took to Kit. Her sister's biting humour and seriousness hid a passionate and loyal nature. Kit could seem aloof, even arrogant to casual acquaintances, but Dierdre and Max saw her heart. This thought made Sondra smile, wanly.

Sondra turned off the heat under the soup and started slicing a baguette. She heard Kit's footsteps coming down the hallway, but still gave a little start when Kit, standing in the doorway said, "Ah, minestrone soup. You do love me."

Sondra made it through the meal, though she ate little, relieved that the children and J-P kept the conversation going with Kit. Kit's frequent concerned glances in her direction unnerved her. Sondra quickly turned to avoid her gaze, afraid she'd burst into tears if Kit caught her eye. And that simply would not do.

Sondra managed to get the children to leave the table by saying, "Maybe your Aunt Kit will read you a bedtime story."

Evidence of Uncertain Origin

She watched them go, each holding one of Kit's hands. Then, Sondra made herself stand and start clearing the dinner things. She caught J-P watching her and lifted her eyebrow at him, why did he look so damned guilty?

"Do you want some help with the dishes, *chèrie?*"

She went over and kissed the top of his prematurely balding head and, putting both hands on his stooping shoulders, said "Shoo, now, J-P, don't you have your lawyer work to do?"

Her husband stood, towering over her, and gave her a quick hug. "*Mais oui, ma petite.*" As the youngest partner in the firm, she knew he carried the bulk of prep work on the cases scheduled for court the following week. J-P hesitated as if he had something more to say but instead retreated to his office off the living room.

Sondra started washing the dishes, comforted by the menial routine and the feel of warm soapy water on her hands.

By the time Kit had read the children to sleep, it was late. She tip-toed out of their room, closed the door as quietly as she could and stood in the hallway. The stairwell opened into deep darkness on her left; the aquarium's faint glow lit the living room in front of her. The susurrating of paper and the scrape of a chair leg meant that J-P was still up and working in his office. So Sondra would be alone. The light under her sister's door to the right told her Sonn was still awake. Kit tapped gently.

"Come on in, Kit, it's my turn now."

Kit took a deep breath before opening the door.

Sondra had her back to Kit and was yanking a brush through her tangled auburn hair. She was sitting at her vanity, the one piece of fancy furniture their grandmother had owned. The face Kit saw reflected in the mirror was pale, and dark, puffy skin encircled Sondra's green eyes; "peaked" Grannie Win would've called it.

Kit plunked down on the bed, rolling over on her side to watch Sondra's nightly routine of brushing and plaiting her curly red hair. Kit was grateful for this small normalcy. Sondra caught her eye in the vanity mirror and said, "So, when did Jean-Pierre phone you?"

"What do you mean?" sputtered Kit.

"Come on, Kit, I know you like the back of my hand. What did he tell you?" Sondra's voice was cool and serene, like moonlight. Unsettled, Kit wasn't sure how to respond.

"I'm sure he was over-reacting, Sondra. He's crazy about you."

"Crazy, eh?" Sondra said with such brutal precision it made Kit scramble up into a sitting position on the bed.

Kit crossed one leg over the other; her foot tapped reflexively on the floor. She patted her jacket pocket, searching out of habit for the non-existent pack of cigarettes, her mind racing.

"Come on, Kit, you can't lie to me." Sondra's demeanor did not change.

Kit debated for a moment, then, unable to keep up the pretense, confessed, "Yeah, you're right. He did call me." Grannie Win had always said that Sondra was *fey*. Kit didn't buy into any of that superstitious nonsense, but she had to admit that Sondra's insights about her were correct ninety-nine percent of the time.

Sondra turned around, so that she was facing Kit. "So, what is the deal between you two?"

"No deal," replied Kit, "no deal at all. I'm not going to report in to him, if that's what you're worried about." Kit said, guilt tempering her feelings of offense. After all, she had conspired with J-P to have Sondra committed to the Douglas.

Placated, Sondra slumped, the imperiousness that had held her body erect drained away. "Well, Kit, no matter why you came, I'm glad you're here." Her dejected look belied her words as she stared at the hardwood floor and shivered.

Kit was up off the bed in an instant, pulling the duvet along with her. She put it around Sondra's shoulders and sat beside her on the vanity's ample bench. "It'll be OK, Sondra, we'll get through this."

"No, we won't," Sondra said. "How can we?" Her fierce tone faded and she leaned against Kit.

"What is the matter, Sonn? I'm no shrink, but maybe if you get it off your chest you'll feel better."

"'No shrink', eh? So you think I'm crazy too?"

"Unless you tell me what's bothering you, I don't know what to think."

"All right, I'll tell you what it's about, but," and here she turned on Kit, "I don't want you to say anything until I've finished. And even then, I don't want you to comment or judge or analyze or, or anything. I just want you to listen to me."

"OK, OK—I promise."

"Alright then. Did J-P tell you I'd been having nightmares?" Kit nodded. "Yes? Well, I've only had one nightmare, and, the trouble is, I don't think it's a nightmare, I think it's more, more of a... visitation..."

Kit tensed, clenching her jaw to keep back the torrent of dismissive words bubbling up in her throat. Instead, she managed to nod at Sondra to continue.

"You see," Sondra began wringing her hands, "Gramps was murdered."

"What?" escaped the blockade.

"And," Sondra took a deep breath. Her words sounded as though they were forced out into the open air against their will. "I could have prevented it." Sondra put her head in her hands and began to sob.

Kit felt as though someone had slapped her. On auto-pilot, she handed Sonn a box of tissue, patted her shoulder and listened while she blew her nose. Even after Sondra's sobs had subsided, all Kit could say was, "Well, Sonn, I am truly flummoxed."

As though reassured by Kit's confusion, Sondra's next words poured out, "I do realize how hard it is, Kit, for you to believe me, but in a way it all makes sense. In fact, you are key to this. I'm sure you are here for a reason."

Kit was alarmed at the feverish glow lighting up Sondra's pale cheeks as she continued speaking. "You are here to help me find Gramps' killer."

Evidence of Uncertain Origin

PART II
Ambiguous

Pseudis paradoxa
Paradoxical or Shrinking Frog

Montréal
Saturday, October 11, 1969

*T*he red mailbox was in the middle of the English enclave of Westmount. It stood at the intersection of Springfield and Metcalfe and was, to the man waiting in the car, a hated emblem of English tyranny over the French Canadian masses generally and himself in particular: a painful reminder of that despised English General James Wolfe's victory on the Plains of Abraham west of Québec City over two hundred years ago. Well, if the army of Marquis de Montcalm had failed and forfeited his habitant ancestors' land to the English crown, then it was damn well up to him and his comrades to get it *back, no matter what the cost.*

He sat smoking a cigarette, keeping his eyes glued to the mailbox's image in his rear view mirror.

At last the street was clear of traffic, but before he could make his move, a young négresse sauntered into sight, coming up Metcalfe from rue Sherbrooke. She approached the box and dumped in a bundle of letters, then continued on her way, pushing a stroller, occupied by a white enfant anglais no doubt. A nanny, Haitian, he guessed, or maybe Jamaican. He couldn't tell. The child must be fussing because she stopped and bent over to say something to it.

"Tabernak!" He slammed his hand on the steering wheel. "Hurry up!"

Finally, she continued on her way, disappearing from view; with no further hesitation he initiated the signal on his homemade radio transmitter. The explosion covered the sound of his car starting. All he could see in the rear view mirror as he sped off was a cloud of white confetti.

Kit had forgotten how draughty the old Montréal flats could be. She had awakened in the guest bedroom off the kitchen to the Saturday morning sound of Deirdre and Max rummaging around looking for something to eat. She smiled at their loud stage whispers; at least they were trying to be quiet for her sake. Eventually, they went to watch cartoons in the living room.

Brilliant red leaves still clung to the maple tree framed by the bedroom window. The backdrop of bright blue sky promised a beautiful day, but Kit wasn't ready for it. She didn't want to budge out from under the warm comfort of the duvet. She had not slept well.

Kit yawned, rolled over, looked at her travel alarm clock ticking on the bedside table and groaned: only seven twenty-seven a.m. and way too early to get up. She plumped up the pillows, lay on her back, stared at the plaster designs in the ceiling and thought back on Sondra's dream.

Kit dismissed Sondra's nightmare as a product of pathological grief, but dared not say so. Everything Kit held to be most true, namely the concrete comfort of material reality, screamed out against the idea that Sondra's dream represented some communication from the unseen world of the dead, yet Sondra was clinging to that exact conviction.

Kit was the eldest, the responsible one, Sondra's protector. If she voiced her opinion, as she usually did, Sondra would shut her out, destroying Kit's hope that she could pull Sondra out of the miasma of her strange depressive imaginings and back to reality.

Kit had sat there, confused and desolate, fearing that any incautious word from her could tip the balance the wrong way.

After what seemed like a long time, Sondra had taken her hand and said, "It's alright, Kit." The gentle pressure of Sondra's hand holding hers had made Kit relax. As the tension had drained from her body, a single word had popped into her mind: *paradoxa*.

"That's it!" she had exclaimed, relieved.

In response to Sondra's puzzled glance, Kit had explained. Carl Linnaeus, the grandfather of taxonomy, was undaunted by the plethora of strange animals coughed up by nature and the eighteenth century imagination. Linnaeus was able to assign these ambiguous specimens to neat categories of genus and species, many still in use today. Doing so, he delivered life from its apparent havoc and mystery, into the order so valued in the Age of Reason.

In fact, she had explained, Sondra's dream reminded Kit of the genus Linnaeus had created for creatures that contradicted the natural laws as scientists of his time conceived them. Some of them were mythical, like the phoenix, but some were animals they had heard of but not themselves seen, like the antelope. Linnaeus was unwilling to leave any organism without a genus to call its own, so he came up with the term *paradoxa.*

"For example," Kit warmed to her topic, "there was *Paradoxa satyr.*"

"Huh?" queried Sondra.

Kit, pleased to have roused a modicum of curiosity from Sondra, went on, "You know, the satyr. Species – *satyr,* Genus – *Paradoxa.* Let's face it, a hairy, bearded animal with a human-like torso and goat-like feet is rather a paradox, wouldn't you say?"

Encouraged by Sondra's smile, Kit continued, "Linnaeus eventually tossed out the genus, but the term, paradoxa, is still used today for animals or plants that are quirky. There's even a frog that's named *Pseudis paradoxa.*"

Sondra piped up, "That's an awfully strange name for a frog. What could be so paradoxical about a little frog?"

"I'm glad you asked." Kit was comforted. *Paradoxa* gave her a framework which kept her grounded and secure in the black and white rational world that was her reality, while it also provided a place to put Sondra's dream and the irrational constructs her sister had invested it with. It allowed her to accept Sondra's view, without compromising her own so that they were on the same page, at least for now.

Kit expanded on her topic. "I like to call it 'The Amazing Shrinking Frog.'" That got an actual laugh out of Sondra. "It confused the early naturalists because the tadpole was larger than the frog it turned into. In fact, they assumed that the frog, because it was smaller, must be the juvenile version while the tadpole, because of its size, must be the adult. They also thought the tadpole must be a fish. So they called it *Rana-Picis* or Frog-Fish. It looked to them like the natural laws were being compromised and a frog was metamorphosing into a completely unrelated animal, a fish. You can see why they included it along with satyrs and unicorns in the genus *Paradoxa,* ambiguous creatures

Evidence of Uncertain Origin

combining characteristics of unrelated animals. Even after Linnaeus threw out the genus *Paradoxa*, taxonomists still named it *Rana paradoxa* or the paradoxical frog. Eventually they abandoned that name and gave it the one we use today—"

"Pseudo frogo!" Sonn chimed in, grinning.

"Ha! Not quite, *Pseudis paradoxa.*"

"I don't know how you keep all those wild names straight, Kit, but I do sort of see your point. Still, I don't think I like the idea of my vision rubbing shoulders with a frog-fish, a unicorn, maybe, but a frog-fish?"

Kit smiled and nudged her sister. Tension drained from her like water out of a bathtub. What a relief to have found a place in her own world of strict categories to sequester Sondra's disturbing dream.

"OK, so explain it to me again, how does this all relate to my vision?" Sondra asked.

Kit took a deep breath. "I do believe your dream is important, Sonn, and conveys a message, we both do, even though we may not agree on what that message is. It has come from somewhere, and it gives us evidence about something. I guess we could call your dream *Paradoxa somnium.*"

Sondra put short shrift to Kit's satisfaction with her clever title. "Sorry, Kit, but I vote for a name I can pronounce and remember. And don't pout; it's my vision so I get a say."

"Oh, alright," said Kit, feigning disappointment. In fact, she was elated that Sondra was arguing with her, evidence of sanity as far as Kit was concerned. "I've got it, Sonn, does 'evidence of uncertain origin' meet your exacting standards?"

To Kit's relief, Sondra thought about it for only a moment before nodding in agreement. "That'll do," she'd said and grinned.

Sondra sat in the kitchen, a large cup of coffee in her hands; she was trying to decide between a bagel and a croissant. J-P had brought them back after his usual Saturday foray to boulevard Saint-Laurent where he also bought the Saturday papers: *La Presse* and *The Montréal Gazette*. He'd already retired to their large central living room, to relax in his favourite arm chair and read all the news he'd missed. The children, chins cupped in small hands, lay sprawled out on cushions at his feet watching cartoons on TV.

Sondra relaxed for a moment, thankful for her home's peaceful atmosphere despite the news of the most recent bombing. Sondra tried not to worry about things she couldn't change, but every time J-P left on an errand and was a few minutes late she started to get nervous. When he had returned this morning, Sondra was so relieved she wondered if she'd been holding her breath all the time he'd been gone.

Sondra, wrapped in one of J-P's old plaid bathrobes, found herself smiling. She'd slept through the night, and miracle of miracles, there had been no disturbing visitation. Now that she had shared it with Kit, the burden was lessened, and she had the energy to move forward.

Sondra picked the croissant, buttered it and took a bite. She knew what they had to do next. She opened one of Deirdre's spare composition notebooks, took another sip of her coffee and started writing out her plans.

The door to the bedroom off the kitchen creaked open and a foggy looking Kit staggered out.

"Hullo, there, you look like the living dead!"

"No thanks to you, kiddo, what a night I've had."

"Here, sit down and I'll pour you a coffee. There're bagels, cream cheese, croissants. J-P went to town in your honour I think."

Half an hour later Sondra, having waited until Kit finished one bagel and was sipping her second cup of coffee, launched into her plan. "Kit, I've got it all figured out, eh?"

Evidence of Uncertain Origin

"Oh?"

"Well, the first thing we have to do is get a hold of the police report."

Kit, mouth full of coffee, sputtered it out all over the table and protested, "Sondra, why would we want to look at the police report?"

Sondra laughed as she dabbed at Kit's spewed coffee with a napkin. "That's where we have to start—at the beginning, with the facts. Every good detective understands that."

"To what purpose, Sherlock?"

"Mrs. Holmes to you, ma'am!" Sondra retorted. "But, seriously, Kit, it's the first step to finding out who murdered Gramps."

"What!?"

"Why are you so surprised? I thought we'd agreed last night: all that stuff about paradoxes and frogs and evidence of unknown origin."

"Uncertain origin," Kit corrected, "Evidence of uncertain origin."

"Alright, Linny," Sondra cajoled.

"Doctor Linnaeus to you," Kit replied in a milder tone.

"*Touché*. But, Kit, we do have to follow up on this." Sondra reached across the table and took Kit's hand, getting her attention and keeping eye contact for a few seconds. "I've got to follow up on it."

Sondra stood and continued, "I understand if you don't want to go with me to the police station, Kit, but that's where I'm headed this afternoon. I'd love it if you'd come with me."

"Oh, alright, how can I resist?"

Sondra smiled; it might be sarcastic and begrudging, but it was a beginning.

And that's how Kit ended up at 1701 rue Parthenais,

standing beside Sondra while the pudgy Sûreté du Québec desk sergeant with stringy hair rummaged through papers looking up information about who had investigated Gramps' death. Kit figured out that the tune Sondra had been humming was Leonard Cohen's "Suzanne" only she'd added her own perky tempo to the melancholy song. The change in her sister overnight was heartening to Kit and if humouring her amateur stab at sleuthing was what it took to keep Sondra in high spirits, then, she, Kit, would participate whole-heartedly, or as close to it as she could manage.

They sat down to wait after the desk sergeant passed on a message from the detective in charge; he would come for them "when he had a moment." The station was abuzz with activity; uniformed policeman rushed in and out; plainclothes detectives conferred at desks and in hallways; technicians in lab coats carried clipboards and looked officious. Kit poked her sister and gestured, what's going on?

Sondra leaned over and whispered into her ear, "Another bomb in a Westmount mailbox."

At last Inspector Perron arrived and ushered them into a small windowless room. This looks like an interrogation room, thought Kit, glancing at the pea green walls, the shabby table with mismatched chairs and the large mirror taking up most of the wall across from her; a one-way window, Kit surmised. An overflowing ashtray and waste paper basket completed the décor. The thought that unseen others might be watching her every move, unnerved her. Kit had to fight the urge to hang her head and stare at the floor.

Sondra amazed her; she seemed impervious to the bleak atmosphere; she had her composition book opened and was already taking notes although Inspector Perron hadn't said anything yet. He had seated himself across the table and was sifting through the documents in the folder in front of him.

He looked up, his face a pleasant mask. His hair was a mousy brown and a little long for a cop, Kit thought. His solid blue tie was askew, a fact that annoyed her. He put his hands, broad and thick knuckled, on the table, eyed Sondra's note taking and then asked, "So, what is your interest in these documents, so long after your grandfather's death?"

They'd agreed that Kit would do the talking. She had convinced Sondra not to request an immediate reopening of the case, because the police might dismiss them out of hand without some additional material evidence to warrant such a move. Kit pointed out that the police might assume they were a couple of "hysterical females," thereby jeopardizing the acceptance of any hard evidence Kit and Sondra might find afterwards.

Kit cleared her throat. "Well, he was our grandfather; he raised us, so we were very attached to him. His death was so, um, unexpected; it threw us for a loop. We couldn't bring ourselves to face what his last moments must have been like until now." Kit hazarded a glance at Inspector Perron, who was nodding for her to continue. "Also, I live in Hamilton and my sister has two children at home and neither of us wanted to do this alone. So, when I came for Thanksgiving, we decided that now would be a good time to, um, find out the details about how he died." Kit looked up into grey eyes that had softened somewhat.

"I see." He paused. "This information could be distressing to you both. Are you sure you want to read through—"

"Yes," Sondra spoke up before Inspector Perron could finish his query. There was no way out at this point. Kit nodded her assent as well.

"OK, then," He collected the papers he'd selected from the folder, tapped them on the table to neaten them, and placed the pile down in front of them. The folder was still open, exposing the papers he had kept away from them. In the split second before Perron closed the folder, Kit glimpsed the photo he had tried to hide. The image of a body sprawled like a rag doll on the side of the road embedded itself in her brain.

The crumpled and lifeless form was her grandfather. She looked away, stifling a gasp.

"I'll be back in half an hour to answer any questions you might have. I have to lock you in, to secure the papers. There's a bell beside the door, ring if you need anything."

With that he picked up the folder, turned and left.

They had agreed not to discuss anything while at the police station, fearful they would be overheard, assuming that the room was wired for sound and conscious that they could be being watched. They moved their chairs closer together so that they could both read simultaneously. The first was the accident report itself.

Sondra copied the times into her notebook, translating from the French as she went. Kit peeked over her shoulder as she was writing:

> 20:20 - Driver (Henri Lalonde) travelling northwest along Senneville Road, passes the lodge, sees movement in the bushes, brakes but says he could not avoid hitting the victim in a wheelchair. Man and chair are separated; man flies through air, hits windshield and lands on the road.
> 20:21 - Driver exits car, checks man, who is not moving, pulls man to the verge.
> 20:22 - Drags the crumpled wheelchair to the verge, drives car off the road.
> 20:30 - Runs to Senneville Veterans Lodge where he finds the administrator (Captain Michel Tremblay) getting into his car. Tremblay returns to his office and calls police. Lalonde returns to scene.
> 20:40 - Tremblay joins Lalonde and identifies victim as John Flanagan, a resident.
> 20:50 - Sûreté du Québec arrive.
> 20:55 - Ambulance arrives.
> 21:10 - Victim proclaimed DOA at St. Anne's Veterans Hospital.

Sondra looked up and whispered, "Poor Henri Lalonde. What an awful thing to happen to him."

"Was the administrator from the Veterans Lodge, the one Lalonde had gone to get, the younger guy who was at Gramps' funeral?" asked Kit.

Sondra nodded.

Kit read as Sondra continued translating the report: an accident, deemed the police. No fault was assigned to the driver. The victim, riding in a wheelchair, had rolled into traffic from a driveway that sloped down toward the road and whose entrance was hidden by bushes. There were skid marks on the road where the car had attempted to stop.

Kit looked up. Something seemed to be missing. She read through the report again and then it hit her: What about the wheelchair? Shouldn't it have left skid marks too? If the wheelchair left no skid marks it means that the brakes had not been used. Why not? Kit had hoped that the hard facts of the case would quiet Sondra's imagination and put her suspicions to rest. Instead, they were posing some disturbing questions. Kit was beginning to have some suspicions of her own.

The coroner's report was tougher to get through, but the long and short of it was that "The deceased, a seventy-four year old Caucasian male," had died when his neck had been broken as a result of being hit by a car. The manner of death was deemed to be accidental. No autopsy had been requested.

Kit looked up and caught her reflection in the mirror. She saw a woman who looked back at her with drab hazel eyes, whose disheveled dark shoulder length hair was dull and whose face seemed frozen in an expression of perpetual numbness. Kit hoped this listless version of herself was due to the fluorescent lighting. Inspector Perron's return abruptly ended Kit's depressive musings.

"Are you finished?"

"Yes, thank you." Sondra had put down her pencil.

He collected the papers into the folder and asked, "Do you

have any questions?"

"Why wasn't there an autopsy done?" Sondra was quick on the draw.

"Well, I was the investigating officer, and I saw no reason for any, and there was no request for an autopsy from the family."

"Who in the family did you ask?"

Inspector Perron checked his case documents. "A Dr. Sean Flanagan, the victim's son." He looked at them. "Your father, I assume?"

Kit's hackles rose and she could feel her face get hot, but she said nothing.

"Yes," said Sondra, checking her notes. "What about this, there's no mention of skid marks from the wheelchair. Why?"

Good question, thought Kit.

Inspector Perron waved his hand. "I could not say for sure why."

"But, what is your opinion?" persisted Sondra. Kit leaned forward.

"You understand that there is nothing to indicate that any of these possibilities is true or even if they are, that they have any significance at all."

Covering his butt thought Kit.

Perron took a deep breath before continuing, "He must have lost control of the wheelchair. The driveway does slope towards the road and it was dusk so he could have miscalculated the speed or distance and, with the bushes in the way, not seen the car until it was too late . . . " Perron's voice slowed to a stop.

"But there could've been other scenarios, right?" asked Sondra.

"I suppose. The wheelchair could've malfunctioned or perhaps your grandfather wasn't paying attention or . . . " Perron paused. His grey eyes zeroed in on Kit's, held hers for a moment then he looked away, shrugged and stood. A band tightened around her chest, did he suspect suicide? Thank God Sondra was busy scribbling in her notebook and did not seem to notice. Murder was bad enough, but if Sondra thought Gramps had committed suicide, Kit was convinced that her guilt for not having visited him would intensify a hundred, no a thousand, fold. It just might kill her.

"Or what?" Sondra queried, looking up.

"I couldn't say." Perron stiffened, looked at his watch and moved toward the door. "I'm sorry but I do have another meeting." He opened it, waiting as they collected their things.

"But what was he doing up there in the first place?" Sondra blurted out as she stood.

"I couldn't say," he repeated.

Sondra pressed her point. "Didn't you interview anyone about the circumstances?"

After a moment's hesitation Kit saw Perron's shoulders shrug before he said, "According to the Lodge Administrator, the victim was an independent sort, and it wasn't unusual for him to go off by himself."

That did sound like Gramps, Kit thought, but what if there was more to it than that?

"OK, thanks, Inspector Perron," Sondra said. She looked pale, but resolute.

They followed the policeman through the door. Kit felt sick to her stomach.

Nikki Everts

Montréal
Sunday, October 12, 1969

Kit awoke with a mind as cloudy as the overcast sky. She had not slept well again, waking in the middle of the night with anxious thoughts around Gramps' death. Did the lack of skid marks from the wheelchair mean that Gramps had not tried to stop himself? Had he driven intentionally into traffic; had he, in fact, committed suicide by proxy?

The image of his body flung on the road kept replaying in her mind, accusing her of neglect. Had he been lonely? Or sick? Or depressed?

And what if Sondra came to the same conclusion? Kit feared that the guilt and remorse would push her sister over the edge into another nervous breakdown or worse.

By three a.m., Kit gave up on sleep, turned on the light and sat up in bed. If indeed they uncovered evidence that might point to suicide, Kit stood more of a chance of redirecting the interpretation if she stayed close to Sondra. She needed to be clever, especially if it turned out that Gramps had killed himself. She'd have to frame whatever evidence they found so that it pointed convincingly to accidental death.

By three-thirty a.m. she had come up with three firm commitments: to find out if Gramps had committed suicide, to at all costs keep even the suspicion of this possibility from Sondra and to divert her sister's attention away from the idea of suicide by joining Sondra wholeheartedly in her sleuthing.

By four a.m., Kit was sleeping.

When, at ten a.m., Kit stumbled, sleepy-eyed, into the

kitchen, she found it in its customary disarray. The welcome smell of drip coffee was promising as were the melted cheese and bagel open faced sandwiches, some half eaten, others still intact and still others reduced to crumbs on the table.

Except for Christmas and Easter they were not a church going family. Gramps, Sondra and Kit had all stopped attending Mass a few months after Grannie Win had died. It had been an attrition of interest rather than a genuine atheism. God's existence and worship seemed optional, irrelevant. Besides, they'd all attended church to please Grannie Win, not God. So, now, Kit reflected as she munched on a partially eaten cheese bagel and sipped pungent coffee, Sunday mornings were pleasant, drowsy affairs, meant for sleeping in, finishing the newspapers, listening to music or relaxing and staring at the ceiling: the sublime ordinary joy of family life.

God, I've missed this! she thought.

That afternoon, clothed and in her right mind, to quote Grannie Win, Kit joined Sondra, J-P and the children on a walk to the sliver of Mount Royal Park a few blocks from the flat. The clouds protected the air from the chill of outer space, holding in what heat there still was in the cooling earth. It may be one of the last days before the snow fell that they could play soccer in the park, J-P had said.

Kit was delighted that Sondra had slept well again and without dreams of any kind. Still, Sonn was jittery as they walked along. She even wanted them to cross the street because a mailbox was in their path. J-P teased her about being fearful for no reason, after all this wasn't Westmount, he'd said.

But Sondra was insistent, and shepherded the kids to the other side of the street. Kit and J-P followed them. Kit was used to indulging her sister, but J-P couldn't help raising his eyebrows, expressing his silent exasperation for Kit's eyes only.

They had passed the dreaded mailbox and Kit had caught up with Sondra. The children scampered ahead of them while J-P brought up the rear. Kit was just turning to ask J-P a question when the mailbox behind them exploded. Deafened, Kit stared, immobilized, as J-P lunged at her, dragging all of them down to the ground. Pushed backwards, Kit bumped her head on the sidewalk, her torso landing heavily on Sondra. She felt rather than heard a dull thud right next to her, must be J-P.

Almost immediately Kit felt Sondra wiggle free. Her ears rang, and confetti rained down on the street around them. The children. Where are they? Kit sat up. She put her hands to the back of her head and felt what turned out to be blood. She turned to look around.

Sondra was on her knees crawling over to where the children sat about a metre away, huddled together under a hedge, their mouths open. They must be crying, and if they're crying they aren't dead, Kit thought. Then she saw J-P. He was lying face down on the ground, not moving or crying. She leaned over to touch him and he shifted, looking up at her.

"J-P, are you OK?" Her voice sounded hollow through the ringing in her ears.

She saw J-P mouth something she couldn't decipher. He tried to lift himself up on his elbows, but collapsed.

Kit spoke, and her words echoed in her head, "The kids are OK, Sondra's with them. What's wrong with your arm?" He had rolled over on his left side and was holding his right arm.

Kit helped him sit up. People were starting to gather around them from the houses on the street. She saw their mouths move as they spoke to her, and noted the concern in their eyes and faces, but she couldn't hear anything. She wondered if some of them were saying just how lucky they were.

Evidence of Uncertain Origin

Later, after ambulance rides, hospital waits, x-rays, bandages, much prodding by doctors, and almost as much prodding by the police, they were finally home, sitting around the kitchen table with their father and his new wife. Sondra glanced at Kit, knowing she was unhappy that their father was here. She almost felt guilty about having called him from the hospital, but, really he was their father. Besides, Sondra was glad he'd come.

Thankfully, they'd all been released. Kit hadn't even needed stitches for her head wound, despite the impressive amounts of blood. The worst off was J-P with a broken wrist. She and the kids had gotten off with a few bruises and scrapes. They really had been very lucky.

"The damned FLQ," her father ranted as he paced back and forth in the kitchen, "you all could've been killed!"

"But we weren't," said Dierdre, clutching her favourite stuffed toy, a blue elephant she perversely called "Pinkie", eyes wide watching her grandfather.

"That's right, my dear," said Marie-Claire, who was sitting beside Dierdre. Her bracelets jingled as she put her arm around the child; a spicy perfume wafted up when she moved. Sondra saw Dierdre's lips curl into the cautious little smile that indicated her daughter was pleased.

Sondra noticed that Kit was sitting as far away from their father and Marie-Claire as she could. Her long legs were stretched out under the table and she was slumped in her chair, arms crossed over her chest, glowering at a spot on the table in front of her.

"Yes, we have you to thank, *chérie*," said J-P. Sondra was standing beside his chair and he caught her hand in his own. He pulled her towards him so he could plant a kiss on her cheek. "I promise I will never, ever again tease you about your instinctive dislike of mailboxes."

Sondra smiled; she really was quite fond of him. He saluted her by raising his other arm, encased in a cast and a sling, but grimaced and returned it gingerly to its resting position.

"Is it painful?" she asked.

"No, no, I'll be fine," J-P asserted almost convincingly.

In an instant her father was in front of J-P. "Let me have a look. If the cast is too tight, the tissue underneath might be swelling and they may have to recast it."

"Anything but that!" her husband protested, but left his arm in his father-in-law's grasp.

"It is a little puffy, but that's normal." Looking up at Sondra, he added, "Give him a couple of aspirins. They should help with the pain and the swelling."

He then turned to Kit. "And you, Katherine, how is your head?" He went to touch her, but she shrank away.

"Fine," Kit muttered. "Just leave me be, if you don't mind."

"Of course, Katherine, as you wish." He withdrew his hand as if he'd burnt it and looked at Sondra, his eyes questioning. Sondra shrugged and cringed inwardly. She could see her father's dismay as he stood in the middle of the kitchen, looking around at them, shoulders slumped and silenced.

A few awkward seconds passed before he took a deep breath. "Well, Marie-Claire, we'd best be on our way." And with that they exited the room and the flat, leaving an uncomfortable stillness in their wake.

It was Dierdre who finally broke the spell. "I like her," she announced.

Evidence of Uncertain Origin

Montréal
Monday, October 13, 1969
Canadian Thanksgiving

Sondra was tying on her apron; it was noon on Monday and time to start baking the four pies that were her contribution to Thanksgiving dinner at J-P's parents' house. Things were mostly back to normal after yesterday's close call. J-P had managed to sleep alright, despite the discomfort of his cast and the broken wrist. In fact, he had left with the children, taking them to a matinee showing of "A Boy Named Charlie Brown." She'd gotten him to promise to avoid all mailboxes there and back again before kissing them all goodbye. Strange, she wasn't as worried about bombings as she had been before actually living through one.

Kit was another matter. She was mooning around in the living room having declined the invitation to join them. Sondra could hear the restless rustle of newspapers half read and set aside. Was it the residual effect of yesterday's injury, or something else?

"Kit, come and help me with these pies."

Sondra heard a mumbled response and a few seconds later Kit appeared beside her. "Present, and ready for assignment, Ma'am," she said, clicking her heels together and saluting, half-heartedly. "No time off for wounded soldiers?"

she added, touching the small bandage on the back of her head.

"Nope, afraid not," Sondra handed Kit an apron, but noticed Kit's reddened eyes. Had she been crying?

"What's wrong, Kit?"

"Nothing, really, we're all alive, aren't we?"

The edge in Kit's voice made Sondra take her hands and look straight into her eyes. "You called Paul, didn't you?"

Kit slumped against the kitchen counter and nodded. "I just wanted to tell him about, about, you know, the bomb and stuff."

"No answer I take it?"

"Nope."

"He's probably exhausted after his classes. Or maybe he's studying."

"Or maybe he's with some fetching female med student."

"Kit! You don't believe that do you?"

"I don't know. Yes, no, maybe so. You know the stats, Sonn. More than half of marriages don't last past the medical student's internship!" Kit looked at her defiantly. Sondra could tell she was holding back tears.

Kit began pacing back and forth, waving her hands. "I don't even know if I still love him, Sonn. I'm so lonely all the time I can't stand it. But I'm too exhausted after working all day to do anything about it."

The dam has been breached, thought Sondra, as the words poured out of Kit. "And our only social life consists of potlucks with his damned friends from school. All they ever talk about is that week's disease *de jour*. I just sit around with nothing to add. I bring up Linnaeus and they look at me blankly. I hear myself talking about the bank and, hell, Sonn, I even bore myself! No wonder Paul isn't interested in me anymore."

Sondra put her arms around her sister; Kit sagged. "I'm so sorry, Kit. Maybe it's just a matter of hanging in there." She stroked her sister's hair. "Sit down, Kit, I'll make us a cup of tea."

Kit sat while Sondra busied herself making the tea. "And working in that bank is mind numbing, Sonn; I'm forgetting who I am and what I love. God, Sonn, I'm throwing away my own life, slaving away to support a man who doesn't even care if I exist. Do I want to be married to Paul at all? I don't think I'm cut out to be a doctor's wife, Sonn, and I wonder if I'll end up like Emily."

Ah, thought Sondra, setting down a cup of tea in front of Kit, that's the grain of sand in the oyster. As adolescents, they'd spent hours analyzing their mother's abandonment of them. They decided that Emily had turned to alcohol to stave off the loneliness and isolation that their father's dedication to his medical career had foisted upon her. They saw their mother as a victim and blamed their father, because after all he had turned to other women. A divorce had been the sorry end to the marriage and the family. Their mother had left them.

"It's better this way," she'd said, her eyes bleary and sad, her body reeking of alcohol. Then she'd staggered down the walkway, carrying her brown suitcase and a train ticket to Vancouver, where she had grown up. She'd left them standing on the front stoop of their grandparents' cottage, two little girls holding hands and crying.

"Well, you're nothing like our mother," was all Sondra could think of to say.

"You mean besides being the 'spit and image' of her according to Grannie Win?"

"That's just the outside, Kit, and you know it." She didn't want to add that on the inside Kit was far more like their father.

"Yeah, I can't stand beer or hard liquor, although there's some hope for me turning into a wino."

Sondra raised her teacup after drinking the last of it. "OK,

Mrs. Almost-A-Teetotaler, we'd better get back to those pies."

"If you say so." They both stood up, and Kit asked, "How do you and J-P manage to be so content together, Sonn?"

"Oh, we aren't happy all of the time; he's so stodgy, but he loves me and the kids and he's kind." Sondra handed Kit a knife, a cutting board and a bowl of apples, then rummaged through her kitchen drawers until she found the rolling pin.

"Sometimes, I think we are so busy trying to figure things out about the children, the home, the career that we don't have time to be mad at each other much." She patted the pie crust dough into eight equal rounds, picked one up and began rolling it out on the floured board.

"Come on, Kit, we're going to have to rush to get these pies done."

"You got it, Sonn," Kit said, brandishing the knife, "but something's missing—the CBC." Kit turned on the radio, then started on the apples.

By the time J-P and the kids returned the house was filled with the smells of baking pies. Sondra and Kit were sitting in the kitchen sipping tea. There had been no dire news of bombings that day, and Sondra smiled at the sounds of music overlaid by the cheerful voices of her family, safely home again.

Kit thought J-P's parents' home was beautiful. They lived along avenue des Pins in a large limestone house overlooking downtown Montréal, far away from Pointe-Saint-Charles, the working class neighbourhood where she had grown up. Giselle and Joseph Foucault were descendants of French-Canadian aristocracy, tracing their ancestry back to 1600's New France. While they no longer ruled over *seigneuries,* they still influenced politicians with the wealth accumulated and managed through Joseph's law firm.

Evidence of Uncertain Origin

J-P's two younger sisters, elegant in high heels and close fitting cocktail dresses, greeted them at the door. Martine kissed Kit on both cheeks and said under her breath, "Thank God you've come, *Maman* has been driving us crazy."

Nicole, the youngest, whispered, "She's been so worried about you all."

Ushered into the living room, Giselle emerged from the kitchen, makeup perfect and not a hair of her upswept chignon out of place despite the fact Kit knew she'd been in the kitchen all day. "My dears, I am so happy you are all OK." She hugged and fussed over them while her husband stood to one side, appraisingly.

After his wife had finished her ministrations, Joseph intoned with deceptive calmness, "This simply cannot continue; bombing Mayor Drapeau's home, the disaster at the taxi company, and now my own family. Bad enough that the FLQ and the *maudit souverainistes* want to ruin us economically and politically by wrenching us away from Canada, now they want to murder their own people!"

Kit saw Dierdre's eyes widen in alarm at her grandfather's subdued rage.

Giselle put her hand on her husband's arm, and said with a smile, "Now, now, Joseph, let's not get into politics before dinner, you know it is bad for the digestion."

With that, they filed into the dining room to a truly sumptuous Thanksgiving feast.

Kit enjoyed the meal despite the awkwardness she felt with J-P's family. They were always very kind and welcoming, even speaking English for her benefit. Languages hadn't been Kit's strong point. Now, of course, she wished she'd become bilingual, like everyone else in J-P's family, including Sondra. It reminded Kit that J-P had been Sonn's French Teaching Assistant during her first year of college. He had pursued her after she'd completed his class. Finding out that she went folk dancing at Mount Royal's Beaver Lake during the summer, he had contrived to "accidentally" run into her up there. And the rest was history.

Looking around the table, Kit saw how light-hearted and gay Nicole and Martine were. Almost birdlike in their colourful dresses they laughed and joked with an ease that often escaped Kit. She felt herself a large, clumsy ox by comparison. Especially dressed as she was in what for her was formal wear: a long charcoal grey woolen skirt, with a tweed jacket and a black turtle neck.

Still, the meal was lovely: turkey and all the trimmings by candle light. Kit was pleased on Sondra's behalf that their pies were well-received. After dinner they all retired to a large living room where they sat sipping cognac and gazing out of floor to ceiling windows at Montréal stretched out below them. The evening was overcast which lent a mysterious aura to the scene. A gentle drizzle made the large boats moored at the docks along the south river look like an old grainy photograph.

Kit saw that even the children were enjoying themselves. Martine and Nicole had brought out a few toys and puzzles kept especially for the times they visited.

The conversation turned inevitably to the political situation and the rise to power of the Foucaults' neighbour. Pierre Elliot Trudeau, their young and newly elected Prime Minister, owned a house just down the street.

"Oh, he'll intervene eventually," proclaimed Giselle. "He just has to bring those *felquistes* to heel."

"I'm not so sure, *chérie*," her husband countered. "You know he has always been a bit wild, traipsing all over the world."

"And, *Maman*," J-P added, "he's always sided with the labour movement."

Kit did too, for that matter, but decided to just listen, interested to hear the Foucaults' points of view.

J-P continued, "And, don't forget Trudeau and René

Lévesque were aligned earlier in Pierre's political career. He may find it difficult to turn his back on his old *confreres*."

"But, Jean-Pierre, that was before René got involved with the *souverainistes*," protested Giselle, "I'm sure they've nothing in common now."

Joseph harrumphed, "René is not just involved, *chérie*, he runs the *maudit Parti Québécois*."

"Still, René is a respectable member of Québec's parliament. It isn't the same as being actually in the FLQ and bombing things." Giselle protested.

"No, but I'm sure Lévesque hears whispers of what they're up to." J-P said.

Joseph nodded his agreement. "Most likely, I'd say."

"What does any of that have to do with Pierre?" Giselle said. "He chose to join the Liberals. If he was truly left-wing he would've gone with the New Democratic Party. No, I think he's matured."

"Well, I think he's quite amazing," piped up Nicole. "Did you see how he stood up to the crowd during the *Fête de la Saint-Jean-Baptiste* parade just before the election last summer? He declared his opposition to Québec separating from Canada right there in front of all those separatists."

"Yes, we were there, Papa," added Martine. "They were yelling abuse and throwing rocks at him, but he just stood there, so proud and brave."

Kit nodded; in fact she'd voted for the Liberals, Trudeau's party, instead of the New Democrats in part because of his courage.

On a different note, as Catholics, Kit wondered what the Foucaults thought about Trudeau's decriminalization of homosexuality when he was the Justice Minister under Prime Minister Lester B. Pearson. Gramps had been disgusted by it and said so to anyone who would listen. Kit kept her ponderings to herself.

The elder Foucault took a sip of brandy and sat back.

"We'll see, we'll see. Pierre is unpredictable but brilliant; I've always thought so. The question is will he have the political will and the strength to rein in the FLQ? He'll have to make up his mind soon, before it's too late."

Returning home and opening the door to the flat, Kit heard the phone ringing. She bounded up the stairs, thankful after all that she wasn't wearing a slinky cocktail dress or high heels. She was too late. The person hung up before she got there. She called Paul in Hamilton right away, but there was no answer. She wandered, desolate, back to the front foyer.

"Who was it?" asked Sondra, standing at the top of the stairs, struggling to remove a sleepy Max's coat and mittens.

"I thought it might be Paul, but they hung up before I could get there."

"It might've been Dad; he had invited us for Thanksgiving dinner."

Kit grimaced, and crossed her arms over her chest. "Great! That's new, isn't it? Whatever you do, don't let him weasel his way into your affections, Sonn."

J-P stumped up the stairs carrying a sleeping Deirdre in his arms. "I forgot to tell you, Kit, Paul called the other day while you and Sondra were at the police station."

"Thanks for telling me." She was in no mood to hide her annoyance.

J-P looked apologetic as he slid past her to deliver Deirdre to the bedroom.

Later on, Kit found Sondra sitting in the kitchen, head buried in her hands. Alarmed she rushed over to her. "What's the matter, Sonn?"

"It's Gramps; it's the first Thanksgiving we've had without him. We used to drive out to Senneville and bring him in to have dinner with us at J-P's parents. Kit, I miss him. I wish I'd listened and gone to visit him last summer. I am so, so guilty: if only I'd gone, he wouldn't be dead. I could've prevented his death."

Sondra looked up, wild despair in her eyes. "Oh God, Kit, it's my fault he's dead. I might as well have killed him with my own hands."

Kit pulled another kitchen chair over, sat and put her arm around Sonn. Sondra let her head fall onto Kit's shoulder.

"Oh, Sonn," was all Kit could say. None of Kit's words would bring Sondra the comfort she needed. Kit had tried in the past to give Sonn logical arguments to refute her sister's dangerous, irrational feelings, but Sondra had only drawn away from her and shut her out. So they sat there, ensconced in silence, listening to the faint sounds of the aquarium burbling and the soothing creaks of an old building settling in for a cold night.

PART III
Hardy

Acer saccharum
Sugar maple

Montréal
Tuesday, October 14, 1969

"*T*abernak!" *The man leaned over and turned off the car's radio, silencing the Radio-Canada commentator.* "Damned traitors!"

"Calm yourself my friend, have patience, some day they will all understand." *The taller man's smile was grim.*

Scowling into the windshield the shorter man was in no mood to appreciate the panoramic view of the city in the early morning light. They were parked at the overlook on Mont Royal. Below them Montréal glimmered through overcast skies.

Evidence of Uncertain Origin

"How could they talk about a hero like Geoffroy like that? Don't they get that he's done it all for them? For us? Pour un Québec libre?"

"I understand. But, Geoffroy is now a martyr, no? They haven't burned him at the stake, but a hundred and twenty-four consecutive life sentences? And martyrs are always good for the cause."

His companion glowered at him, unconvinced.

The taller man continued, "Come on, it's ridiculous. Vaillières and Gagnon bombed La Grenade shoe factory, killing a secretary, and they got nothing in comparison."

"The secretary should've been at home," the shorter man growled. "Not working late, licking the boots of those dirty English bosses . . . they wouldn't have paid her overtime for it if she'd lived."

"Chut, such harshness does not advance our cause, my friend. We aim to free the workers, not damn them." The taller man sat up straight, warming to his topic. "We want to break the stranglehold of the damned English, to halt their plunder of our heritage, self-respect and rights."

His companion nodded, placated for the moment. "What's our next target?"

"No more mailboxes; we will make this one really count. This one will be for Geoffroy."

"So you say, but bigger plans cost money, money we don't have. And your clever plan almost exposed us."

The taller man stiffened, but remained silent. He looked away from his comrade.

His companion shifted, uncomfortable. "I say we rob a bank—it's worked for the other cells, why not us?"

"You think so?" the taller man's tone like ice. He stubbed out his cigarette, furiously. "My plan is working, the money is still coming in, and, if you recall, I have taken care of our past 'exposures' as you so elegantly put it, so I suggest you leave the thinking to me."

52

Kit raised one eyebrow. She was used to being the rational, logical and well-organized one, and was surprised that Sondra, her artsy-craftsy sister, had planned their day so efficiently. Sonn had arranged for Deirdre to go home with her friend Alexa after school; Max would spend the day with J-P's mother, and J-P had even promised to be home in time to warm up the turkey leftovers for dinner.

They took the family car. Kit enjoyed driving, and, after dropping Max off, they headed out west along Highway 2 & 20 towards Sainte-Anne-de-Bellevue and Senneville Veterans Lodge.

Sondra had insisted that visiting Senneville Lodge was the logical next step since they needed to gather information about Gramps' last days, and any possible enemies or conflicts he might have had. Sonn believed this information would direct the course of their investigation. As well, Sondra was convinced Gramps' papers were there to be found.

Of course, they had two other legitimate reasons for a visit: until now Sondra had been unable to bring herself to go to the lodge to pick up Gramps' things, and they both wanted to thank his friends for coming to Gramps' funeral.

Kit hoped their conversations with Gramps' friends would provide the evidence she needed to prove that Gramps' death was in fact accidental. This would put to rest Sondra's belief that his death was murder, and quiet her own unnerving suspicion that he might've committed suicide.

"Kit, I'm sure Gramps was hiding something from me. When I visited him in June he had that glint in his eye. He was teasing and evasive, hinting at something, but avoiding giving any information. Remember how he'd get when he had a secret of some kind?"

Kit nodded. "What did you think he was up to?"

"Oh, at the time I thought he was planning a surprise for Deirdre's birthday, but I guess not." Sondra sounded sad.

Evidence of Uncertain Origin

"So, what do you think it was?"

"I've been mulling it over a lot, Kit. Gramps was always fighting the good fight. He loved to champion the cause of the underdog. He took his responsibilities as the Chairman of the Residents' Committee very seriously. I think it kept him happy or at least not so lost after Grannie Win died, having someone other than himself to take care of. Anyway, he had been talking a lot about how the 'boys,' as he referred to his fellow veterans, were being hard done by. When I asked about it, he got that conspiratorial gleam in his eye and changed the subject."

"It could've been anything."

"I know, I know, but I do think he had some secret mission. He seemed so down right cheery. Like a dog with a bone."

Sondra was silent for a bit, and when she spoke again her voice was low. "That was my last visit, end of June. I called him once a week during July, and the last time we spoke he asked me to come out. He never did that. He never wanted to impose on our 'family time' as he put it." Sondra gulped. "Gramps told me he was going to send me a key to something important. I mean, he'd already given me a key to his trunk, so this must've been a different key. But I never received it, and two days later he was gone."

"Jeez, Sonn." The now familiar confusion and alarm started up again in the pit of her stomach when Sondra spoke about Gramps' final days. She noticed that Sondra was wringing her hands. "What's wrong?"

"I can't help thinking that if I'd gone out to see him, he'd be alive right now." At this she began to cry.

Oh God, thought Kit, maybe he was lonely enough to kill himself. "Sondra, don't think that way; how could you have known what was going to happen? And what makes you think visiting him would've changed anything?"

"I know, I know, but even at the time I felt guilty, like

there was something he wanted to tell me, but I thought we had all the time in the world."

Kit reached over with her right hand to touch Sondra's arm. She thought about Paul, of all the times he hadn't been around and how none of that could be relived, and she wondered, in a self-pitying sort of way, if Paul would regret this and have awful dreams about her if she were to die. This idea pleased her, but was countered by an inner voice chastising her for being both juvenile and foolish.

Kit's musings ended as she navigated the exit to Sainte-Anne-de-Bellevue. She liked being back in the picturesque little college town perched at the westernmost end of Montréal island. She'd enjoyed pushing Gramps in his wheelchair to see the boats going through the locks. Kit remembered the quaint church and the sprawling grounds of Macdonald College, the agricultural arm of McGill University. In fact, Kit used to daydream about living here. She loved the way the students livened up the place, helping to ensure the village's continued survival and quaintness.

Kit guided the car through the narrow streets, gratified that she still remembered the route through town and the turn off to Senneville Road. Once out of the crowded village, Kit smiled. She enjoyed this part of the drive most of all, loved the mansions snugged in behind stone walls and surrounded by magnificent old trees.

Ten minutes later they drove through the gates and into the parking lot of Senneville Veterans Lodge. Getting out of the car, Kit stretched and took a deep breath. This was as close to the country as she had been in ages. She looked around. Behind her was the neat, white-washed administration building. It ran perpendicular to the parking lot so that windows and doors opened on a view of Senneville Road and the shoreline beyond. Well-trimmed lawns and hedges surrounded the building, and Kit remembered that a nine-hole golf course lay out of sight, somewhere behind the Lodge buildings. A large tree stood to the right of the parking lot; its flaming leaves repeating the motif of the flag waving from the pole nearby.

Kit scrutinized the tree: one of the *Acer* species, a maple, the quintessential Canadian tree, for sure, but not *saccharum*. The leaves were reddening but they only had three lobes, not five like the sugar maple. It's probably an *Acer rubrum* or red maple, Kit thought, and a much better choice for placement in a lawn. *Acer saccharum* was great for syrup and hardwood but not the best choice for lawns and gardens. Their roots were shallow, dense and fibrous sucking up so much water only the hardiest plants could survive under their canopy. Kind of like Gramps, Kit mused; he was a hard man when standing up for his principles and his country, but sweet and kind to those he loved. Still, like the *Acer saccharum*, he wasn't always the easiest person to live with. His strict sense of right and wrong offended some, but she certainly could understand the comfort to be had from clear categories. We sure shared that approach to life, didn't we Gramps, Kit thought.

Kit looked across the road at the entrance to a small, enclosed park with paths and benches. Decked out in toques and scarves, a couple of hardy veterans were taking a bit of air, sharing the shoreline and view with their rich neighbours. Ironic, thought Kit, they fought and were wounded to protect the right of some to live a life of luxury. She wondered if any of them ever regretted their service to Queen and country.

A slight movement drew Kit's attention back to the maple. A tall, stooped man had stepped out from behind the tree. He was dressed in coveralls and held a rake. He was staring at her with eyes that were such a light blue they looked almost colourless. Kit nodded at him and smiled. The man frowned and kept staring at her, ignoring the rake and the small pile of lawn detritus at his feet.

"Come on, Kit," Sondra took Kit's arm and directed her toward the steps up to the white washed administration building behind them. "That's just Serge," she added in a whisper. "Remember Gramps complaining about him? He's the grounds man that wouldn't let Gramps dig up a patch of his precious lawn to plant a vegetable garden that first year Gramps came to the Lodge. They disliked each other ever since."

Kit nodded. "Yeah, he's kinda creepy. I'm sure he's still staring at us."

"He always does every time I visit; guess I'm used to him by now."

They climbed the two short flights of stairs to enter at the main doors in the middle of the sprawling building. The Lodge Administrator's offices were to the right. A sign informed all visitors that they'd have to "report" to the administrator to request a day pass.

Once seated in the familiar waiting room Kit noticed that the receptionist wasn't the friendly blonde that Gramps had liked to tease. Instead a dour, middle-aged woman with short business-like greying hair sat behind the desk. She looked up from her work at them, frowned and asked unconvincingly, "May I help you?"

"Where's Annie?" asked Sondra. Kit noted her surprise and realized with a pang that Sondra had visited Gramps often enough to be on a first name basis with the secretary.

"Annie?" The woman replied; she pursed her thin lips, making it clear she could care less about Annie. She gave them a penetrating look. "How may I help you?"

"I'm sorry," said Sondra, "I didn't mean to be rude, could we have a visitor's pass for the day?" The secretary nodded and bent to pull out a form.

Sondra turned to Kit and whispered, "How odd, Annie was an institution around here."

"With whom will you be visiting?" Watery brown eyes

peered at them over glasses that seemed to be slipping down a long nose. Kit almost expected her to neigh.

"Oh, we'd like to visit two of our grandfather's friends," Sondra explained.

"Not a relative?" Her eyes narrowed.

"Our grandfather died, and we wanted to visit with the two men who came to his funeral, to thank them for coming." Sondra's voice faded out.

"I see." But Kit wasn't sure that she did. "I'll need their names."

Kit watched Sondra rummage through her bag; then, reading from a scrap of paper, Sondra said, "Robert Brault and Fred McIntyre."

The secretary spent a few minutes looking through her files. "I'm sorry, but I don't see either of these men listed."

Surprised, Kit said "But that's impossible, we saw them two months ago; the administrator brought them to our grandfather's funeral."

"I wasn't here at the time; all I can go by is the paperwork, and they are not listed." She replied, her voice clipped and brittle.

"Please check again, there must be some mistake." Sondra tried a more reasonable approach, but the secretary, after another, lengthier look, shook her head.

"I am sorry, but they are not listed. Is that all for today?"

Kit exchanged glances with Sondra and took up the ball. "Is the administrator in? We need to arrange to pick up some of our grandfather's things."

The woman nodded, picked up a phone, confirmed that the administrator could see them now. She got up, opened the door to the right of her desk and gestured them to enter.

Before they stood up to follow her, Sondra whispered into Kit's ear, "Whew, glad we got past the Dragon Lady!"

Kit smiled and whispered back, "Now we get to meet the dragon."

Kit recognized the man behind the desk who rose and stepped forward to greet them. This is the younger man who brought Gramps' friends to his funeral, she remembered. He limped, supporting himself with a silver-handled ebony cane. Dressed in a well pressed uniform, Kit noticed that he was a head taller than she and moved gracefully despite his uneven gait.

"Hello, please come in. How nice to see you again. I fear the last time was under very unhappy circumstances."

Kit was surprised that he remembered them and struggled to retrieve his name. She tried to read it off the framed certificates on the wall, without being obvious about it. Yes, Michel Tremblay, that was it, confirming that his very slight accent was *Québécois*. She shook his proffered hand. "Thank you for seeing us on such short notice. It's Monsieur Tremblay, right?"

"Captain Tremblay, actually." He shrugged and smiled. Kit looked up at him; he had deep set dark blue eyes, high cheek bones, and an aquiline nose. His somewhat sallow complexion was balanced by raven black hair, and the hint of a dimple softened an otherwise stern and patrician face. Now, if I were a student of physiognomy, mused Kit, that full mouth would suggest a sensual nature behind that crisp military stance. She smiled back at him as he guided her to sit beside Sondra in one of the leather upholstered chairs. He settled behind a large oak desk.

"I hope we aren't disturbing you," Sondra said.

"No, no, it is my pleasure, as you can see, my work will still be waiting for me," he gestured at the neatly stacked piles of folders, "and you bring me a nice diversion. Now, what can I do for you?"

"Well," Sondra began, "we'd like to pick up our grandfather, John Flanagan's, personal effects."

"But of course, they should still be in his locker. I believe we put it in storage after his accident." He paused. "I will ask

Evidence of Uncertain Origin

our gardener to help you carry it. But you could have called us, and we would have sent it to you. You did not need to make the long trip out here."

"Thank you," said Kit. "You're right, of course, but it is a lovely day, and we wanted to visit our grandfather's two friends, the ones you brought to the funeral. We were rather surprised when your secretary couldn't find their names. We were hoping you'd be able to solve the mystery for us." She smiled in what she hoped was a winning way.

Kit watched Captain Tremblay lean back in his chair, put his two hands together, finger tips touching, and gaze past them at the back wall. "It is always a sad affair to lose a comrade, but the men who come here are old and have been through a lot in their lives." He sat forward and looked at them. "I am sorry, but Corporal Brault passed away shortly after your grandfather's death, and Private McIntyre has had to be transferred to the Ste. Anne's Veterans hospital. He is not doing at all well I'm sorry to say."

This was not what Kit had expected to hear and she sat for a second in stunned surprise. "This is terrible."

"Yes, it certainly is," he agreed, pausing slightly before continuing. "I'm sorry to be the bearer of bad news. Perhaps you will join me for lunch in the canteen? It's the least I can do."

Sondra would've preferred to lunch alone with Kit and discuss the significance of Brault's sudden death and McIntyre's equally sudden illness. But Tremblay had been an agreeable enough companion, favouring them with wine for lunch, not something usually on the menu, as they discovered rather unpleasantly.

This request had brought the chef from the kitchen. Claude Leduc, according to the name tag pinned to his clean but threadbare white jacket, was a tall, bulky man, with long blondish hair kept back in a tidy pony tail and further restrained by a hair net. He strode to their table and bent over to address only Tremblay, refusing eye contact with her or Kit.

Flushed, with indignation Sondra supposed, his tone was chiding as he bent to speak in a harsh whisper to the administrator. She caught a few words, *vin* and *cher*. Sondra looked at Kit who raised her eyebrows and nodded towards the *fleurs-de-lis* pin on the chef's lapel. Sonn's eyes widened. Was he a *separatist,* maybe even a member of the FLQ? Was that why he'd ignored Kit and her?

Meanwhile, Tremblay calmed the large man with a few well-chosen words. Leduc stood, apparently mollified, wiped his long, be-ringed fingers on his apron, and glared in their general direction before stalking back to the kitchen.

"What was that all about?" asked Kit.

"I don't think he was happy about serving us wine," replied Sonn. Then, turning to Captain Tremblay she asked, "Is it us, the fact we're English, or the wine he was most upset by?"

"A bit of all three, I'd say." Tremblay regarded them coolly.

"He's a *separatist* then?" asked Sonn.

"Many *habitants* are," replied Tremblay with a smile.

"Do you think he's a member of the FLQ?" Kit blurted out.

Tremblay shrugged his shoulders. "I'm sure I have no idea. Do you think he would tell me if he was?"

"I guess not," said Kit. Sonn saw her sister turn away and knew she was hiding a blush. Kit had always hated sounding like a naïve school girl.

"Chef Leduc has to guard the food budget; so any extras, like the wine, have to be accounted for. This makes more work for him and he is already short staffed. We had our *sous-chef* quit recently."

"And— ?" Sondra queried, wanting to know the third

possibility.

"Ah, yes, we come to our Claude's complaint against your grandfather. Do not take his displeasure personally, you cannot help but inherit both the good and the bad from Corporal Flanagan, *comprennez-vous?*"

"Oh," said Sondra, remembering. "Was he the cook that Gramps took to task around the plum pudding last Christmas?"

"*Certainement.*"

Kit was looking confused so Sondra filled her in. "You remember how Gramps used to take hours to steam the plum pudding for Christmas? And how proud he was of serving as a cook in the navy during the war? Well, there was some debate about the length of time the pudding should be steamed and whether or not to use suet instead of lard. Gramps claimed it was not 'up to snuff' as he put it and, apparently, chef Leduc took great exception to this."

Captain Tremblay added, "That wasn't the only disagreement they had had—your grandfather was cook in the Navy and Leduc had served as a chef in the Army—neither one wanted to disappoint their 'brothers-in-arms,' so it became a larger issue than just the suet or lard debate. Once they almost got into a fist fight. Your grandfather's friends tried to convince him to apologize, but instead he continued to criticize Claude about it whenever he had the chance." Here the administrator shrugged his shoulders. "Your grandfather was not one to let go of an issue if he was convinced he was right."

Kit annoyed Sondra by laughing. "That's Gramps alright. You seemed to know him well, Captain."

Sondra stiffened. Glaring at Kit, she said, "Well, of course, that was Gramps. He had integrity. It's nothing to laugh about. It's a good thing."

Kit touched her arm. "I'm sorry, Sonn."

"No offense meant," added Captain Tremblay. His

sympathetic smile did little to allay Sondra's indignation on Gramps' behalf.

Kit found Tremblay gallant and conciliatory; she was touched by his concern at their distress about Gramps' two friends. After lunch, he had insisted on helping them locate Gramps' trunk. Displaced to make room for a new resident, it had been moved from the foot of Gramps' bed, ending up in a storage closet.

Sondra retrieved the key from her purse and opened the trunk. Almost a fourth of it was filled with several different types of toilet paper rolls.

"I never knew Gramps was such a pack rat!" Kit had exclaimed.

"He wasn't." Sondra jumped to Gramps' defense.

"These old fellows develop some amusing but harmless little habits as they age." Captain Tremblay leaned on his cane and peered into the trunk.

Kit hadn't wanted to look too closely into the rest of the contents. On first glance, it bore the sparse tidiness that had characterized her grandfather's possessions: tools, shoes, paperwork, had always been neatly arranged in the small bungalow they'd grown up in. Kit noticed that even the numerous rolls of toilet paper were organized in careful rows.

Glimpsing Gramps' familiar old shaver and toiletry bag almost undid her. Sondra and she had pitched in to buy it for him when they were just into their teens. He had scolded them with shining eyes for their extravagance while Grannie Win had winked at them and smiled from behind his back.

But Sondra, single minded, had squatted down and rummaged through it, dry-eyed, while Kit and the administrator stood watching. After five minutes, Sondra had stood, muttering, "Where are they?" in a frustrated tone of voice.

Tremblay looked at Kit and inquired with raised eyebrows, "Is something missing?" Kit shrugged and felt her face get hot.

Before Sondra could answer, Kit said, "No, no, nothing really, my sister thought there might be some of Gramps' personal papers in the trunk, that's all." She glared at Sondra. "Right, Sondra?"

"Yes, yes." Distracted, Sondra kept searching through the trunk. All Kit could do was stand there and watch, embarrassed by her sister's persistence in what was obviously a futile task. It took another five minutes before a face-flushed Sondra stood up and accepted defeat.

A concerned look on his face, the administrator stated in a gentle voice, "I asked Serge to help take the trunk to your car. He'll be here in a minute."

The last thing Kit wanted was a face to face encounter with creepy Serge. "Is that really necessary? I mean Sonn and I can handle it, can't we?"

But Kit's attempt to avoid another encounter with the groundsman's unnerving gaze was thwarted by Sondra who said "Yes, please."

Footsteps and voices heralded Serge's approach. Through the storage room door Kit saw a short stocky man with a greying brush cut talking and gesturing in French to Serge as they walked together down the hallway. Serge was listening, head bent towards his companion and nodding, face as expressionless as Kit remembered it. Before they came into hearing range, Serge's friend glanced up at them. The man caught Kit's eye and scowled straight at her before turning on his heel and stalking off. How odd, thought Kit. Not another *separatist,* she hoped.

Tremblay's presence ensured that Serge kept focused on the task of loading the trunk onto a trolley, barely glancing at them and saying nothing at all. He'd changed out of his coveralls and Kit could see another *fleurs-de-lis* pin on his jacket. Kit wondered idly if the Lodge was a hotbed of separatist support. She joined Sondra and followed Serge as he threaded his way back to the front entrance, trunk in tow.

With the trunk stowed in the car, Captain Tremblay dismissed Serge and suggested a walk around the grounds. The weather was brisk and bright. The grass was still green despite a few frosts and unadorned with fallen leaves. Evidence of Serge's prowess with a rake, thought Kit.

"Could you show us where our grandfather died?" Sondra asked. Kit froze and Tremblay was silent for a moment.

"I will, but are you sure you want to see this?"

Kit was sure she did not; she wasn't ready for this, had not even thought about it, but Sondra was emphatic. "Yes, we do."

So, Tremblay led them to the road where they turned right and walked about a hundred metres before a row of trees and brush marked the Veterans Lodge boundary. In contrast to the groomed lawns and shrubbery of the Lodge grounds, the property next door was still undeveloped and wild although a driveway extended back into the bush, indicating that someone had plans for it. Kit could see how a car traveling at dusk would not have seen a man in a wheelchair careening down this driveway until it was too late.

In silence Kit and Sondra turned to follow Tremblay up the driveway. It had a definite incline, leveling off as the asphalt petered out into gravel about twenty-five metres from the road. Once they'd reached the top, Sondra nudged Kit and pointed to a path through the trees angling back toward the Lodge property.

They both stopped. "Gramps?" Sondra whispered in Kit's ear.

Kit nodded. It would be a tight fit for someone in a

wheelchair but it could be done. She looked around for some evidence of Gramps having been there. The gravel revealed nothing except for a few random cigarette butts and Gramps didn't smoke. Kit figured this must be a popular spot with the Lodge residents. It wasn't the most scenic place, but it did give people privacy, where you could be alone with your thoughts.

Sondra bent over, picked up one of the cigarette butts, wrapped it in a tissue and put it in her coat pocket. Kit frowned at her then glanced at Tremblay who was watching them. He probably thinks we're nuts, Kit thought. Sondra grabbed her hand and pulled her around so that they were both looking at the bottom of the driveway where the car had hit Gramps' wheelchair. Kit was glad the administrator was behind them, she could almost imagine that they were alone.

Kit wondered what Gramps had been thinking as he'd looked out at the road from this same vantage point only a few months earlier. Had he realized he'd be dead in a few minutes? Why had he come there in the first place? Was it to watch the water and trees across the road, or to get away and think? About them, Kit wondered, about ending his own life, about how to make it seem like an accident, to spare them? She shook her head, trying to throw off these disturbing thoughts, but she couldn't. Instead, dread and despair clenched her heart. She shivered.

It was late afternoon and the driveway was in shadow. Kit heard a match strike behind them. There was a sulphurous smell and the sound of Captain Tremblay inhaling. She squeezed Sondra's hand. "Let's go," she murmured, her voice swallowed by the surrounding bush.

They walked down the hill, tracing the path Gramps' wheelchair had taken as it carried him to his death. Sondra began humming something dirge-like. Kit thought she should cry but she couldn't.

They halted at the end of the driveway. Sondra stopped

humming and they stood in silence there, waiting. For what? Kit wanted to know. She sure wasn't expecting any thunderous revelation from the great beyond. Still, a comforting thought would be nice, even if it was from her own mind. But nothing came to her. She glanced at Sonn whose eyes were closed and head bowed. Could she be praying?

Tremblay cleared his throat, and said, "I think it's time to leave."

No one spoke on the way back to the Lodge.

Later, after they signed out at the office, Kit and Sondra were standing on the front steps with Captain Tremblay. Kit had just thanked him for all his help when Sondra demanded, "Who do you think killed my grandfather?"

"Sondra!" Kit blurted out.

Tremblay turned to Sondra and asked, "Pardon me?"

"You heard me," Sondra said. Kit's jaw dropped and she stared at her sister. Sonn ignored her and continued, "Was there any one with such a strong dislike for my grandfather that they might have wanted him dead?"

"What an odd question. Why do you ask? Your grandfather's death was an accident."

"Really, Sonn, we should get going." Kit's cheeks were hot with embarrassment. She touched Sondra's arm, hoping to get her attention and make her stop this ridiculous conversation, but Sondra shook off her hand.

"Well, did he have a fight with some one?" Sondra paused for a moment, took a breath, and said, "You see, I know his death was not an accident."

Kit wanted to sink into the earth; instead she held her breath and waited.

Captain Tremblay leaned on his cane and tilted his head, as though considering the possibility. Kit let out her breath slowly, relieved that he had not taken offense. She looked more closely at the tall lithe man, thinking that a less sensitive person would've dismissed the idea, if not laughed outright at such a supposition.

"He was not always on the best of terms even with his friends. As you saw, there was his disagreement with our Claude. And, that incident about the garden did not sit well with Serge." Tremblay looked towards the maple tree flaming in the afternoon sun. "Then, there was outright antagonism between your grandfather and Roger Dufresne."

"Oh, I'd forgotten about Dufresne," Sondra said.

"That was Roger Dufresne, the one talking with Serge in the hallway," said Tremblay.

"Really?" Sondra said.

Kit looked at Sondra quizzically, so Sondra explained, "I'd never met Roger Dufresne before, but Gramps sure had a lot to say about him. They'd both been nominated to head up the Senneville Lodge Residents' Committee last year. Gramps won and Dufresne had accused him of stuffing the ballot boxes, calling him a *maudit anglais tricheur*. Gramps did not appreciate anyone accusing him of being a cheat, much less a 'damned English' one."

Captain Tremblay nodded then added, "Even so, I cannot imagine anyone planning to hurt your grandfather. Like all of us he was his own worst enemy. As these men age, they change, sometimes they get depressed, they can lose their *joie de vivre*, you understand?" He paused for a second and Kit paled at his words, visualizing her grandfather poised at the top of that dark and wild driveway, lonely and depressed.

Captain Tremblay continued, "Do you have any reason to think as you do?"

Sondra bit her lip then squared her shoulders; looking Captain Tremblay in the eye she said, "Yes, I do." Her words hung in the air for a moment before she pivoted and almost ran to the car. Kit could hear impending tears in Sondra's voice.

"Is she alright?" Tremblay asked Kit.

"She'll be OK. My sister's taken our grandfather's death very badly. She's not been herself." Kit fumbled for words and watched as Sondra got into the car.

"Does she really think that your grandfather was murdered?"

Confused and miserable, Kit shrugged. "I'm sorry we're rushing off like this. You were kind to usher us around today. Thank you." With that Kit retreated to the car, awful thoughts clawing at her heart, wondering what else Captain Tremblay could tell her about Gramps' state of mind before his death.

Sondra shivered as she slid into the car, waiting for Kit to join her. The sun, no longer overhead, couldn't prevent the open sky from sucking the heat from the air and land. She was crying, out of frustration and renewed guilt. She was disappointed not to find the papers; once again she'd failed Gramps. On top of everything, she was mad at Kit for her obvious embarrassment.

Kit got into the driver's seat. "You OK?"

"I'm *fine*."

"You don't sound fine," Kit replied. The car started and Sondra folded her arms across her chest and stared fixedly out of the window as Kit backed the Volvo out of their spot.

As they turned left onto Senneville Road, Sondra sighed, reached over and turned on the radio. John Lennon's voice wafted into the car; "Give Peace a Chance" he crooned. Could it have been only six months ago that he and Yoko Ono had graced the Queen Elizabeth hotel in Montréal with their "love-in"? She relaxed a little and decided to let Kit off the hook. "I'll live, just a little overwhelmed, I guess."

By the time the song was finished they were both singing along, the mood in the car brighter.

"I wonder what happened to those papers, and that key

Evidence of Uncertain Origin

Gramps had wanted to give me." She dug out the composition book, recorded the date and started writing down pertinent facts, talking aloud as she tried to write legibly in the moving car. 'Annie—missing, Robert Brault—dead, Fred McIntyre—in hospital.' Odd, don't you think that all of Gramps' friends are out of the picture?" Sondra looked at Kit, waiting for her response.

"Jeez, Sonn, I have no idea, coincidence?"

"I don't think so. It's suspicious, and we'll need to investigate." She retrieved the cigarette butt from her pocket and almost shoved it under Kit's nose. "And what about this?"

"What about it?" Kit asked.

Why was Kit being so obtuse Sondra wondered? She sighed. "Well, Gramps didn't smoke, so this butt proves someone else was up there with him who did!"

"Not necessarily," Kit commented. "We have no way of knowing when it was left there. It could've been left long after Gramps, or long before."

"Or it could have been left by his murderer!" Of course, Sondra conceded to herself, Kit always had to be right; they had no way of knowing for sure. She shoved the wrapped cigarette butt back into her pocket and looked at the trees and houses of Baie-d'Urfé as they whizzed by. Kit was taking the scenic route back home along the lakeshore. Sondra stared out the window, catching a glimpse here and there of the water.

"Did you notice that almost everyone we met seemed angry at us? Was it because we are related to Gramps or that we're English?" Kit asked. "I wonder if any of them are *felquistes*? Wouldn't it be weird if there was an FLQ cell operating out of the Senneville Veterans Lodge?" she mused, a smile in her voice.

Sondra looked at her. "Outrageous as it seems, Kit, you may be on to something." Sondra thought about it a moment. "Although I'm not sure how they'd be able to make bombs or rob banks without it being noticed."

Kit guffawed, but took the idea one step further. "Well, there are all of those outbuildings. And it would be a great cover. After all, who would ever suspect a bunch of doddering old veterans?"

"I'm going to write it down as a possibility," Sondra said, "even though it doesn't make any sense: why would anyone want to violently separate from a country they'd risked their lives fighting for?"

"Well," said Kit, always the devil's advocate, "maybe that's exactly why they'd want to separate. If you'd fought a war on behalf of Canada, then came back and felt you were treated like second class citizens because you were French, it might make you mad enough to want to set up your own government."

"Good point, Watson," said Sonn, happy that Kit was engaging with her. "Guess it does get included in my little evidence book after all." She licked the tip of her pencil and started to write, muttering to herself as she did, "No key, no papers..."

"Unless you count the toilet paper," interjected Kit.

"Ha, ha, no, seriously, Kit, we do have to count the toilet paper as some form of evidence, again 'of unknown origin'..."

"'Uncertain origin', Sonn."

"Alright, smarty pants." Sondra was almost elated. Even if Kit didn't believe Gramps was murdered, yet; at least she was contributing to the investigation.

Sondra bent back to her task. "As for suspects, there are Roger and Serge, both of whom disliked Gramps. And what was the cook's name?"

"Claude Leduc."

"Right," Kit always had had a good memory. Sondra paused, stared out the car window. "What if the murderer didn't just dislike Gramps, what if he was part of an FLQ cell and Gramps found out about it? That would give him a motive to kill, wouldn't it?" Sobered by the possibility, Sondra put down her pencil.

Neither sister spoke for a minute. Finally, Kit said, "Sondra, that's, I don't know, scary, improbable, incredible, don't you think?"

"I know, but is it any more incredible than being murdered because of an argument about plum pudding or gardening or a lost election?"

"I guess not."

"It would mean Gramps' death was premeditated, not just spur of the moment." Sondra continued, thinking out loud, "Of course, if it were spur of the moment, it might've happened almost accidentally, an argument gone awry, which means we can't rule out even his friends."

"Isn't that stretching it, Sonn?" Kit seemed startled.

"Well, sometimes friendships turn sour, or a friend betrays you, or you have an argument that gets out of hand. It might have been accidental or in the heat of the moment. So, I think we need to include Robert and Fred."

"You're the expert."

"And, don't you find it suspicious that Annie is gone? Right after Gramps dies?"

"I guess."

"So, I'm putting her down too."

"You might as well put down everyone in the Lodge at this rate!" Kit declared.

"Brilliant, Kit!" Sondra looked at her sister.

"What do you mean?"

"Well, maybe there's some other person that could've had it in for Gramps that we don't know about yet."

They drove together in companionable silence while Sondra mulled over her list. "It's getting a little unwieldy."

"What?" asked Kit.

"The Suspects List."

"Okay, I see your point," Kit conceded. "It's just you and

me and we only have a week or so to work on it."

"Exactly, so, I was thinking we ought to concentrate on investigating the major suspects. We should eliminate them before we start digging into the others. And, hopefully we'll find out enough that the police will carry on the investigation for us before you have to leave."

"Now wouldn't that be nice."

Montréal
Wednesday, October 15, 1969

At ten a.m. Kit and Sondra were again heading west along Highway 2 & 20 on another glorious fall day with clear blue skies and air as crisp and refreshing as the first bite of a Macintosh apple. Kit was driving. She found this kind of weather invigorating and loved it. So she couldn't refuse Sondra's plan to visit a sick Fred McIntyre at Ste. Anne's Veterans Hospital, despite her own dread of hospitals and all they implied.

Sondra had been enthusiastic and cheerful and that alone was motive enough to tag along, playing Dr. Watson to Sondra's Sherlock Holmes. In any case, Kit figured she might pick up something in McIntyre's conversation that would tell her about Gramps' mental and emotional state prior to his death. Their discussion about possible motives for murder the day before had been unsettling, but it fit in well with Kit's plan to keep Sonn's attention away from any suspicion of suicide. The idea that the Veterans Lodge could be home to an FLQ cell was far-fetched but worthwhile to hang onto since it kept Sonn thinking murder not suicide. So she wouldn't discourage it until they dug deep enough to satisfy Sonn that Gramps' death was an accident. Kit set aside her worries about how to navigate the situation if the facts pointed to suicide. One thing at a time, she thought, no sense brooding about what hasn't happened yet.

They exited the highway before the bridge to L'Île Perrot and turned onto rue Saint-Pierre, following the narrow street until it ended at rue Sainte-Anne. They turned right and wound along Sainte-Anne-de-Bellevue's main street as it curved northeast after the locks. Driving past the road they'd taken the day before to Senneville Veterans Lodge, they continued on another 500 metres until they turned right into the Ste. Anne's Veterans Hospital grounds.

Kit slowed down to ogle the huge barrier surrounding the ruins of the new hospital. No sooner had it been completed than it had burned down, putting the project back to square one. Unnerved, Kit wondered if this too had been done by the FLQ, although she couldn't for the life of her figure out how burning down a hospital could further their cause. She dismissed the thought and, following the signs, found the old hospital's parking lot.

Standing beside the car Kit looked around, waiting for Sondra to join her. Which of the clustered low lying wood and stucco buildings housed Private McIntyre? They headed toward what looked like the main entrance and found the gift shop where they bought some flowers. After wandering down a few corridors they came to a nursing station where they asked for Private McIntyre.

A young round-faced brunette was sitting at the desk, writing furiously. She looked up, smiled, checked the roster and nodded them down a hall towards room 187. An austere older nurse was standing behind her and gave them an appraising look.

Kit, fighting the knot in the pit of her stomach, asked "How is he doing?"

The brunette glanced up at the older woman who gave her a stern shake of the head before responding, "I'm not supposed to discuss the patient's medical status unless you're family. Are you family?"

"No, he was a friend of my grandfather's. We wanted to thank him for coming to our grandfather's funeral." Sondra said.

"Oh." The brunette nodded approval and smiled at them,

signaling their conversation was ended. Kit noticed the older nurse scowling at them as they turned to walk down the hall.

Room 187 was darkened; hesitating in the doorway they peered in, but couldn't see much. A male orderly whisked by them into the room. He was of medium height, well-muscled and dressed in whites, a *fleurs-de-lis* pin graced his uniform. The gurney he was wheeling contained an old man who leaned over to make a grab for Kit as he passed by, garbling and grinning all the while.

"Now, now Sergeant Mallory, we keep our hands to ourselves," said the orderly in a sweet sing-song voice.

"Shud-dup, ya f'ing *separatist* fairy," said Sergeant Mallory making an obscene gesture as the orderly winced and smiled apologetically at Kit and Sondra who stood rooted to the ground.

"Tsk, tsk, try to behave, you old fart!"

Sergeant Mallory chortled, while the orderly lifted his frail body into the bed. "Keep yer hands to yer self, André, ya bleedin' frog cock — oof!"

His insult was cut short as André slipped him into bed, and clanged the side bars into place. Before the sergeant could muster another round of taunts, the orderly had fluffed his pillow, covered him with a sheet, turned on his reading light and tossed a final, "Behave yourself!" over his shoulder as he rolled the gurney out of the room.

"*Vous devrez excuser le sergent, mesdames,*" whispered André as he passed them, "*il est tellement taquin!*"

Kit looked at Sondra whose eyebrows were raised. Sondra returned her gaze; Kit could see that the corners of her mouth were twitching, a sure sign that Sonn was fighting back laughter.

"What on earth did he say?" Kit asked, amused by the performance they'd just witnessed.

"He said we'd have to excuse the Sergeant because he's 'such a tease!'" Sonn's eyes twinkled.

Kit looked away, fearful that she'd collapse in inappropriate hilarity and bring down the wrath of that banshee of a head nurse upon them.

Kit leaned over and asked Sondra, "That's not McIntyre, is it?"

"No, no, McIntyre's a Private and a whole lot less..."

"Salty?"

Sondra nodded then gestured to the bed almost hidden by mounds of equipment on the other side of the room.

"You won't get much outta that fella," commented Sergeant Mallory hitching a thumb at the other bed. "Come over here and visit with me. I've still got a few kicks left."

"Ah, thanks, but we're here to visit Private McIntyre."

"Yer loss, lasses," said the Sergeant and turned his attention to the bowl of orange gelatin wobbling gently on his bedside tray.

As Kit's eyes became accustomed to the dimness, she could see a small form outlined under the bedclothes. Wires and tubing seemed attached to, or extruding from, most of Private McIntyre's exposed fleshy surfaces. They looped up to connect with monitors and bags arrayed around the head board. He looked so helpless in that huge bed. Kit heard the mechanical ticking of the machines he was attached to and smelled disinfectant overlaid by whiffs of nameless bodily fluids. The familiar knot in her stomach tightened and all she wanted to do was run away from the sad horror of it all. What the hell were they doing here, anyway, disturbing this poor man?

Sondra grabbed Kit's elbow as if sensing her intentions and guided her into the room as though she were an unruly child. Kit thought of Paul and regretted her ongoing resentment of his studies; she had to admire his willingness to spend his life with sickness and death.

"Private McIntyre?" Kit heard Sondra whisper as they neared the bed.

Evidence of Uncertain Origin

The response was a faint groan and the shifting of bed sheets.

"Fred McIntyre?" Sondra repeated and reached out to touch him.

This roused the wizened shape in the bed and he turned his head towards them, barely opening his eyes.

"It's Katherine and Sondra Flanagan, John Flanagan's granddaughters—"

Before Sondra could finish her introduction, McIntyre's eyes widened in what looked like terror and he struggled to bring his hands up. Was he trying to ward them off? Kit noted Sondra's surprised little gasp as she stepped back, shoving the carnations towards Private McIntyre in a placating manner.

When they didn't turn to leave, he started mumbling, "No, No, No," or maybe it was "Go, Go, Go." Kit couldn't be sure; he was almost incoherent. McIntyre was shaking his head and shooing them away with his hands. His eyes were squinted shut, as if against some dreaded outcome.

Kit feared his violent activity would dislodge all those tubes and wires. A buzzer went off on one of the monitors and the banshee nurse came rushing in.

"What did you do to him?" She accused.

"Nothing, nothing at all," Sondra sputtered.

"You must've said or done something to upset him. He is usually so peaceful and calm." She checked monitors, twisted knobs, took his pulse and pulled his eyelids back to check his pupils.

"I think you'd better leave now." She pulled out a vial and hypodermic needle, upending the vial, sticking the needle through the rubber stopper and pulling back the plunger. She had already given Private Fred McIntyre the shot before Sondra had time to set down the carnations on his side table and back toward the door with Kit.

Kit caught one last glimpse of Private McIntyre's eyes.

They were fixed on her and wild with what? Fear? Worry? She couldn't tell. He shook his head at her and she thought he mouthed "No" or "Go" before closing his eyes and letting his head fall back against the pillow.

Sergeant Mallory's "Told yer so," followed them out the door.

Once out of earshot of the nursing station, Sondra turned to Kit, her eyes gleaming. "So, what do you make of that, Kit?"

"Who knows? We have no idea why he's in here; it could be he's psychotic, or paranoid, or senile like that Sergeant what's-his-name." She caught Sondra's pitying glance. "OK, so what do you think?"

"Well, I rather doubt he'd be hooked up to every possible monitor if senility was his only problem. And did you see how alarmed he got when he recognized us? He did not want us staying in the room with him."

"Yeah, I got that message loud and clear." Kit did worry about this. Had he been fighting with Gramps, like Captain Tremblay had intimated? Had that pushed Gramps over the edge? Was a guilty conscience driving his erratic behaviour? Or was it just all the drugs he was obviously being given?

"He was terrified of something," continued Sondra. "I can't figure out whether he was afraid *of* us or *for* us. Do you think he might've been warning us off?"

"Maybe we startled him," Kit knew she was wrong as soon as the words came out of her mouth, but she wanted to downplay the situation, trying to put the most innocent face on things.

"Startled!" Sondra harrumphed "Certainly, but it was a far more extreme reaction than simple surprise."

They'd arrived at the front doors of the building. Kit took a deep breath, preparing for Sondra's onslaught once they would reach the relative privacy of the parking lot. Sondra, ahead of her by a few feet, was giving the doors a vicious shove when they were pulled opened and Sondra almost fell into the arms of a large man with a blond pony-tail.

"*Merde!* What are you doing here?" He asked, frowning down at Sondra who had regained her balance.

"It's a free country," Kit retorted, taking Sondra by the arm and striding by him. "Who was that rude guy, anyway?"

"Didn't you recognize him, Kit? That was the chef from the Lodge."

"Claude Leduc? Monsieur I-don't-need-suet-for-MY-plum-pudding? The maybe-I'm-a-card-carrying-member-of-the-FLQ suspect?"

"Yep, I vote for his being a *felquiste*; I can't believe that plum pudding would leave such a bad taste in someone's mouth for so long."

Kit groaned at the pun, and punched Sondra, relieved that the chef had come along in time to deflect Sondra's annoyance away from her.

As though reading her mind, Sondra said, "I'm still mad at you, Kit. I hate it when you contradict everything I say. It sounds like you think I'm an idiot!"

Maybe I have been a little too dismissive, thought Kit. So far, every bit of new information only muddied the waters further, and this lack of clarity made Kit want to cling to her convictions even if it meant criticizing Sonn's. By the time they reached the car, Kit's remorse had kicked in, remembering how close Sondra had seemed to another breakdown just days ago.

Sliding into the driver's seat, Kit said, "Listen, I'm sorry I was so snooty. I guess I'm really bothered by the whole thing. You know how I get sometimes."

"You mean rigid and inflexible?" Sondra asked.

Kit cringed; Sondra was always accusing her of being pigheaded. "I prefer 'uncompromising', if you don't mind. It sounds better. More like Gramps."

Sondra softened. "I do understand, Kit. This is all hard to take; believe me, I get it. I've been living with this confusion and mystery for a while. You haven't. I understand. Of course you're not going to believe he was murdered, to begin with anyway."

"But, Sonn, do you think Fred McIntyre, that poor little man in the hospital, could've—," Kit paused, finding it difficult to speak about Sondra's dream, "—could've, um, killed Gramps?"

"Well, he was in the army. They were trained to kill. And who knows how much strength a person has when he gets angry."

"But why would he get that angry with Gramps? Weren't they friends, didn't he come to the funeral? It doesn't make sense to me."

"Yes, but look at his reaction to us. Maybe now that he's so close to death he feels guilty and haunted by what he did, and fearful of, well, meeting his maker."

Kit turned to her sister. "Sondra, please tell me you don't believe there's a big old guy with a long white beard sitting on a throne passing judgment on dead souls."

"Maybe, maybe not, who's to say." Sondra wouldn't look Kit in the eye, which was worrisome. "But it isn't what I believe or not that's at issue. It's what Private McIntyre believes, isn't it?"

"Yeah, I see your point."

Sondra went on, "Well, if you want to think about someone acting suspicious, why was that Claude guy so mad when he saw us?"

Kit's stomach growled. "Can we put this on hold, Sonn? It's lunch time. Let's go into Sainte-Anne-de-Bellevue and grab a bite to eat."

Sondra perked up at this. "Great idea! I wonder if that little tea shop along the main street is still there. They used to read tea leaves when we were younger, remember?"

Kit nodded and started the car.

Evidence of Uncertain Origin

The tea shop was comforting and familiar to Sondra with its quaint frilly cloths covering the odd assortment of tables, each surrounded by three or four mismatched chairs. Large wooden planks, smoothed by many feet, made up the floor, which tilted slightly toward the back. The rear of the shop was curtained off, but through a side window you could catch a glint of sunlight on water. The tea house perched on a retaining wall beside the St. Lawrence River. A heavy scent of lavender and sandalwood bespoke both the elderly shop owner and her youthful wait staff. Sondra figured they'd been culled from the undergraduate agriculture students attending MacDonald College.

They sipped chamomile tea in china cups, and nibbled at fresh scones, served with butter in a little pot and elderberry jelly with its own tiny spoon whose handle advertised the distant port of Marseille. Sondra relaxed as they reminisced about prior visits with Gramps to the very same tea shop.

Out of the corner of her eye Sondra saw the shopkeeper, Mrs. Grady, amble over to their table, a friendly smile on her face.

"My dears, I couldn't help but overhear you chatting. Please don't mind an old busy body, but I thought I recognized you both." She waited for them to reassure her and invite her to continue. Sondra did so in an instant, glad to accommodate the eccentric old lady. She glanced at Kit who frowned at her, always so impatient, thought Sondra.

"Well, I don't mind if I do, the old dogs get plum tuckered out by the end of the day, I don't mind telling you." She sat with a grateful little wheeze. "So, it's been awhile since I've seen you and your old Pappy."

When Sondra told her that Gramps was dead, Mrs. Grady's face clouded over. "I am so sorry to hear that." She waited a considerate moment or so before continuing. "He was quite the talker, wasn't he?"

"You knew him?" Kit sounded surprised.

"Well, sure, honey, I knew him. I just didn't figure it was him that had died! Never even occurred to me that he'd be taken by an accident. So careful he was, so proud of himself, and all like that. Not one to let things happen, if you know what I mean."

Sondra nodded at Mrs. Grady, encouraging her to continue and willing Kit to relax.

"I'd heard in the village that two of the old soldiers had died. Tsk, tsk. And I must've seen him shortly before it happened. Sometime in July it was if I recall correctly."

"Really?" said Sondra, attentive. She saw that Kit had stopped fidgeting with her tea cup and sat up, eyeing the proprietress with interest.

The old lady seemed gratified by their heightened attention and continued in a conspiratorial manner. "Yes, and he looked like he was the cat that ate the canary, now."

"Why's that, do you think?" asked Sondra.

"Well, I expect it's because of that sweet young blonde he had with him. No fool like an old fool, they say."

Sondra and Kit shared a confused look.

Mrs. Grady cackled and her eyes crinkled merrily. "You young folk don't think that anything much happens for a body past oh about forty or so. But, just because we look old, doesn't mean we feel old." She paused, lost for a moment in what appeared to be a pleasant memory.

"Do you remember much about her, like maybe her name or something?" Sondra leaned in toward her intently.

"Me? No, I'm not that nosy. I did look, mind you, because I recognized your old Pappy, and at first I'd thought it was one of you. So I did stare some at the get go. When I took on to the fact that t'weren't neither of you, I kinder backed off some. But I did keep my eye on them, that I did. And I'd swear on my own mother's grave that those two were up to something. Planning something, I'm sure of it. Thought at first they were sweet on each other, and maybe they were, but t'was more to

Evidence of Uncertain Origin

it than that!"

"So, what did they do?"

"Just talked, far as I could see, no smooching or anything like that. I'd not allow it in my place. I'd have tossed them out for sure and certain. 'Sides, come ta think on it, I don't rightly figure they were sweet on each other, though your old Pappy mighta bin. She just wasn't interested in that way, you could tell, and nervous as a cat, that one. Always lookin' over her shoulder, thought at first she was afeared of her husband or boyfriend or someone, afeared they might catch her out with your old Pappy. But then I said to myself, 'Thelma, that don't figure. Here's a nice young woman, don't seem right she'd be sippin' tea at my shop with this elderly gent if her intentions weren't honourable.'" Mrs. Grady grinned at them and winked.

"So did you ever figure out what was happening?" Sondra asked.

"Don't rightly know. I was in and out at the back, but there weren't many people in at that time of the day. Near closing time it was. So I did spend some time tidying up in here."

The old lady paused, put a finger to her temple and continued. "Come ta think on it, an odd thing did happen just before they left: your young woman there got up, went to the door, opened it and looked up and down that there street. I did worry for a moment that they might've been skedaddling without paying, but your Pappy was still seated and she comes back in, serious as anything. Mind you, she hadn't eaten a bite since she got here. Then she goes and pulls out one of them briefcase thingummies from under the table, turns plum near white as a ghost, holds the blamed thing tight against her chest then puts it in your old Pappy's lap, grabs her purse and high tails it out of the shop. Strangest darn thing I ever did see."

Walking back to the car Kit wondered if, as bizarre as it seemed, Gramps had fallen in love with the young blonde. Had she involved him in something illegal to do with the contents of the briefcase? Had she then broken his heart?

"So, what do you make of that?" Kit asked, worried that Sondra might be thinking the same thing.

"You know very well what I think of it. I think the papers from my vision were in the briefcase and that the blonde was Annie and that Fred McIntyre knows something he's afraid to say and that Gramps was murdered and maybe poor Robert Brault, too!"

They were just half a block from the car when Sondra stopped and pulled on Kit's arm. "Wait a minute, Kit. Look in there." They were in front of a seedy looking bar; the lights were on inside so the denizens were visible through the smudged window.

Kit peered in and saw a couple of men playing pool. She turned to Sondra and shrugged. "What's so interesting about some old guys playing pool?"

"Didn't you see the two men sitting at the back?"

Kit's second look surprised her. "Isn't that Serge and—"

"Yes, and Dufresne," Sonn said in an excited whisper. "See? There are papers on the table, and," Sonn craned her neck for a better look and pointed, "look, they're counting money."

One of the pool players looked up at them, and smiling, gestured to them, inviting them in. Kit said, "Let's get out of here, Sonn. What if Dufresne and Serge see us?" She looped her arm in Sondra's and tried to drag her sister the last few steps to the car.

Too late, they were seen. Before they could retreat Roger Dufresne burst out of the bar and stood, his bandy legs apart, face red, arms stiff at his side and hands clenched into fists. "And what in hell do you think you two are doing here, spying on us?" he demanded.

Evidence of Uncertain Origin

"Just passing by, honest," sputtered Kit.

Sondra shook off her sister's arm. "And what in the world are you doing in there, Mr. Dufresne, counting money? Whose money is it anyway? I bet it isn't yours." Kit felt like sinking into the sidewalk.

"Sergeant Dufresne to you, Mme. Flanagan," he said icily, "and it is none of your damned business what we are doing. You're just as bad a snoop as your grandfather. Be careful that it doesn't get you into trouble." With that he spun around on his heel and went back into the bar. The door slammed behind him. Kit could see surprise on the pool players' faces as they watched Dufresne stalk back to the table, making sure to get out of his way.

Elated, Sondra said, "See, I'm sure they are up to no good, Kit! Otherwise, why would he take such offense?"

"Maybe he just doesn't like being spied on?" offered Kit and was rewarded for her efforts with a pitying glare.

"Don't you see, Kit, this is one more piece of the puzzle," Sondra gushed as they got into the car. "I mean, could those papers be linked to the ones in the briefcase? And with money involved, that could be part of the motive." She immediately pulled out her notebook while Kit pulled out into traffic.

Although curious about what Serge and Dufresne were doing and taken aback by Roger Dufresne's extreme reaction, Kit was silent as she drove them out of Sainte-Anne-de-Bellevue and back onto the 2 & 20. She couldn't get rid of the thought that maybe her upright grandfather had been so smitten that he'd aided and abetted thievery, if indeed the contents of the briefcase had been obtained illicitly. He'd have been distraught by his own actions. And if the blonde had then abandoned him, would it have driven him to suicide?

Kit turned on the radio; the news was a needed distraction. She glanced at Sondra who was scribbling in her composition notebook, and felt hugely thankful that her sister's perceptive gaze was not focused on her.

Sondra closed her notebook. "Let's try to get more information about Serge and Dufresne although I'm not sure just now how to go about that. In the meantime, I want to speak to Robert Brault's wife. I think she still lives around here. I also think we should try to track down Annie."

"Good idea, but how will you track them down?" Maybe we'll be able to put both of our suspicions to rest, Kit hoped.

"The phone book for Robert's wife, but I'm not sure how to trace Annie. I never knew her last name, but I could call Senneville Lodge to find out."

Kit wanted more than ever to talk to Captain Tremblay, wanted to ask him about Gramps' state of mind, but without Sondra around. She decided to beg off. "Well, you've got to do what you need to, but I think I need a break. The last couple of days have been pretty intense."

Kit avoided Sondra's steady gaze, concentrating on navigating the car through traffic.

"Oh, Kit, I've been so caught up with Gramps and my own guilty conscience I haven't thought much about you. Are you still worrying about Paul?"

"Oh God!" Kit said, relieved to have the subject changed. She turned onto Sondra's street and found a parking spot close to the flat. Kit turned off the engine, and took a deep breath. Turning to Sondra she said, "You know it's not just Paul, Sonn. I've hit a wall.

"I mean five years ago I was sure of the plan, sure I could fit myself into it. But now I feel more like a unicorn or a fish-frog, as vague and imaginary as the one and as confused as the other." Kit shook her head. "I mean, Paul and I agreed that I'd support him through his pre-med studies and medical school then he'd support my PhD field work. But I wonder if we'll even be together by then, or if I want to be with him, or if I'll even want to go back to school."

characterization; reader sympathy

"But, Kit, it's always been your dream, ever since you were little." Kit saw Sonn's brow furrow. "I mean, when every other girl was playing with dolls, you were out turning over rocks in the back yard, collecting who-knows-what awful creepy-crawly."

"Well, that was then and this is now, Sonn." Staring out the windshield, Kit continued. "Sitting on that damned uncomfortable stool in that god-awful, stifling bank, waiting for the next customer, I used to comfort myself by imagining I was a research scientist traipsing through a tropical rainforest, any tropical rainforest." Kit turned to Sondra, "Now, I just sit there, waiting for the next little old lady to deposit $1.53 in her savings account. I don't even daydream anymore. It's like I'm just fading away. Why can't I keep my focus on the plan?"

They got out of the car and walked in silence up the wrought iron stairway. Sondra stopped before opening the door and turned to Kit. "Listen, we don't have to be joined at the hip. I can carry on with my sleuthing on my own. Why don't you take a day off, hang around town and relax." Kit saw the sweet smile on her sister's lips. "And maybe even let yourself dream a bit."

PART IV
Agitating

Coffea arabicus
Coffee

Montréal
Thursday, October 16, 1969

*T*he man in the black sedan finally found a parking spot downtown. He stepped out into the chilly, overcast day and shook his head in disgust. He had forgotten his gloves again.

Cursing under his breath he lit up a cigarette, flicking the burnt match into the gutter. This earned him a disapproving look from a mink clad dowager exiting Holt Renfrew onto rue Sherbrooke.

Maudite anglaise-damned English, he thought to himself, *shrugging into his overcoat to simulate a nod and hide his* angry frown from the woman in front of him. He'd been warned not to draw attention. He strolled past her and inhaled, comforting himself with images of this very store, dedicated to the expensive clothing tastes of the hated English, collapsing into a pile of rubble, and this very woman, so smug and secure in her mink wrap, running shrieking with terror into the street.

But first things first: he paid close attention to the foundations, looking for cracks and crevices big enough to hide explosives, noting as he did the doorman watching him. He took one last puff on his cigarette, dropped it to the sidewalk and shoved his hands in his pockets. There were other suitable targets. Turning right he headed towards the Gare Centrale.

He and his comrade weren't murderers; revolutionaries had to keep the end in mind, and sometimes the means involved death. A sudden chill penetrated his chest, though the day was windless. He shivered and picked up his pace.

Kit spent the afternoon meandering amongst the stores on boulevard Saint-Laurent. Cooler and cloudy, the grey city streets were punctuated by the orange, red and yellow leaves littering the sidewalks and beginning their slow metamorphosis into the decayed, sodden slippery mess that was their destiny. Despite these somber thoughts, Kit was beginning to unwind from the rigours of the last few days and months. She had succeeded in contacting Captain Tremblay while Sondra and Max were walking Dierdre to school. She had arranged to meet him at a café on rue Saint-Denis.

Kit found the place and arrived a half hour early so she could sit back and enjoy her purchases—her birthday was in a few days so she'd bought herself a few gifts. Kit laid out the tomes she'd found at a second hand book store. All were related to her key interest. Taxonomy was not a popular topic these days, but one she thought fascinating. She was glad to have found Edmund Otis Hovey's *The Bicentenary of the Birth of Carolus Linnaeus,* the 1908 biography of the great taxonomist. She'd also acquired an English translation of the 4th edition of Linnaeus's *Systema Naturae,* and a small treatise on *Unreason in the Age of Reason.*

She settled in to the pleasurable task of deciding which book to read first. It gave her such comfort to think that everything had a place, a neat and tidy category. Life was so much more manageable when you knew where everything belonged; she sighed, almost happy.

The café was small, lit only at this hour by the big windows which let in the fading afternoon sunlight. The perfect atmosphere for a "penny university," as the English called coffee houses in the 17th century, Kit mused. In those days coffee cost a penny, and the high caffeine content of *Coffea arabicus* stimulated social activity and communication. Kit noticed the political posters on the walls. Not much has changed, she thought as she sipped her café latte, except the prices.

The lull of voices speaking French, the smell of fresh coffee and croissants—this was the life. She had decided to start reading the biography when a shadow blocked out the light from the window. She looked up and at first did not recognize the man standing before her.

"Katherine? Katherine Flanagan?"

"Yes?" she peered up into the long sallow face of Captain Tremblay.

"May I sit?"

"Of course, yes, thank you for coming."

He sat across from her, his head haloed by the light behind him, his face in shadow. "My pleasure, how may I help you?"

Kit heard the sound of a smile behind his words. "Um, I'm not sure that you can." She hadn't thought this out very well, she realized. It was too late now to pull back so she might as well plunge ahead. "There are some things that don't add up around my grandfather's death."

"Oh?" Captain Tremblay leaned forward.

"It may not make sense to you why I'm worried, but my grandfather was not accident prone; he was a very careful man. There were no skid marks from his wheelchair, so the brakes had not been engaged. It makes me wonder. Could there have been anything wrong with his wheelchair?"

"It's possible, I suppose, although unlikely. We do have them serviced regularly." A cool caution had crept into his tone.

"I don't mean to imply that you or Veterans Affairs were responsible or anything."

"You would be surprised what relatives accuse us of."

"I'm not accusing you of anything, Captain Tremblay. Damn it all! I'm getting this all jumbled up. I thought you might remember something about his last days: who he spoke with, what his state of mind was, you know.

"My sister is convinced that he was murdered. I think she feels guilty about not seeing him as often, and he'd wanted to talk to her about something important. Do you know anything about that? Did he talk to you about any of this?"

Tremblay sat back and sipped his espresso. He drew out a packet of cigarettes and offered her one. She was almost tempted to take it but declined. She crossed her right leg over her left, and her right foot started swinging as though it had a mind of its own. He tapped the cigarette on the table before lighting it and inhaling. It was unfiltered, she noticed, Gauloises by the pungent smell.

He blew a smoke ring before replying. "Yes and no."

"What do you mean?"

"Just that: yes, he did speak with me the week before he died, but no, I do not think it related to his death."

"What did he say?"

"Do you think he was murdered?"

"No," Kit shrugged. "Mainly, I'm worried about my sister. That's why I'm here in Montréal and why I've been humouring her, and yes, even encouraging her. If we sort through all her suspicions, compare them with the facts, then I'm sure she will realize that that's all they were, nasty suspicions, and she can get back to her life."

"Ah," he interjected, smiling as he pointed at the book on Linnaeus with an elegant finger, "I see you are taking a scientific, perhaps even a taxonomic approach."

"Are you mocking me?" Kit's face heated up and she bent down to return the books to her shopping bag, hoping to hide her discomfort.

"*Mais non!* I noticed your books and well . . . " He shrugged and let his words drift away.

They were silent for a minute, and, recovered, Kit sipped her café latte.

"Well, I guess I hadn't thought of it that way, but, yes, perhaps I am approaching this taxonomically. Anyway, I want to get to the bottom of it, for her peace of mind."

"What about your own?"

"Mine?" She gulped.

"Your peace of mind, your worries." He waved his hand in the air. "They appear larger than simply those surrounding your sister."

His tone of voice was sympathetic, and she realized how alone she felt. It would be such a relief to be able to talk to someone about her fears. She began to tear up.

He reached out and touched her arm. "It is alright to cry, I too have lost loved ones; I know it is difficult."

Kit sat immobile, staring into the dregs of her café latte, her foot, swinging under the table, increased its tempo.

"I've upset you," he said.

"No, no, it isn't your fault." She shook off her agitation, blew her nose on her napkin and uncrossed her legs. She put both arms on the table, and leaned forward to say, "In fact, you are right; I am worried. If there was nothing wrong with the wheelchair, that means Gramps didn't even try to save himself."

"Are you saying you think he might have let himself be hit by the car, on purpose?"

Unable to speak, Kit nodded.

"Yes, I can see how that would worry you. I had not known about the lack of skid marks. Perhaps, it was, how can I say this, an accident of a different nature?"

"Like what?"

"Well, I don't mean any disrespect to you or your family, but you may not realize that in the last few years, your grandfather had begun to drink a great deal." Anticipating her protests he put up his hand. "Please understand, I do not condemn him. It is not his fault. Many veterans drink, perhaps more than is good for them. But, they have suffered much and sometimes alcohol is a good medicine, a good friend, a comforter."

Kit made two fists, her eyes narrowed and she said through thin lips, "My grandfather was not an alcoholic! Are you insinuating that he was drunk at the time?"

"I insinuate nothing; I look at all possibilities. And it is one, *n'est-ce pas*?"

"Well then, so is suicide, or, or even murder!"

"But who would want to murder your grandfather? Or why would he want to kill himself?"

"I don't know." Confused and miserable, Kit went on, "That's what I wanted to ask you about in the first place. What was his state of mind? You spoke with him, what did he tell you?"

"He was concerned that someone was stealing from him."

Kit sat up straight; their conversation with Mrs. Grady sprang to mind, and her thoughts began to spin like a dozen different coloured spinning tops set off all at once and bumping into each other until they all blurred together in a chaotic mess. Could the blonde woman Mrs. Grady had seen with Gramps be involved? Was she returning something that belonged to him already? Did it have anything to do with the papers and money Serge and Dufresne had? Did this somehow involve the FLQ? Was there something else in the briefcase Mrs. Grady had seen exchanged? Was the blonde woman Annie? Her head was beginning to throb.

"You are not well." Tremblay announced, touching her hand and signaling to the waitress. "*De l'eau, s'il vous plaît.* You, Mme. Flanagan, you look like a ghost."

"I'm sorry, I hate to be a bother," Kit said, watching the waitress rush over with a glass of ice water, eyebrows furrowed with concern. "*Merci,*" she said as she took the glass. Sipping the cool water soothed her.

"Better now?"

"Yes, thank you, Captain Tremblay," Kit murmured, embarrassed.

"Please, call me Michel." He made a slight, mock bow, hand on his heart and a half smile on his lips.

"OK, Michel, thanks," she raised her glass to him.

"It was nothing. So, what happened just now?"

"I don't know. Really, sometimes it just all seems too much."

Michel nodded as though he understood; his raven black hair glinted, iridescent in the afternoon light. Kit hoped he did understand. That would make one of us, she thought.

Kit cleared her throat, remembering what she wanted to ask him. "Did my grandfather know who was stealing from him?"

"He suspected someone but did not want to point them out before being sure, and giving them a chance to pay him back themselves. He was an honourable man, your grandfather." A wry smile flitted across Tremblay's lips.

"Yes, he was." Kit felt suddenly tired and sad. She sipped her water. "Did he tell you who he thought it might be?"

"No, but he had made some enemies."

"Yes, you told us about them the other day."

"Your grandfather was somewhat, how can I say this?" Tremblay circled the air with his hand looking as if he expected to snatch the right word out of the ether. "Inflexible, yes, he was inflexible in his attitudes. If he thought he was right, he did not hesitate to share his convictions with others. Not everyone appreciated this quality."

"Who in particular?" Kit leaned forward. "That chef?" she guessed.

"Claude did not enjoy your grandfather's *effronterie*, but somehow I doubt this would drive him to murder, although—" Michel looked at her as if gauging how much he could tell her. He twirled his cigarette before tamping it out. "Please understand, I do not mean to imply that anyone I mention would want to kill your grandfather; harm him—perhaps, frighten him—maybe, bring him down a notch or two—definitely."

Kit nodded. "I don't like to hear it, but I do understand."

Michel sat back, lit another cigarette before continuing. "Claude, of course, was unhappy with him, as was Serge around the incident of the garden and then there is Roger Dufresne, who lost the election to him. They disagreed on other matters as well—"

"Like, what, for instance? Politics?" She leaned forward and looked directly into Tremblay's face. Her wild theory about an FLQ cell based at Senneville Veterans Lodge popped into her head.

Tremblay sat back as though pushed away by her intense stare. "I think I've said enough. I do not want to, what is your cliché? Ah, yes, I don't want to 'air our dirty laundry' in public. Besides, I'm sure none of it is a motive for murder."

Tremblay's reply assuaged Kit. His tone implied conflict of a more personal than political nature. "But you said he came to talk to you about a theft, of what? And why did he want to speak to you about it?"

"He did not say what had been stolen. He just wanted to find out if anyone else had complained of theft."

"And had anyone?"

"No."

"Was he afraid, or worried?"

"Not exactly," He paused. He seemed hesitant to continue. "Perhaps I did underestimate his state of mind at the time."

"Go on."

"He was very upset about the whole thing. It depressed him to think a 'brother in arms' might have stolen from him."

"Oh no," Kit groaned; she covered her face with her hands. The idea of Gramps at the top of that long driveway, discouraged, disillusioned, maybe even heart-broken, brought the fear of suicide back full force. When she looked up, she asked, "Do you think he might have committed suicide?"

Captain Tremblay shrugged his elegant shoulders. "I do not know." He touched her hand; his sympathy moved her. "I see your distress; perhaps I can help you. Would you like me to check the wheelchair's service record?"

"Yes, please do. Thank you."

"You are most welcome." He stood to leave.

Kit reached over and put her hand on his arm. She'd thought of one last question.

"Captain Tremblay?"

"Please, call me Michel."

"Sorry. Michel, then, what was my grandfather's relationship with your blonde secretary like?"

She felt him stiffen and immediately removed her hand from his arm as he asked, "Annie?"

"Yes, Annie." She looked up at him.

"I'm not sure I understand what you mean." He remained standing, his tone was neutral.

"I mean, do you think there might've been any—" Kit felt

embarrassed on her grandfather's behalf, but pressed on, "any romantic feelings on his part towards her?"

"Who can say? Annie was friendly with all the men; your grandfather might've mistaken this for something more."

Kit's heart sank.

Captain Tremblay put his hand on her shoulder. "As pleasant as this interrogation has been, I am late for another meeting."

"I'm so sorry." Kit stood and extended her hand. "Thank you for coming, Michel."

He took her hand and kissed it. His lips were cool and firm, and Kit thought he held her hand a little longer than need be before releasing it. He shrugged into his overcoat, retrieved his cane and was about to leave.

"Um, Michel, when do you think you'll have the information about the wheelchair?"

He smiled. "Will tomorrow be soon enough for you?"

"Of course, that would be great!" Kit thought a moment then added, "Could you please not call me at my sister's house? I don't want her to know my concerns, or that we've met. It would only worry her more."

"Then, shall we meet back here tomorrow at the same time? I should have the information for you by then."

"I'll be here. Thanks again, Michel."

"I hope our next coffee will be more enjoyable for you." She watched him limp to the counter where he paid his bill and exited.

Kit saw him through the large window as he made his way down the street; he walks as if he owns the world, she thought, and smiled.

"He likes you, *je pense*," said the waitress with a sly smile as she came to clear their dishes. Startled by her boldness, the woman's words sent a small jolt of enjoyment through Kit's body. When she grabbed a two dollar bill from her jeans pocket, the waitress shook her head, no, and said, "*Il a déjàs payé*—He's already paid."

Kit walked back up the street towards her sister's house, her steps jaunty. The grey sky now seemed muted and mysterious instead of dull and depressing as it had before her meeting with Michel. An agreeable agitation coursed through her body. It must be due to the caffeine from the *Coffea arabicus*—certainly not Michel's touch or the waitress's comments. She tried to slot the information and events of the afternoon into tidy categories, but they were as mischievous as Michel's smile and as elusive as Paul's attentions. She decided to dump them all into the "uncertain origins" box for future consideration and ruminated over how crowded that particular, personal and paradoxical taxonomic category was getting these days.

Sondra closed the door behind her and stood just inside Kit's bedroom eyeing her sister who was scrambling to sit up. The book Kit had been reading thudded to the floor.

"What is the matter with you, you've been somewhere else all evening, you've barely eaten a thing. Are you alright?"

Kit was now sitting cross-legged; elbows on her knees, she rested her face in both hands. "I'm just tired, I guess."

Enthusiasm damping her reproach, Sondra sat next to her on the bed. "I've got so much to tell you, Kit! I couldn't wait for you to get home. You were late and I almost went mad with impatience and worry! I couldn't bear to lose you to a bomb, Kit, and that's where my mind goes every time someone is a bit late getting home."

"OK, OK, calm down, I'm fine, just feeling a bit strange. Coming home to Montréal always has this impact on me. Besides my birthday's coming up, and, turning twenty-six, well I'm now on the downward side of my twenties. It's a slippery slope, Sonn; I'll be thirty before you know it." Kit shifted to sit on the edge of her bed, one leg crossed over the other.

"Oh, Kit, I'd almost forgotten. It's the day after tomorrow, right? We'll have a party or something. The kids will love it!"

"Don't do anything too over the top. I'm not sure I want to advertise my age that much."

Sondra snorted her amusement, and saw Kit relax a little. "Don't you want me to tell you what I found out today?" Sondra asked, elbowing her sister for emphasis.

"Ow, that hurt, Sonn," Kit replied, sitting up a little straighter but without sufficient enthusiasm in Sondra's opinion.

"Well, almost nothing and a lot!" Sondra bragged. She was pleased to see that Kit's curiosity was piqued. "Listen, Kit, I found Robert Brault's wife, or rather ex-wife, in the phone book and called her. She was pretty wary until I told her who I was and that I wanted to talk to her about Robert's death."

Sondra laid the whole matter out for Kit, detailing the Braults' marital unhappiness and eventual divorce. Louisa and Robert Brault had remained on amicable terms; she had loved him but in the end had put her foot down: "Bobbie, it's the booze or me." He'd chosen the booze and Senneville Veterans Lodge. They had one son who had moved to Edmonton, married and was raising his own family so had little time to be concerned with his aging parents, besides regular filial phone calls.

Louisa had known Bobbie would die before her, probably of cirrhosis, but had been surprised that a heart attack had taken him so soon. He hadn't seemed at all ill the last time she'd seen him. He had called her a few days before his death.

"And this is where it gets interesting, are you paying attention, Kit?" Sondra poked Kit again.

"Ouch, cut that out," Kit said, rubbing her shoulder.

"Then quit swinging your leg and listen!"

"I do that when I'm concentrating."

"No, you don't, you do it when you're bored or nervous."

"Same dif," Kit retorted and ducked away from Sondra's punch.

Sondra stood and stomped her foot. "Kit, this is serious. Come on, quit fooling around."

"Alright, alright, don't throw a tantrum. I'll try, but honestly, Sonn, I am tired."

Sondra yielded to Kit's words and let herself be pulled back down on the bed beside her sister.

She continued. "The call came the day after Gramps' funeral. Louisa said Robert seemed confused and had been drinking. He wanted her to come get him and take him back to her house. He wanted to get away from the lodge for a while. And get this, Kit, Louisa thought he sounded frightened, but when she asked him if he was scared about something, he brushed her off.

"Anyway, Robert did sometimes visit her at her home, but she didn't want him around when he'd been drinking, so held him off and said she'd talk to him again soon. The next thing she knew he was dead."

They sat together for a few moments. Sondra took Kit's hand and tried to shake off the passing sadness of this stranger's death.

"Were there any details about the death?" Sondra was gratified that Kit was engaged enough to ask questions.

"No, he'd died during a walk on the grounds, apparently of a heart attack, not unusual in drinkers. One of the grounds keepers had found him. Do you want to guess which one?"

"Not Creepy Serge."

"Yes, indeed, your favourite."

"My favourite what?"

"Suspect, of course."

"Oh, right." At this Kit jumped up and started pacing the room, bent over in a Groucho Marx imitation, flicking ashes off an invisible cigar as she went. "But why not Claude the chef, or Roger, Gramps' political rival, or that awful 'Dragon Lady' of a receptionist who replaced Annie, or Annie herself, or Private McIntryre or poor Henri Lalonde or—am I forgetting anyone?" Kit came to a stop in front of her, hands on hips. "So?"

Sondra crossed her arms and struggled to glare at Kit, trying hard not to be amused by her sister's shenanigans. She failed, and with a wry smile, asked "So, Kit, can't you see why my suspicions are heightened by all this?"

"A little, but I'm not sure that it isn't just what it seems to be," said Kit, plopping down on the bed.

"Which is?" Sondra hated it when Kit trivialized her thoughts.

Kit paused then said, "Some fellow who has spent a life of dissipation finally dies of it." She turned to Sondra and shrugged as though that were the end of it.

"Yeah, but, Kit, he died while on a walk." Sondra wanted to win Kit with reason.

"Lots of people with heart problems die during exertion, what's the big deal?"

"Kit . . . come on, don't play dumb." Sondra crossed her arms over her chest.

"Oh, I get it; you think there is a connection between Gramps dying in a freak accident while out in his wheelchair and Robert Brault dying of a heart attack while on a walk. Sondra, it is illogical to think they both have the same cause because they both happened out of doors."

"Poop on you and your logic! I look at the whole picture, smarty pants. The Gestalt of it all."

"Bless you! Or should I say *gesundheit!*"

"Kit, I'm serious."

"I can see that. Still, try to stay a little objective, won't you, Sonn?"

"Forget objectivity! That's what you're good at, Kit. Not me, I'm all for intuition and subjectivity."

"Tell me something I don't know."

"If it were only that he died on a walk outdoors, I wouldn't be so suspicious of it, Kit. But when you add in his fear, well that makes me sit up and take notice. Why the fear ahead of time? What did he have to be afraid of?"

"Maybe the doctor had given him bad news about his health."

"Or, maybe he knew something. Maybe it was the same something Gramps knew! Maybe there is an FLQ cell at the Lodge and Gramps told him about it; in fact I'm beginning to suspect that this is the case."

Sondra paused to let Kit digest this before continuing. "And, Louisa said that after he hung up that last time, she thought she heard a second 'click,' as though someone had been listening on an extension!"

Sondra was gratified to see the flippancy drain out of Kit's expression. "Kit, what if Gramps had told him something before he died, something to do with the reason Gramps was killed, and whoever did it, was watching Robert, listened in on the conversation and decided to get rid of Robert Brault before he could tell anyone else about it. Some drugs can mimic a heart attack. I think some heart medications, if given in an overdose could induce a heart attack."

"Dad would know." Kit said in a leaden voice.

Sondra stared at Kit. "You're right! I'll have to ask him about it." Sondra pulled a pencil and the now well-worn composition book out of her apron pocket. She looked into space, tapping the pencil against her bottom teeth, and then wrote for a few moments.

"What on earth are you writing, Sondra?"

"Oh, I've got to keep track of the ideas and evidence that we've collected so I don't forget the details."

"A regular Nancy Drew, I see!" teased Kit.

"Humph! Madame Holmes to you, my dear Watson!"

"Oh, yeah?" Laughing, Kit threw a pillow at Sondra. "Take

that 'Holmsie'!"

Sondra returned fire and soon they were both on the bed laughing while trying to get the upper hand. The conflict ended as quickly as it had started, and they both fell back on the bed, breathless, flushed and laughing.

Not more than a minute later, Sondra rolled over and looked at Kit. "Come on, Kit, aren't you the least bit curious about the rest of my investigating?"

Kit groaned and sat up. "Alright, but I am getting tired, Sonn."

Sondra grinned. "OK, OK, but there's still a lot to tell." She sat back against the head board, legs pulled up to her chest. "I called the 'Dragon Lady' and asked to get Claude's and Serge's home addresses and Annie's forwarding address."

"And?"

Sondra raised her eyebrows, put her hands behind her head and smiled, like she imagined the Cheshire Cat in Alice in Wonderland had. "It did take some finesse, I must admit, to get the 'Dragon Lady' to cough up the information. She was hesitant at first to give it out to just anyone."

"And...how did you convince her?"

"I played up the fact that we were pals with the good Captain; in fact I asked her to thank him for lunch the other day."

"You did?"

"Oh yes."

"Still, what reason did you give for needing that information?"

Sondra leaned forward. "Honest, Kit, I took your advice, I said nothing at all about murder or anything. I agree we have to play our cards close to the chest until we get enough evidence to bring in the police."

"But what reason did you give for wanting Annie's and Claude's and Serge's information?"

"Oh, I told her Gramps had mentioned them in his will and

that there was a small gift for each of them."

Sondra loved the look of astonished admiration on her sister's face. "Good grief, Sonn, what an adept liar you are!"

"Well, we all have our little gifts; besides, anything in the pursuit of justice." Sondra blew on her fingernails and made as if to buff them on her sweater.

"It's a good thing the 'Dragon Lady' is so new or she'd have smelled a rat right away. Imagine, Gramps giving Serge anything besides a dirty look!" Kit guffawed.

Sondra nodded, smiling, and consulted her composition book. "Well, she gave me the information I asked for. Get this—Serge's last name is Schultz, spelt like Charles Schultz—like 'Peanuts', Charlie Brown, get it?"

"Yeah, yeah, you were losing me there for a moment."

"So, Schultz lives in Sainte-Anne-de-Bellevue, Claude Sequin lives on the Plateau, not far from here, should be easy to find both of them. In fact, get this, Kit; I called Claude's home and guess who answered?"

"Santa Claus?"

Sondra kicked at Kit with her slipper and was rewarded with a baleful look.

"Ha, serves you right—pay attention!"

"OK, OK, I give up, who did answer the phone?"

"Mr. 'He's-such-a-tease'," Sondra replied in a sing-song voice.

"Not the orderly from the hospital!" Kit snapped her fingers a few times, her standard gesture when trying to remember something. "André?"

"It sounded just like him," Sondra was gleeful, relishing in the triumph of knowing something her older sister did not. It still gave her a thrill.

"So, they're roommates, what's the big deal."

"I think they may be a little more than that, Kit."

"Oh?"

"Well, he didn't sound so pleased to hear who I was or

that I wanted to talk to Claude. A little more involved than someone who is 'just a friend' ought to be. Don't you think?"

"Maybe, what did Claude have to say for himself?"

"He wasn't very pleased to talk to me either, but I was amazingly persistent, if I do say so myself. Anyway, he agreed to meet me next Tuesday afternoon."

"How did you get him to agree to that?"

"Oh, I told him Gramps had left him something in his will."

"You lie like a rug."

"Yeah, well, I had to say something that would get him to see me. I explained that Gramps wanted to make amends for giving him such a hard time about his cooking." Sonn laughed to see Kit's eyebrows rise in surprise.

"And he believed you?"

"Don't know for sure, but he's definitely curious." Sondra tapped the end of her pencil against her teeth. "I want to see his face when I ask him my very pointed questions."

"Like, 'Hello, thank you for seeing me, did you kill my grandfather?'"

"Give me a little credit, Kit, I'll warm up to that gradually."

"Sure, sure you will." Kit grinned and ducked as Sondra whipped a pillow at her. "So, is that all, She-lock?"

"Of course not," Sondra couldn't help smiling. "When I asked about Annie's forwarding address, the 'Dragon Lady' didn't have it which is surprising, don't you think? Don't you have to submit paperwork to the government or something when someone quits? Anyway, I asked if she would ask Captain Nosy Parker about it."

"When did you call?"

Sondra looked at her, a little surprised by Kit's question, and said, "I called first thing this morning, before I tried to track down Mrs. Brault. I asked the 'D.L.' about her too, although to no avail. Thankfully, Louisa's name was in the phone book, and she still lives in the area."

"Have you heard back yet about Annie?"

"No, not exactly—the 'D.L.' did cough up her last name—Desrocher—but the Captain hasn't gotten back to me yet." Sondra noticed Kit sitting up straight. "I'm glad to see you are finally taking me seriously."

"I always take you seriously, Sonn."

"Since when?"

"Since forever, kid, since forever," Kit winked at her.

Sondra smiled. "You haven't heard the best part yet."

"Oh?"

"Indeed. The 'D.L.' actually put me through so I got to speak with Roger Dufresne."

"About what, what did you say to him?"

"Well, I told him I'd like to come out to meet with him because I had some questions about Gramps' death."

"Now that's *chutzpa!* I didn't know you had it in you, Sonn!"

"Well, he didn't sound too happy about the idea, but he agreed. I played up the grieving granddaughter bit, and I asked him very nicely in French. He's definitely a separatist."

"Really?"

"Well, why else end the conversation with '*Vive le Québec libre!*' before slamming down the receiver."

Kit snorted and shook her head. "That's going to be some conversation, Sonn. When are you going in to meet him?"

"He said he's available Wednesday or Thursday next week. Honestly, Kit, I'm a little nervous. He might be Gramps' murderer."

"Do you want me to come with you?" Kit always was her defender.

"Maybe, I don't know yet. But I've decided not to let him know exactly when I'm coming, just show up Wednesday. That way, he can't plan any kind of surprise attack. Kit, maybe you were right about an FLQ cell, as improbable as it seems. Those old guys can be pretty fierce about things."

"Gramps sure was," added Kit. Sondra wondered if her

sister's incredulity was finally wavering.

"Anyway, the threat of exposure is more of a motive for murder than losing an election. And I'm thinking that the money and papers we saw with Dufresne and Serge in that tavern could be a part of it all."

"So, that leaves the chef off the hook?"

Sondra shrugged. "Maybe, maybe not. Claude and André might turn out to be the FLQ murderers; after all André would have access to hospital drug supplies which he could have used on Brault and McIntyre." Sondra tapped the pencil on her teeth then put it behind one ear. "Really, Dufresne, Claude or Serge could've murdered Gramps since all three were military-trained, so knew how to kill by hand." Sondra glanced at Kit who was watching her intently, brow furrowed.

"So are you proposing, one killer or two—one for Gramps and one for Robert Brault?"

"It could be two separate killers with totally different motives, or it could be two separate killers with the same motive, or it could be one killer. Or maybe, they're all in—"

Kit chimed in with Sondra, "—an FLQ cell."

"I'm getting a headache just trying to follow your reasoning." Kit put her hand on Sondra's arm. "Really, Sonn, we should be looking for the simplest explanation, that's what makes a good theory, not the most complex."

Sondra pulled her arm away. "Yes and your simplest explanation is: none of this is connected, Gramps' death was accidental and his friends' death and illness are both due to natural causes." Kit nodded as Sondra stood up, faced her sister, and pointing a finger at her, said, "But you are forgetting the evidence suggesting otherwise."

"Your dream?" Kit asked.

"Yes, but not just that, Kit." Listing each item on a finger she went on. "Why weren't there any skid marks on the road? Who left the cigarette butts at the top of the driveway and when? Why was Brault so afraid before he died? What about the click just before Louisa hung up? Why did Annie suddenly quit her job? And why is there so much hostility towards Gramps?" Finishing she put her hands on her hips and looked at Kit who was staring into space, foot swinging back and forth.

Kit sighed and said, "None of this amounts to proof, Sonn, but I get why it increases your suspicions." With a tired smile she added, "I guess that means we'll just have to keep 'investigating'."

Kit's reply softened Sondra and she relaxed a little. "Okay, Okay. Guess I can't expect you to jump on board all at once." Relenting a little more, she added, "And you do look tired."

"Well, I am. Now, shoo, I've got to get some beauty sleep. Very important for us aging divas, dontcha know?" Kit stretched and yawned.

Sondra bent over her sister's head, parting the strands. "I don't see any grey yet, just a few white hairs." She turned and made a mad dash, closing the door behind her just as the pillow hit it.

Evidence of Uncertain Origin

Montréal
Friday, October 17, 1969

*H*e had found the address easily enough, circled the block and chosen a spot to park and watch; across the street a few houses from the flat and far enough away that he could not be seen from their front windows. The morning was damp and grey. He shifted; he was stiff and his feet were cold. He blew on his hands and checked his watch: 10:06. He'd been there since 8:45.

He cursed himself for not bringing a scarf or a flask or his damned gloves for that matter. He lit his last cigarette. He crushed the package, rolled down the window and tossed it out. No one had come or gone since 9:03 when a tall slouching man had dashed down the wrought iron stairs and crossed the street fifty metres in front of him, briefcase swinging with his hurried stride, head down, unseeing.

He'd watched the man lope towards avenue du Parc, probably trying to catch a bus. What a fool, he'd thought, here's this guy going about his tedious daily routines, like a rat in a maze, oblivious to the danger a few feet away from him. But then most people were stupid. Couldn't even see what was good for them. He'd comforted himself with the thought that it would all be changing soon.

He had made up his mind to leave his post once he'd finished his smoke. His comrade would have to understand that he too had other, important things to do with his time. They'd argued about it and although he was the logical choice for this job, he resented it. After all it wasn't his 'clever plan' that had necessitated this extreme measure.

He'd flicked the stub out the window, was hashing out his

rationalizations and had turned the car back on, when he saw them. The red headed one slammed the front door behind her and was heading down the stairs; a small child was with her. He didn't like that at all.

He gritted his teeth, like it or not, sacrifices had to be made for the greater good: to create a better world for everyone, sometimes the few had to be forfeited. As the article in La Victoire had stated, "we tried to make people understand."

"It's not my fault," he growled under his breath, his anger now shifted from his comrade to the English stubbornness that was forcing his hand.

He waited until they were a block ahead then put the car in gear and pulled out to follow them.

Kit spent the morning before her twenty-sixth birthday indoors. The overcast sky echoed the grey mood she'd woken up to, her elation of yesterday chased away by her conversation with Sondra the night before. When Kit started to think about Gramps' death those multi-coloured, spinning tops just kept bumping into each other: the possibility Gramps had committed suicide by proxy, the confusing assortment of accumulating facts, the police's assertion of accidental death, Sondra's conviction he had been murdered, her theories about it. Layered over it all was her own malaise, Paul's distance and Michel's attentions. Kit just had to stop thinking about it or end up courting another headache.

Unfortunately, sleeping in after a restless night was impossible on a busy Friday morning. She had tried, but Sondra's breakfast preparations meant pots and pans crashing, yelled commands for everyone to hurry up and house-shaking stomps of many feet rushing about. Kit had staggered, largely unnoticed, out of her room and sat hunched over her coffee at the kitchen table, doing her best to stay out of the way. At least it made avoiding discussion with the other humans in the household easy.

Kit had to stop watching Sondra bustle cheerfully around the kitchen. Her sister's energy exacerbated her own exhaustion. Well, one of us had a good night's sleep she thought dolefully and sipped her coffee.

By the time Sonn had gotten Deirdre ready to join Alexa and her mother for their walk to school, Kit had finished her coffee and was leaning against the front room door frame observing Sonn struggle with a wiggly Max. Just getting him into his coat and boots was a major accomplishment. They were heading out for brunch with Jean-Pierre's mother. Later on they'd pick up Deirdre from school and then go shopping. Their secretive little titters and furtive sidelong glances over breakfast let Kit know that they would be looking for her birthday present.

A couple of hugs and waves later, Kit went to stand at the window in the children's room, pulling back the curtain to watch the two walk down the street. Kit shook her head; Maxie made her smile in spite of her dark mood. Twice before they turned the corner and disappeared from view Sondra had had to retrieve him: first from climbing a neighbour's steps and then from chasing a cat into the street.

Kit was stepping away from the window when she noticed a dark sedan passing by. She shrugged, let the curtain fall and went downstairs to check the mail.

Only bills and fliers littered the floor behind the door, nothing for her, no birthday card from Paul. She sat for a long time on the inside stairs, debating. Finally, she trudged up the flight of steps and to the phone.

Kit tensed up as the tinny ring brought the image of her cramped little apartment to mind: the kitchen with its black and white checked linoleum, mismatched chairs, Formica-topped table and the sad geranium pressing its spindly flowers against the small gritty window that looked out onto a brick wall. She let it ring twenty times before she hung up.

She sat in the silence and stared at the sink. The lonely sound of those rings echoed the confused emptiness inside. What did you expect, Dummy, she thought, he's likely in class or at the hospital or having coffee with that cute blonde.

A shadowy smallness, like the beginning of her own personal Dark Ages, was sucking all the good and happy things out of her. Already she felt like a hollow husk of a person. Kit sighed, stood, gritted her teeth and began cleaning the flat. The only antidote to depression she had available.

"Max, leave that poor cat alone," Sondra snagged him by the collar of his coat as he was about to pounce on the large orange tabby trying to hide itself under a thorny hedge.

"Titty, I want titty."

"Come on, dear, we've got to go see *Grandmaman*. She's promised *tourtière*, Maxie." She succeeded in drawing his attention away from the cat for a few minutes. Why on earth the huge orange tabby had followed them despite Max's attempts to strangle it made Sondra shake her head at the mysteries of cat behaviour. They had come to an intersection and would need to turn onto the cross street. Sondra herded Max toward the right, preparing to step off the curb, cross the street and continue on their way.

"Now, hold my hand, Max. What do we do before we cross the street, Max? We stop and look both ways." She saw that Max wasn't paying attention. He was more intent on the orange cat who had emerged from its hiding place and was sitting on the sidewalk beside them cleaning its whiskers. Oh well, she thought.

A dark sedan slid to a stop and seemed to be waiting for them to cross in front of it. Had the car been behind them all along, Sondra wondered? She'd been so busy restraining Max she had not noticed it before.

The car was signaling a left turn. So Sondra waited for the car to proceed since it would have to cut directly in front of them. The windows were foggy, but she could see the outline of a man at the wheel. She nodded at him to go, but the driver shook his head and gestured for her to cross the street first.

She waved back and smiled. "Let's go, the car's waiting for us." With that, Sondra, Max in tow, stepped off the curb.

They got to the middle of the street, and were even with the driver's side headlight when the driver gunned the motor. At the same time Max yelled, "Titty!" and yanked Sondra back towards the sidewalk so hard that it threw her off balance. She stepped backwards to regain her equilibrium but tripped and fell, pulling them both out of the car's path as it roared by.

Sondra scrambled to her feet, dragging Max to the curb. Stunned, she didn't think to look for the car's plates. All she could do was stare at the dark sedan as it zoomed to the end of the block, turned right and disappeared out of sight. She collapsed on the curb and hugged Max close to her, kissing his head and shaking. The large orange tabby paced back and forth beside them, tail held high.

"Thank you," Sondra said under her breath to the cat, her voice quavered and she squeezed Max tighter. She closed her eyes. "And thank You too, Whoever You are."

By the time she had collected herself enough to get up and head off to her mother-in-law's house Sondra was downright cheerful: nothing like a close call with death to make the rest of your life seem amazing. It wasn't until later that she started to put two and two together.

Kit put away the mop and pail; the clock on the stove, always at least five minutes fast, displayed 12:13. The cleaning proved but a brief respite from the black mood she was falling into. Baths usually soothed her, so she ran one and eased herself into the ancient, claw-footed tub. The water's heat sent a pleasurable tremor through her body as she submerged. Vapour rose around her; she watched it condense on the mirror, collecting until water droplets ran like tears down the chill surface.

Kit lay there for a long time, letting the warmth wash away all her dire thoughts, almost wishing that this comfortable oblivion could go on forever. If this was what death offered—a permanent letting go of all that burdened her, her losses, uncertainties, responsibilities, guilt—then she figured Gramps now had the better deal. The water began to cool and, sighing, Kit clambered gracelessly over the tub's high sides.

"Not quite Aphrodite on the half shell," Kit said to herself, smiling grimly. Her wet foot slipped on the tile and she caught herself by grabbing the tub's curved edge. So much for courting death, she thought, guess I'm still pretty attached to this life whether I like it or not. Kit shivered as she toweled off, then stalked into her room to find some warm clothes.

At two p.m. Kit stood at the top of the stairs by the coat rack. She had dressed in a pair of black jeans, topped by a black turtleneck sweater accented by a green vest with the Flanagan crest. She had scrounged it from her grandfather before he moved into the Lodge. Kit waited there for what seemed like a very long time, teetering on the edge of something. Waiting, for what she did not know, Paul's phone call, maybe, divine revelation, hardly.

Finally, Kit put on her coat and boots, pulled on her mittens and a hat, opened the door and stepped out into the dim, chill afternoon. She bent her head into the wind as she navigated the wrought iron staircase.

Approaching the café, Kit could see that Michel was seated beside the window at what she thought of as "his table." Kit stood for a minute and watched him. He had slung his fur-lined trench coat on the chair beside him, his long legs stretched under the table, while he leaned back in the chair, staring at the door and smoking.

He's waiting for me, she thought, and a *frisson* of something vaguely sexual passed through her. Get a grip, you dummy: go in, get the information you need and leave. With that she strode to the door, pushed it open and entered the café.

"Ah, Katherine." He pulled himself up to stand leaning on his cane and made a mock formal bow to her. She felt her face heat up in spite of herself, looked around to see if anyone had noticed and caught the eye of the waitress beaming at her from behind the cash register. She slumped, trying to reduce her visibility, and almost slunk over to sit in the chair unoccupied by his coat.

"I see I have made you embarrassed. You English are so easily flustered, yet rarely offended. We French on the other hand have the *sang-froid* but will shoot you down if you dare to sniffle at us! With us it is always the honour!" He said this in such a self-deprecating way that it made Kit smile at him. She relaxed, determined to enjoy the moment no matter what. After the day she had had, she deserved it.

"No books today?"

"No."

"You have perhaps read them all already?" He was teasing her.

"No." How silly to be answering in monosyllables, but Kit couldn't think of anything witty to say.

He eyed her and said, "Forgive me, I have forgotten myself. You must be chilled; a *café latte* will warm you up." He turned and waved to the waitress placing the order in a gay and lively manner.

Kit watched him. There was something so graceful in his movements, languid and economical at the same time. She averted her eyes to study the posters plastered on the bricks of the café's back wall before he could catch her watching him. There were the usual psychedelic advertisements for local rock bands, a few sleazy ones with nearly naked girls leering seductively, and one promoting an anti-Dominion day rally. She caught him out of the corner of her eye looking to see what she was regarding.

"So, you are interested in our local political concerns?"

"Michel, they are mine as well. Remember? I was born here too."

"*Peut-être,* but what do you actually know about the situation here? Haven't you been living in Ontario?"

Kit looked at him. "How do you know where I live?"

Michel shrugged. "I make it my business to know who visits my Lodge."

"*Your* Lodge?"

"Yes, *my* Lodge." Fierceness flitted across his face. He reached out for her hand. "You see, I take my responsibilities very seriously. I need to know everything that goes on. These are dangerous times, my little Anglophone friend."

Kit pulled her hand away, alarmed and curious. "Are you referring to the FLQ attacks or something else? Do you think the Lodge will be bombed?"

"Ha! No need to worry about the Lodge, there will be no attacks or fires there while I'm in charge, that's for sure."

The image of the burnt down hospital in Sainte-Anne-de-Bellevue rose in her mind. "How can you be so confident? It all seems so unpredictable, so random. Even the new hospital was burned down. And we almost were killed by a letter bomb over the weekend!"

"*Non!*"

His shock sounded exaggerated, disbelieving almost sarcastic. "Yes, we were." She couldn't help sounding defensive and offended.

"I guess it was a matter of being in the wrong place at the

wrong time." Michel regarded her, eyebrows raised.

"Well, in our case, it was the right place at the wrong time."

At this, Michel smiled. "True."

"So, what can you tell this little Anglophone girl from Ontario about the political situation, oh great and wise uncle Michel." Kit decided that two could play at the sarcasm game.

"That depends on what you want to know," he said, voice as smooth as chocolate.

"Well, I don't understand the FLQ's thinking. I mean, what's the point of bombing stuff, for one thing, and why aim to kill people? How will that advance the cause of separatism? Won't that just alienate people?"

"Depends on who you want to alienate, doesn't it?" He leaned back in his chair and blew a smoke ring into the air.

Kit was on a roll. "And who are these people anyway, these *felquistes*?"

"People just like you and me, I suppose," Michel replied, sitting forward. Kit saw him watching her. "Whatever your opinion of them is, they are, I think, people who see themselves as heroes, who are willing to sacrifice for the greater good of the workers."

"Well, I grew up working class, Catholic and Irish, which isn't so different than growing up working class, Catholic and French-Canadian. Especially when the industrialists are almost all English and Scottish Protestants, and those who own the land are feudalistic French aristocrats. Neither group shows much sympathy for workers. But all the same, I wouldn't want to kill them."

"Maybe not, but maybe you don't know how bad it really is for some of them. Try reading Vallières *Les Nègres blancs d'Amérique*; it might give you some insight into who the good guys and bad guys really are."

"You're sounding like a separatist, Michel." Kit looked at him directly. "So, are you a member of the *Parti Québécois*?"

Michel laughed. "Not yet, Katherine, not yet." He reached over, pulled her hand to his lips, a glint in his eyes.

"Cut that out!" She pulled her hand back, though she'd allowed it to linger long enough that he must know she liked his touch. He intrigued her, in spite of herself.

Damn! I'm crummy at this stuff, Kit thought. She glanced at him and saw his expression of feigned offence and amused *savoir faire*. Kit felt she was way out of her league with Michel.

She was rescued by the arrival of their coffees. The waitress brought two lattes and left a plate of chocolate croissants.

"How did you know? I love these," she exclaimed. The flakey rich pastries were one of the things she often yearned for in her dingy little kitchen in Hamilton, along with bagels, smoked meat and friends.

It seemed that she was acquiring at least two out of the four, she thought as she stared into the broad white ceramic cup cradled in her hands. She sipped the hot bitter liquid, grateful for its comforting heat. Smiling, she looked up at Michel and replaced the cup in its saucer.

He smiled back at her, then reached over and, before she could flinch away from him, swiped the bit of foam that clung to her upper lip and sucked it off his finger.

She started and he laughed. Kit put down her cup and sat up straight. She had to cut the crap and get to the point. "So, what did you find out about my grandfather's wheelchair?"

"Ah, so much for the enjoyment of the moment, Michel, you have been put in your place."

"I didn't mean to be harsh about it, but that is why we are meeting. Isn't it?"

"Yes, so it is." He sounded wistful, which pleased Kit. "I checked our records and found that the wheelchair was due in for servicing the week after your grandfather's death." He looked at her and shrugged. "They are serviced every six months, so something could have gone wrong with the brakes, I suppose."

Kit grasped at this information with relief. "Michel, what company services your wheelchairs?"

"You do not trust me?" Michel asked, tilting his head and affecting a grimace that Kit could not interpret.

"Why should I?" She retorted without thinking.

"Good point, although I had hoped I'd won your confidence." He smiled and sipped his coffee.

Embarrassed by her apparent suspicions, she said, "I'm sorry if it seems I doubt you."

"Well, to prove my trustworthiness I will tell you the name of the company: 'Réparations Robinson & Le Blanc.'"

Kit frowned as she wrote it down on her napkin then shoved it into her purse. "Thank you, Michel. Really, it's for my sister; she'll ask me what company for sure, when and if I tell her about this."

He leaned back in his chair and watched her, his smile a little crooked. "And why should this detail interest your sister?"

"It will take a lot to convince her Gramps wasn't murdered."

"She still believes this?"

"Yes, wholeheartedly."

Michel sat back up and rolled a cigarette between his thumb and middle finger. "And why would she believe such a thing? It seems preposterous, ridiculous to me."

Kit wished she'd said nothing about Sondra to this man; she felt disloyal and, besides, it wasn't any of his business. She sprang to Sondra's defense and blurted out, "Well, it isn't that ridiculous! I mean what if there were an FLQ cell operating at the Lodge and my grandfather found out about it. That would be reason enough to murder him, wouldn't it?" She crossed her arms and glared at Michel.

"You don't really believe that, do you?"

Of course she didn't, but she was damned if she'd give him

the satisfaction of admitting it. Kit squirmed in her chair and looked up at him unhappily. "I'd rather not talk about my sister, if you don't mind. She's had a lot to deal with in her life and she is still very upset about our grandfather's death."

"And you, how are you feeling about his death?" He reached over to touch her hand.

Kit withdrew her hand from his in confusion. "I'd better go, Michel," but she didn't stand.

"I don't think you want to, Katherine, do you?" He took a puff on his cigarette and watched her.

The truth was Kit didn't want to leave the warm closeness of the café and his company. She looked at the crumpled napkin in her lap, hoping to hide the colour that must be flooding her cheeks.

"I apologize for asking about your sister and grandfather, I was looking for conversation that is all. I did not realize it was such a, *comment-tu-dis?* 'sore spot' for you."

"That's OK, Michel, I didn't mean to overreact," and here, Kit prevaricated. "I'm just a bit on edge."

"Ah, the famous feminine nerves!"

Kit sent him a glare at which he laughed. Kit relaxed a little, now that she had the information she'd come for, she could maybe allow herself to enjoy this game of flirtation. Just for a few more minutes.

"So, now, tell me your tale of woe."

"You're being condescending."

"Well, yes, but you are being mysterious."

"Perhaps."

"So, of course my curiosity is piqued."

"Well," Kit shifted in her chair. "I haven't told my sister about our meetings, so . . . " She hoped she looked sheepish as she shrugged and looked into his face.

He nodded at her, encouraging her to go on. She wasn't sure she wanted to tell him anything more, wasn't sure she should. She began to perspire and her heart raced. She looked at the dark and handsome man sitting across from her. She felt weak and a bit breathless.

"I'm sick and tired of taking care of everyone else!" Her words surprised and shamed her. Were they betraying Sondra, Paul, her grandfather, everyone? She shot a horrified look at Michel who moved his chair closer to her. She could smell him: a faint muskiness mixed with Gauloises.

As though he had read her mind, he finished her thought saying, "And no one to take care of *ma pauvre* Katherine." At this her eyes welled with tears, and worried she might start sobbing, she held her breath. The tears fell, but silently at least. All she needed was to embarrass herself completely by what Granny Win would certainly have called self-pity.

Michel said nothing, but put his arm across her shoulders and patted her. She allowed herself to enjoy the sensation and was surprised that it actually did comfort her. She let out her breath in a long sigh. Michel took a napkin and wiped the tears off her face handing it to her so she could blow her nose. He removed his arm and shifted the chair so that he could face her.

"I must look awful. Paul says I look terrible when I cry." A far distant part of Kit observed this confession with disapproval.

"And Paul is the husband?" Kit nodded. "And does this Paul give you much occasion for tears?" Again Kit nodded. "*Quel monstre!*" Michel intoned in a gentle, teasing way. She smiled at him, relieved.

He stroked her cheek, pushing a lock of her hair neatly behind her ear; this time she did not pull back from his touch. Instead, to her surprise she said, "Maybe I'm feeling sorry for myself because it's my birthday tomorrow, Michel."

"Then we must celebrate!"

She stiffened a bit. "Sondra and the kids will be expecting me."

"For the whole day?"

"No, probably not."

"Then let me take you for a drive up north. The trees are still beautiful, and I know a place we can have a meal."

Kit, as though observing this exchange from a great distance, heard herself say, "I'd like that."

"*Merveilleux!*"

They arranged for her to meet him in front of the café at ten the next morning. They'd be back by four in the afternoon, in time for any evening celebrations.

Elated, Kit walked back to Sondra's. She climbed the stairs to the flat and let herself in at the door. She could hear voices above her and swore to herself when she recognized her father's loud baritone in the mix. She closed the door quietly, and leaned against it for a moment. Like a diver rising to the surface from a dark and mysterious seabed she feared an emotional version of "the bends" should she ascend too rapidly to the bright joviality of her family's conversation.

"Is that you, Kit?" Sondra called out.

"Yes, just a minute, I'm coming." Kit hoped her breathlessness wasn't too obvious; she didn't want her sister to find her in this state alone: it would be all too easy to blurt out everything. Kit clumped up the stairs, wanting to buy time, but Sondra bounced into view before she could get to the top. Sonn ran half way down the stairs and hugged her.

"At last, you've come! I was beginning to worry and we've all been waiting for you. Dad's dropped by a day early; he and Marie-Claire have tickets for "*Les Grands Ballets Canadiens*" tomorrow so won't be able to come to your party." They'd reached the top of the stairs and Sondra leaned against the wall watching while Kit removed her outer wear.

Kit threw a disgusted look at Sondra.

Sondra hissed at her, "Stop it, Kit. He is trying, so you'd better be nice to him."

"Or else what? You'll spank me? Since when are you on his side, Sondra?" Kit hissed right back.

Evidence of Uncertain Origin

"Since Gramps died, Kit, he's tried to be more, more, involved, I guess."

"Well, I don't give a shit," Kit stood with her arms folded, glad that she could focus on her intense dislike of her father, rather than her intense attraction to Michel. "It's too little too late and as far as I'm concerned, he should've . . ." She was interrupted by Sondra who stepped right up to her and pushed her finger against Kit's chest.

"Look, Kit," Sondra whispered, "you may want to hold a grudge, but I've got the children to think about. They like him, and they adore Marie-Claire, and I want him to be involved in their lives. Maybe he can do them some good, so please, for the kids' sake, pretend you like him. A little bit?" Sondra's tone gentled and she placed her hand on Kit's arm.

Kit relented somewhat. "OK, I'll be good, for the kids."

"Thanks, Kit."

Before they could turn to join the others, Kit's father marched into the foyer. "So, what's taking you so long?" Kit was surprised at how much he had aged, even in the months since Gramps' funeral. His curly brown hair was edged with white, his goatee too was paler, not the dark ruddy colour she'd remembered. His compact frame had become softer, pudgier.

"Father," Kit nodded in his general direction, helpless, hands at her side.

"Oh, come on, Katherine, give your old man a hug!" he held open his arms and waited for her to step into them.

"I'm too big for hugs," she walked past him and tried to smile but it felt more like a grimace.

Kit did her best to behave well, but the children seemed to notice her coolness and turned their attentions to the other adults. Kit noted with a pang that Max had climbed into Marie-Claire's lap, and Deirdre was shyly fondling the suede cuff of her father's jacket. Sondra kept casting significant glances at her while Marie-Claire entertained the group with humorous anecdotes about the back stage goings-on of the other actors in her most recent play.

God, Kit thought, she's even an actress. Kit could not stomach the familiarity and comfort her father and his most recent marital acquisition had gained within Sondra's home. Kit felt betrayed by this, as though she no longer belonged here.

She managed to receive her father's birthday gift with a modicum of grace. It surprised her by being suitable for a change. Usually, her birthday was observed either not at all or with a belated card and money. The last actual gift her father had given her was juvenile and off the mark: a Barbie doll for her sixteenth birthday. She'd hated dolls even when she was ten. Kit decided that Marie-Claire must've had a hand in choosing the lovely abalone shell earrings. Her father had caught her pleased look when she opened it. Kit was mad at herself for so unguarded a moment. She replaced the gift in the box with a tense smile and a curt thank you.

Later on, in Kit's room off the kitchen, Sondra immediately regretted broaching the topic of their father.

Kit turned on her in a fury. "That man has an ego the size of Canada and the morality of a rutting pig!"

"Kit, don't you think it's possible for a person to change?"

"Not him," Kit crossed her arms, face flushed. They stood facing each other.

"Well, I think he's changed." Sondra slumped down to sit on the bed. "Or maybe he's not the way we thought he was. I know it didn't mean much to us at the time, but he supported us by giving money to Gran and Gramps. Maybe that was the only way he could."

"So what, that's the least any human being, no, any mammal, would do for its offspring," said Kit. Her voice was cold and she was pacing back and forth. "How could you, Sonn, after all he's put us through, you especially."

Sondra, her head in her hands, replied, "I've been so distracted and upset, Kit, that I haven't had the energy to fend him off, like I have in the past, and, well, he and Marie-Claire have helped out."

"Does that make up for the past, Sonn? Really? I don't think so. Anyway, I don't understand how you manage to tolerate them, Sondra. I'm just relieved they won't be here tomorrow."

"Well, they won't be."

"I'm exhausted." Kit had stopped pacing.

"OK, I get the hint," said Sondra and rose from the bed.

"Good night, Kit," she said, standing at the door, hand on the door knob. Frustrated and close to tears, Sonn turned and said, "Oh, by the way, you might want to know that Maxie and I were almost killed today."

"What!?" Kit's face paled and she sank down onto the bed.

"Oh, so you do care about us."

"That's not fair, Sondra." Kit patted the bed next to her "What in hell happened?"

Sondra relented, walked back over and sat beside her sister.

"Come on, Sondra, tell me; don't torture me this way."

Sondra related the near miss in graphic detail.

"That idiot! What was he thinking? Did you get a look at the driver? Or the license plate?"

"No, no, it happened so fast and I was focused on getting us to safety, not on the car. I don't even remember what colour it was, though I think it might've been dark blue or black. And I think the driver was a man. That's about all I remember."

"I think I saw him," Kit gasped.

"What?"

"It must've been him, Sondra; I saw a car drive past right

after you left the house. He was going in your direction. I didn't think anything of it at the time, but I wonder; could that have been him?"

They sat together in silence for a few minutes. Kit was shaking, and Sonn turned to hug her.

"It's OK, Kit, we are all OK. Don't worry."

Kit began to cry, then pulled away from her sister's embrace. "I'm so sorry I gave you such a hard time about Dad back then. Almost losing you and Max kinda puts things in perspective. If you want him in your life, Sonn, I'll try to understand. I don't get it, but I'll try."

PART V
Bittersweet

Theobroma cacao
Chocolate

Montréal
Saturday, October 18, 1969

*T**he tall man was taking his daily early morning walk, a self-imposed discipline. He had a lot on his mind today. His comrade had failed, so, as usual, it fell to him to deal with their problem. He needed the clarity of mind these walks gave him. If he could only stay focused on the over-riding goal of a free and sovereign Québec, he believed the answers would follow.*

He'd found his purpose in life as a felquiste. A cause he believed in wholeheartedly and a place where he could put his skills and training to worthwhile use. His minor successes assuaged the pain and disappointments he'd sustained during a lifetime of being told he was flawed, damaged; that the way he was made him less than others.

The memory of those indignities rose unbidden out of the depths of his being, like some prehistoric sea creature whose gaping maw threatened to drag him back into the darkness he'd worked so hard to escape. He quickened his pace as if he could outrun this particular personal demon, but came face to face with a Canadian flag flapping sporadically in the morning breeze. Familiar rage flared, its intensity closed the monster's maw shutting the trap door on his discomforting thoughts.

As the wave of anger subsided, focus replaced agitation and the tall man composed himself, donning the persona he would need for the day's work.

Kit dressed carefully, even deigning to add the new pair of earrings to her outfit of jeans, hunter green blouse and one of Gramps' old tweed jackets. She looked at her reflection in the mirror. The earrings peeped alluringly through her dark hair, and her cheeks had more colour than she'd seen there in a while. For once she didn't find anything to criticize in her features, not even her large mouth or "patrician" nose. Today her deep set hazel eyes, reflecting the greenish tint of her sweater, made her look mysterious, instead of nondescript.

Kit brushed her wavy brown hair until it shone, turned her head to each side and smiled. The new earrings gentled her strong features into something approaching attractiveness. A bittersweet glimmer of gratitude towards her father and Marie-Claire flickered and was extinguished.

Kit knew she wouldn't be able to escape without some sort of investigative planning this morning, although she hoped to minimize her contact with Sondra. She could hear her sister puttering around in the kitchen. Kit took a deep breath and opened her bedroom door.

Sonn was at the sink washing up the breakfast dishes,

Evidence of Uncertain Origin

Dierdre had left for Alexa's hours ago, and J-P was busy in his home office. Max sat at the kitchen table with crayons and paper. As soon as he saw Kit, his mouth rounded in surprised alarm and he scrambled to cover his artwork. Kit smiled at him and ruffled his hair, pretending not to notice his dismay. She knew he must be working on a birthday card for her. Sondra turned around, and Kit could see that she hadn't slept well. Her blue eyes looked pale and red rimmed, though she tried to smile. A familiar guilt welled up in her, but Kit pushed it back down, way back down.

"Hey, Sonn, isn't it a wonderful day!"

Kit was pleased that Sondra seemed to rally with this and smiled at her. "The weather's a little dull for your birthday, Kit, but I'm glad you are here for it. Happy Birthday!"

Kit gave Sonn a big hug. "Thanks!" She spoke into her sister's wild auburn hair.

"So, Kit, what would you like for your birthday breakfast? I can whip you up anything your little heart desires: Pancakes? Waffles? French toast?"

Without having planned exactly what she'd say, Kit blurted out, "Oh, I'm sorry, Sondra, I've already made plans for the day, but I'll be back by four."

Sondra couldn't have looked more shocked, disappointed and disapproving. Spluttering she said, "But, who? Why? What do you mean you're going out?!"

"I forgot to tell you, I ran into an old friend yesterday and he invited me to go for a drive in the country." She tried to keep her voice light and easy.

"And who is this 'friend'? I know all of your friends, Kit, and you haven't lived in Montréal for a very long time—what's going on?"

"You don't know him, Sonn, he was more of an acquaintance at university than a friend, but he recognized me and we got to talking at the café around the corner." A part of her could not believe that she had lied to her sister.

Another part hoped she'd be able to bluff her way through it without getting caught.

Sondra seemed somewhat mollified. "Does Paul need to worry?"

"No way, Sonn, his girlfriend is coming with us too."

"So does he have a name?"

Thankfully, Kit had sorted this out in her mind ahead of time. She replied, perhaps too quickly, "His name's Martin and his girlfriend is Françoise." Kit was beginning to feel warm and had to avert her eyes, reaching past her sister to grab up a left over piece of French toast from one of the breakfast dishes. She shoved it in her mouth, and mumbled through the crumbs, "I can't stay long, Sonn. I told them I'd meet them at ten at the café."

Sondra wiped her hands on her apron and pulled out her little notebook along with a chewed-up pencil from her apron pocket before sitting down at the table across from Kit. She tapped the pencil point on her front teeth a few times before saying, "Then, we should spend a few minutes talking about the attempt on my life!"

Kit sat too. She tried to keep the exasperation from her voice. "What do you mean, 'attempt on your life'? It was probably somebody who was lost in their own thoughts and didn't see you."

"Come on, Kit! We've been making inquiries into a suspicious death. How could it be a coincidence? We have to list who would've had the opportunity to run me down." Sonn opened her notebook.

"Let's see, it could've been Serge, Roger, one of Private McIntyre's family, or Claude or someone still unknown to us." Sondra paused for a breath then added, glancing at Kit, "I'm sure the driver was a man, so that eliminates Annie, the 'D.L.,' Brault's wife and McIntyre's female relatives." She bent her head and began writing.

"Sondra, don't you think you're taking this a little too far?

Evidence of Uncertain Origin

It must have been an accident, pure and simple. They happen every day. Scary and awful as it was, don't make more of it than that."

Kit was shocked at Sondra's gaze of pitying contempt. "Really, Kit, you are SO naïve."

Kit sputtered in indignant protest. "I am not!"

"For all your being older than me and more educated, you don't have a clue about things sometimes." Sondra was very calm. "Look, Kit, I was there, I experienced it; it was no accident. The person in the car saw us and waved us across. That driver tried to kill Maxie and me." With that she closed her notebook, replacing both it and her pencil in her apron pocket.

Kit glanced down at Max; he was watching them, eyes round with concern. Kit put her hand on his shoulder, wracking her brain for something reassuring to say.

"Oh, Maxie, I'm sorry," Sonn went over to his chair, knelt, and took his little face in her hands. "Don't worry Maxie; you are safe now—that bad man can't hurt you."

"Well," Kit said at last, "I'm glad you both escaped unscathed." Max looked up at her, puzzled, so Kit added, patting him on the shoulder, "I mean 'unhurt'. I'm so happy you are both OK." At this he smiled and she kissed the top of his head.

"Look, I've got to go, Sonn. I'll see you by four. Don't go overboard on the celebrations, OK?"

Sondra nodded, in the same calm way that so unnerved Kit. "Have a good time, Kit. See you later."

She left Sondra and Max at the kitchen table and hurried towards the front door. Pulling on her coat, boots and mitts, a familiar worry gnawed at her gut. Sondra spoke with the same damned calm, distant, untouchable assurance that had preceded her nervous breakdown. Would it grow into another detachment from reality like the one after Max was born? Sondra was as confident then in her conviction that

God wanted her to die as she was now in the truth of her "vision." If things worsened, Kit would have to break her promise and talk to J-P. But, there wasn't anything she could do about it right now. Besides, today was her birthday and she had an adventure to go on. One she did not want to be late for.

Kit hurried towards the café; she was determined to enjoy her day, no matter what. She smiled, a small grim one, as she forced herself to slough off the nagging whispers of guilt trying to gain a foothold in her mind. She told herself Sondra would be OK for the day, and the lies she told Sondra were little white ones, for Sondra's own good. After all she didn't want Sondra to worry about her. Besides, things had changed. Sonn had allowed their father to come between them. That was a greater betrayal than a slight and temporary diversion from the path of complete honesty.

Kit indulged in the luxurious feeling of being a little miffed. After all, she shouldn't have to lie to Sondra. She, Kit, was an adult and able to take care of herself, and should be free to decide where and with whom she went without unnecessary concern and questions. By the time she reached the café she had rationalized away her guilt and worry, replacing it with a small dose of self-righteous indignation.

Michel was there ahead of her, must have seen her approach through the window because he was already out the door grasping her arm in a firm but light grip.

"Well, well, well, happy birthday my little huntress," he bent his raven black head to her and brushed his lips on both her cheeks.

They walked the block or so to his car, an older model beige Mercedes Benz. He opened the door gallantly and was waiting for her to step into it. She hesitated a moment, wondering at the oddness of her behaviour, the strength of the pull she felt from this stranger, the ease with which she'd sidestepped her own conscience. She almost turned away from him, but did not.

What the hell, she thought, it's my birthday, and I'm tired of always doing what everyone else thinks I should. And with that she eased herself in and smiled at Michel as he shut the door.

"Where are we going?" she asked after he'd slid into the driver's seat and pulled out of the parking spot.

Michel smiled at her, his dark eyes glinting with something like mischief. "I am taking you to my chalet up north where I will treat you like royalty for your birthday." With that he turned and was silent.

They drove through Montréal and headed up north towards the Laurentian Mountains and cottage country. Kit noticed that Michel kept his car in excellent condition; the leather seats were still smooth and resilient, the heater's warmth releasing a faint odor of lemon. The engine hummed flawlessly.

They exchanged small talk. Kit found out that Michel shared the chalet with a friend and went up whenever he could because the beauty of the wilderness took his mind off of his work. Kit spoke little of her family, sticking to information relevant to her own life. How she'd graduated from McGill with a Bachelor of Science, specializing in Biology and that she found taxonomy fascinating. Kit was gratified to hear that, unlike almost every other *Homo sapiens* she knew, Michel also found taxonomy interesting.

Or perhaps he found her interesting. This thought silenced her and she settled into the sheer physical pleasure of the car's interior, its speed and the bright autumn palette passing outside her window as they drove along.

"Michel, I never would have guessed that you were a career soldier."

At this he put his head back and laughed. "But I'm not!"

"If you weren't in the Canadian forces, how did you end up working at Senneville Lodge? And how come you're a captain?"

He glanced at her and smiled. "This calls for a cigarette, do you mind?" He pulled the package from his jacket pocket, shook it until a cigarette appeared, and offered her one.

Kit looked at the cigarette longingly, but said, "No thanks."

Michel grasped the cigarette in his lips, then lit it with the car lighter and inhaled. Pungent smoke filled the confined space of the car as he exhaled. Then holding the cigarette between his first two fingers he used thumb and third finger to meticulously pick a stray piece of tobacco from his tongue.

"And now you want to know my story, *non*?"

"*Oui!*"

"I am not a soldier in the Canadian Army," he said, with some rancour. "No, I was with the US 5th Special Forces in Vietnam."

"Weren't those the Green Berets?"

"Well, done, my little friend, not everyone knows their origins." He smiled at her and went on. "*De Oppresso Libre* is our motto: To free from oppression."

"Yeah, and then murder those you were sent to free!" Kit blurted out.

"Ah, you've been reading about my old commander, Colonel Rheault, no doubt: The 'Green Beret Affair'. You do know that the man they said he killed was a double agent."

"So says the CIA, but I don't trust them to tell the whole truth and nothing but. Do you?" Kit looked at him, incredulous.

He shrugged. "It's complicated."

They drove on in silence for a bit before Kit's curiosity got the better of her. "So, why on earth did you join the US Special Forces? Wasn't the Canadian military good enough for you?"

"Ah, *voilà le hic*! All the Canadians were doing when I wanted to join in '56 was keeping the peace. No glory in that. Not good enough for the son of my father." His voice was cold.

"Did your father want you to join up?"

"I don't know. My father had fought and been decorated in World War II. I was three when he joined *Les Fusiliers Mont-Royal* in 1939. He was wounded at Dieppe and sent home, bitter that he didn't get to finish out the war with his buddies. To hear him talk about it, all that mattered to him were his deeds of bravery and idealism for King and country." He spat out the words.

"If you had such contempt for the armed forces, why did you join?"

Michel's expression froze and he was silent for a while before answering her. "Oh, I believed him when I was a child. I even believed him when I was an adolescent. My father had won medals in World War II; I wanted to do the same, maybe to impress him, maybe because I wanted adventure. One is never sure after the fact."

"And did you?"

"Did I what?"

"Win medals, impress your father, have an adventure."

Michel reached past her to open the glove compartment, pulling out a small hinged box and handing it to her.

"What's this?" Kit asked.

"Open it and see."

Kit pried open the shallow box to find a heart shaped cameo of George Washington against a purple background attached to a purple ribbon. "What is this?"

"My Purple Heart," His voice was flat.

Kit stared at the medal. "What did you do to earn this, Michel?"

"Ha. Good question. Poor payment I'd say for five years in a green hell, a heroin addiction and this," he was vehement as he tapped his lame leg.

Kit sat up and stared at him, all civility had drained out of his face and the man she saw looked raw and fierce. A mixture of sympathy and admiration for him welled up in her. The bitterness in Michel's expression hinted at terrible things in his past. Yet there was strength; after all he must have overcome his addiction. He didn't seem like any heroin addict Kit had ever heard about. There's more to this man than I'd expected, thought Kit.

"Tell me about it."

"What are you, my psychiatrist?"

"No, but I'm interested; I've never met anyone who fought in Vietnam."

"Technically, we didn't fight. Technically, we were there to train the ARVN, the South Vietnamese Army, at least at first. The 1st Airborne were happy to have me when I joined; for a change being francophone was an advantage. It felt pretty good to a guy from Saint-Henri to have a bunch of *anglais* falling all over him because he spoke French."

He'd finished his cigarette, pausing to fish out and light another before continuing. "Then, in '61, with Kennedy, it all changed, that's when the 5th was formed, the Green Berets. I could've gone home then, but didn't. Got sent to Laos, with a Military Training Team; we ended up doing a lot more than that." His voice trailed off.

"Is that where you were wounded?"

He nodded and shifted his leg as though it too were remembering the event.

"Is that when you returned to Canada?"

"You mean when I was kicked back to Canada, broken and used up. I felt like a pile of shit. I was barely fit enough to travel when the US military pinned a medal on me and booted me out. No medical help, no nothing. And Canada did no better."

"What do you mean?"

"Canada did not recognize me as a veteran so I had no access to the very services I administer now. Ironic, isn't it?" His voice carried more venom than irony.

"But your family, your father, he must have been proud of you?"

"You know nothing! He hated me. In his eyes I was a weak fool."

"Why?"

"Why?! Because I came back with more than an injury, I wasn't home for long before he found out that I was too weak to be a son of his. I'd gotten hooked during my recovery period, first I took it for the pain, then—" Michel shrugged. "—then it became my only friend. More like a demon lover to be honest." He laughed, and it sounded hollow to Kit. "It drove me to do some bad things, things my father fixed for me. Not out of concern for me, mind you, but for his own damned reputation."

Kit saw his lips thin and his eyes narrow. "Of course he made sure it cost me. He wanted his pound of flesh, so in the end, he disowned me. All ties severed. He wouldn't even let my mother speak to me on the phone."

Kit was all too familiar with the arrogance of fathers. "What a damned jerk!"

Michel looked over at her, surprise on his face. "If it weren't for my friends, I'd be dead or worse." He glanced at her, his smile crooked, daring her to pity him.

All Kit could do was shake her head. "It's just all so unfair."

Michel's voice took on a philosophical tone. "My father was a product of his time. He believed what he was told. Actually, it is our political system that taught him to be unfair, *ma petite amie*," he said. "We can choose to be squeezed to death by them, or . . . " Kit saw him look at her, as though assessing her reaction to his words.

"Or find a way to work around them to get what we want." She replied. "Like you did by using your military experience to get a job as the administrator at Senneville Lodge."

"Exactly!" Michel's affirmation sounded tinged with a triumphant bitterness Kit did not understand.

Michel signaled the end of the conversation by turning on the radio. *"Mon pays ce n'est pas un pays, c'est l'hiver."* Gilles Vigneault's anthem to Québec filled the space between them. Kit remembered the first time she had heard his song: mid-winter in Montréal with snow drifts piled a metre high around cars and buildings. The words in English weren't as lyrical as the French, but she still loved the nostalgic patriotism they called out in her: "My country isn't my country, it's the winter; my garden isn't my garden it's the snow." She looked at Michel and saw his fierceness had melted away, replaced by his usual expression of sophisticated irony.

Kit spent the rest of the journey watching the passing vistas of stark rock, small pristine lakes and the riotous colour of autumnal deciduous forests giving way to the deep evergreen darkness of the north.

They turned off Highway 15 and drove about fifteen minutes before passing a sign that said, *Ville-du-lac-Sainte-Thérèse*. The small village perched beside a lake. On the left was a rocky shoreline with a small marina, on the right sat a corner store with a sign which would need a new coat of paint before next year's tourist season. A gas station down the street still advertised *"vers frais*/fresh worms"; beside it lounged the village inn and a few shuttered shops. Catering to the whims of the casual vacationer Kit deduced. A handful of older model cars were parked outside the inn and an elderly man sat in front of the gas station taking in the autumn sunshine. He nodded to them as they drove past.

Michel pointed across the lake where Kit could see the steep "A" frame roof of a cabin fronting on the lake and set off against a backdrop of pine trees and rock. "That is our destination." Kit stared at it until the road left the village and evergreen trees blotted out her view of the water. Michel drove another few minutes then turned left onto a dirt road.

They bumped along through thick forest before he pulled

over and parked. The car's wheels crushed the pine needles covering the shoulder releasing a pungent and spicy aroma that assailed Kit as she rolled down the window. They seemed to have stopped in the middle of nowhere.

Where are we? Kit wondered, a little alarmed.

Michel announced, "We have arrived!" As he waved his arms in presentation, Kit looked more closely and saw the tip of a shingled roof just visible through the trees. They had come up behind and above the cabin. Relieved, Kit exited the car and stretched, inhaling the chill freshness of a pine forest on the verge of winter.

The top of a steep set of stairs was partially hidden between a boulder and a large cedar. Kit wondered how anyone would ever be able to find the place. Michel led the way, hopping down the stairs, cane tucked into his belt, one hand steadying himself along a smooth log balustrade and the other carrying a grocery bag. Kit followed with the second bag. The stairway was cut into the side of the hill, each step a sawn off railway tie. She could see light glinting off the lake through the trees; a cool breeze ruffled her hair. Kit smiled; it was beginning to feel like a perfect day.

The steps ended a few metres behind the cabin which had been built on a large rock cliff overlooking the lake. A slate path led to a door; Kit figured it must open into the kitchen since the door was between a stack of stove wood and two garbage bins. Another slate path branched off to the right, disappearing around the side of the chalet. I wonder where that goes, thought Kit. She hadn't remembered seeing a dock or swimming area from across the lake.

Following Michel into the chalet, Kit was struck by its sparse orderliness. To the left of the door a red and black plaid jacket and cap were hanging on one of a series of hooks. A pair of rubber boots sat in a box which fit into the angle made by the roof and the floor. To the right of the door and a few feet from the wall was a chrome plated wood stove.

Michel put his groceries on a solid wooden table in front of the stove. He pulled a milk bottle out of the bag and placed it in the small white fridge nestled against the slanted roof. Kit noticed that the kitchen had a ceiling; stairs to what must be a loft above it formed a storage space occupied by a locked chest. She set her bag of groceries on the kitchen table as Michel had done and found a hook for her coat.

"It's lovely, Michel. Do you mind if I look around?"

"Go ahead, be my guest. You can light the fire while you are at it."

Kit walked past the stairs into a large living room. The loft ended and the peaked roof rose high above the rough-hewn boards of the floor. A sliding glass door opened onto a balcony that took up most of the wall facing the lake. Two sofas were angled so that those seated could look out at the view; the bold stripes of a Hudson's Bay blanket thrown over the back of one of the sofas added colour. Built into the room on the left was a field stone fireplace in which the wood for a fire had been laid. Kit found a box of wooden matches tucked behind a rounded brass carry-all filled with wood to the right of the fireplace. She lit the paper and kindling and leaned back on her heels for a few minutes, enjoying the flames as they licked up through the kindling and split logs. She inhaled and sighed with pleasure. The logs must be pine, she thought.

Kit stood, dusted off her hands on her jeans and looked around. An easy chair, a wooden coffee table, a desk, a TV with a radio on top and a bookshelf completed the furnishings. A few magazines lay scattered on a coffee table; a carved owl perched on the bookshelf, and a calendar with the distinctive abstract art of Paul-Émile Borduas decorated one of the walls. A rag rug covered the distance between window and sofas softening the décor. Kit noticed that, unlike most cabins she'd visited, it did not smell musty. She figured Michel must spend a lot of time up here.

Evidence of Uncertain Origin

"Welcome to *ma petite chalet*," Michel called from the back. "Go ahead, you may explore while I heat our meal. Don't be shy."

Kit went to look at the view from the sliding glass door. Beyond the balcony, through the tops of pine trees, she could see the lake glinting, its dark surface reflecting the late morning sky and beyond, the small village hugging the opposite shore. She buttoned her tweed jacket; the fire had not yet taken the chill from the air. When she turned toward the back of the chalet she saw Michel standing in the doorway, watching her, a wooden spoon in one hand.

"Ah, you look cold, come here by the stove. This place takes a while to warm up."

Kit returned to the kitchen area and sat in the chair closest to the wood stove, glad for the crackling warmth of its fire. "This is so beautiful, Michel. How can you bear to leave?"

"Well, I come as often as I can." He'd been heating milk on the stove. "*Chez Michel* does not have *café au lait* on the menu, would *chocolat chaud au Michel* do?"

Kit laughed and nodded. "Ah, *Theobroma cacao*, my favourite!"

Michel grinned at her, his right eyebrow raised. "Oh?"

Kit leaned back, watching Michel stir the pot of hot chocolate on the stove. "Well, we aren't the only ones to value the humble cacao bean; the Aztecs required them as tribute from those they conquered. In fact, our word chocolate comes from the Nahuatl word meaning 'bitter water.' You might not know this, but the seeds have to be fermented to remove their bitter flavor." Kit paused. "Am I boring you?"

"Only a little," he smiled as he stirred.

Determined to engage him, she dared to say, "You do realize you are treating me like a goddess, don't you? The Aztec and Mayan priests used to offer the seeds from cacao plants to their gods." Kit intended her tone to be both teasing and imperious.

"Just before they ripped the living heart out of their human sacrifices?" Michel turned to look at her as he spoke. His eyes sparkled without warmth and Kit shivered. Her discomfort must've been apparent, because she saw a self-satisfied grin spread on Michel's face.

"Should I worry?" Embarrassed by her momentary fear, Kit shifted in her chair, found a crack in the table top and traced it with her forefinger.

"Probably, not," he said, clearly amused. He turned back to the stove. "Remember, *ma belle*, you are my goddess, the one receiving the sacrifice, not the victim, *n'est-ce pas?*"

Regaining her humour, Kit added, "Well, you're torturing me right now, Michel; it smells wonderful, and I'm *dying* to try your concoction!"

"Well then, I'd better put you out of your misery." Michel reached over to pluck two mismatched ceramic cups from the counter and poured the steaming liquid into them. He added a dollop from a small bottle of brandy to each one, asking "Do you mind, my goddess?"

"Too bad if I do, eh?" she replied. "I wonder if alcohol enhances the mood elevating properties of chocolate or counters them?"

"Ah well, the scientific approach demands that you try it to find out."

Kit acceded to his point by smiling, tilting her head and reaching for the proffered cup.

Michel suggested they sit in the living room so Kit brought the steaming mugs and set them on the rustic coffee table. She held her mug with both hands, and blew on the liquid before sipping at it. The brandy had a very pleasant warming effect. Michel limped over to the sofa, his cane hanging from his belt, his hands full with a baguette, knife, cheese, *pâté* and plates.

"Our birthday feast," he announced and set about tearing

chunks of bread and cheese. He must've noticed her rather surprised look because he added, "The knife is for the *pâté*," then laughed. Kit wondered if he was laughing at her consternation. In fact, the primitive act of ripping the bread had stirred her, but before she could think about it much, Michel was holding up a bite-sized piece of bread and cheese intending to hand feed her. Though taken aback, she opened her mouth to receive the tidbit. They both sat down.

When she copied his act, Michel caught her hand and kissed her fingertips. Kit pulled back, as though she'd touched a hot stove. This made Michel chortle, and he leaned towards her, kissing her on the lips. "Is that better, Katherine?"

Kit realized that it was, and, though she said nothing, she hoped he'd kiss her again. Dimly, she also knew it probably wasn't a good idea. His dark beauty, almost feline in its sleekness, thrilled her.

Michel regarded her. Kit's face was getting hot; it seemed he must know what she'd been thinking.

"You are very beautiful when the colour rises to your face." His voice had thickened somewhat and she looked away from him so he would not see that this too moved her.

"Ah, come back, my friend, don't turn away." He began to twirl her hair in his fingers. "Your hair, it is so soft." His fingers grazed her ear and he began to fondle the lobe. A tremor passed through her.

"You are shivering; come closer to me and let me warm you." Michel put his arm around her and pulled her toward him. She complied, and the sensation of his thigh against hers did nothing to calm her.

She had no chance for second thoughts as Michel, turning her head towards him, kissed her long and fervently. Her body responded to him, while her hesitations weakened. Now his hand was touching her breast; she gasped but did not pull away. Then he took her hand and held it so that she felt him harden. His heat seemed to radiate through her. Her heart raced as he pulled her sweater over her head.

She pulled his sweater off and they fell back onto the couch, he on top of her, nuzzling her neck and breasts till she was breathless. He leaned back enough to unzip her pants and she helped to pull them down and off until all she was wearing were her socks. Blood pounded in her ears; from a great distance she heard herself moan.

From a much closer distance she heard the sound of the door opening with a bang. Kit froze.

"Michel!" A deep, masculine voice called out as she heard heavy boots stomp into the house.

"Jean-Marc?!" Michel leapt back from her and she grasped at the blanket to cover herself. Her French was not good enough to catch what "Jean-Marc" said, although his voice was exultant and excited at first then, as Michel responded, the voice became angry.

She shrank into the couch with the irrational hope that maybe Jean-Marc would not notice her. Michel bent down and gathered her strewn clothes from the floor and thrust them at her. His eyes had gone dark, like a northern sea on an overcast day.

"Go," He pointed to the stairs that led to the loft above the kitchen area. "You can get dressed there." He stood, pulled on his sweater and limped towards the kitchen while she tucked the blanket around her and stood. She glanced at Jean-Marc before fixing her stare on the floor in front of her. He was leaning against the door watching her, arms folded across his chest, a medium sized man, medium brown hair, cut short. He was wearing black predominantly, toque, sweater, pants. Kit noticed his eyebrows which were heavy and furrowed, seeming to radiate contempt and annoyance. His thin lips were pursed and he glared at her before continuing to lambaste Michel.

Kit stumbled; her face felt hot, her hair was askew and she

wanted to shrink into the woodwork. Somehow she made it up the stairs and into the loft where she sat on one of the two single beds trying to catch her breath and herself.

Although she could make nothing of the words, spoken low, fast and in anger, their meaning was clear from the tone and delivery. The invective Jean-Marc hurled at Michel seemed the equivalent of, "What the hell do you think you're doing!" Kit struggled to get her clothes on, as her body shook, readjusting itself to the current situation. She wasn't sure what to do next. She heard Michel's quiet voice, speaking now and calm though she couldn't make out his words.

She looked around the loft, hoping to find a mirror and a hairbrush. She had to restore some semblance of order to her disheveled self and combing her hair was all that her addled mind could come up with.

One large window overlooked the hillside throwing a dim and flickering rectangle of light on the floor as the pines outside blew in the freshening wind. Under the window was a wooden set of drawers strewn with books and papers. They seemed to be diagrams though all was in French, and she noted them only in passing. No mirror or brush here.

She opened the top drawer hoping to find some toiletries there, but only saw more papers: receipts held together with paper clips, a few folders, a calendar and a tin box, probably holding money, but no brush or mirror. Tucked underneath the box was a stained yellow silk scarf. She moved the box and scarf aside to see if there was a comb beneath them.

The sound of steps clumping up the stairs made her start, fearful that she'd be caught prying. The thud of the cane identified them as Michel's. She pushed the drawer shut and whirled around, hoping that the sounds had been muffled by his footfalls. She moved forward to meet him, self-conscious and humiliated.

He did not come all the way into the loft but stood still on the steps, so that his head was a foot or so below hers. When he looked up at her, it seemed to Kit, in her heightened state of perception, that he had composed himself to look cavalier and remorseful.

"*Ma petite belle amie.*" He tilted his head and spoke this with a wry smile. Extending his hand to her, he said, "Come, let me introduce you to Jean-Marc. He shares this chalet with me; his arrival was, *comment-tu-dis*, unexpected?" Kit looked into his eyes. Although he looked back at her, they told her nothing.

"I, I don't know what to say to him," Kit stammered. Or to you, she thought.

Michel shrugged his lithe shoulders. "It is not necessary, we are adults; we come and go as we please."

"But he was so angry, so disdainful."

"It was only his surprise; he is a very impulsive fellow, from the country, *tu sais*. Not worldly. He is calmer now." Michel spoke as if Jean-Marc were a large unruly dog he had managed to subdue.

"Besides, we will leave right away, now that the *ambience* has changed." At this his eyes glinted, Kit looked away, her face flushed with heat. "Ah, *charmante*," he said, almost to himself. It sounded wistful to Kit. "*Prête?*"

Kit nodded and followed him down the stairs, passing her fingers through her hair in an attempt to instill some order to it. She was loathe to meet Jean-Marc appearing as disheveled as she felt.

Jean-Marc stood silent, arms still folded across his chest. Tight lipped and frowning, his eyes assessed her with a knowing look. Thankfully, he said nothing to her, just nodded. Numb, Kit nodded back at him then stumbled into the kitchen. The aroma of hot chocolate lingered there. Bittersweet certainly sums up this experience, she thought. Outside, she trudged up the railway tie steps to the car. I hate irony, she grumbled to herself, panting a little from the exertion.

Evidence of Uncertain Origin

In the car on their way back, Michel broke the silence by apologizing. Kit countered with what she hoped was a gracious disclaimer. Michel reached his hand out for hers, the touch of his long fingers reminding her of their near intimacy. The atmosphere, easy and pleasant on the ride up, was awkward and forced now. The day had become cloudier and the grey light chilled her.

"So, how did you meet Jean-Marc?" Kit took a stab at what she hoped was a neutral topic. Michel withdrew his hand from hers.

"Oh, we were friends growing up," he replied, his tone cool.

"Where did you grow up, Michel, Saint-Henri?" Kit soldiered on, still trying to avoid the silence. This was the conversation we should've had on the trip up, she thought.

"Yes, Saint-Henri in Montréal mostly, but we traveled a lot. My father loved the military so much he became a career soldier. My mother was from Chicoutimi, so I was born up there, and I visited a lot in the summers. That's where I met Jean-Marc. But we lived in Nova Scotia, British Columbia, all over the map."

"Is that where you learned to speak English so well?"

"I suppose, although I perfected my accent in Vietnam." He sounded as bitter as raw cacao beans.

"Oh, of course," Kit thought for a bit then asked, "How exactly did you end up at Senneville Lodge, then? And you are a captain in the Canadian army, right?"

"Again, that is thanks to Jean-Marc. He convinced me to go back to school and take business administration. With my military background and *diplôme*, I was, as you say, a 'shoe-in'. All I had to do was join the reserves; they made me a captain. What a joke, my buddies in the Green Berets would get a real laugh out of that one!"

"So, you've done well for yourself."

"You think so?" His tone was sardonic.

"Well, haven't you?"

"Not if you aspire to greater things. Being an administrator for aging soldiers isn't what I'd call heroic or—" He stopped abruptly as though unwilling to continue his train of thought.

"So, you want to save the world."

"Well, don't you think it needs saving?"

"Sure, it's a noble goal, but don't you think it's a bit grandiose?"

"Maybe," Michel shifted his lame leg. "So, let's talk about you for a while. I'm boring myself."

"OK, what do you want to know?"

Michel reached for her hand again. Kit noticed the strange soft firmness of his grasp as though he were trying to read her mind through her skin. "Why are you so curious about your grandfather?"

She bristled. "Why shouldn't I be? He was more than a grandfather to me. He raised my sister and me when my parents divorced. Neither of them had the time or inclination to." Her rancor surprised her. Michel's grasp tightened and he glanced sideways at her.

"I am sorry, then, for his death." She turned to look at him, his wording seemed odd. His eyes stayed on the road and after a moment she relaxed. The strangeness was likely due to those malapropisms non-native speakers often fall prey to. "We share a common dislike for our fathers," he added.

"I suppose," Kit answered.

"You are married," he said with something of a smile in his voice. Stricken, Kit turned to look at the scenery. "It is not a shameful thing, *ma petite*, many are so entrapped. His name is Paul?"

"Don't remind me, please, I don't want to think about him just now." Kit's words were rushed, cramped.

"Well, it is hard to have a conversation with you. We must not discuss the husband or the grandfather or the father. May we discuss the sister, at least?"

"Sondra? Why her?"

"She is something of a sleuth, *n'est-ce-pas*?"

"What do you mean?"

"Come now, she has been asking my secretary questions, you both have gone to the hospital to speak with Private McIntyre, you have spoken with the tea room lady—yes, do not be surprised, it is my job to know what happens under my roof." He squeezed her hand and she tried to pull it away. He looked at her for a second before releasing it, emphasizing his control of the situation.

"So? Why wouldn't we want to learn about our grandfather's days before he died?"

"Of course, but you understand that I must protect those under my care, including my groundskeeper and my chef, not to mention our veterans. Your sister has asked after them all."

"Well, you have to admit, Serge does act a bit weird, staring at Sondra and me without speaking."

"Maybe he is taken with your beauty."

Refusing to be placated, Kit retorted, "Or maybe he is a homicidal maniac."

Michel guffawed. "I doubt it; he is so shell-shocked he can barely manage to rake the lawn, he'd never be able to plot a murder."

"It could've been a spontaneous act, an argument of some kind, about gardening? He and Gramps had a falling out when Gramps first arrived."

"Perhaps, but what does your sister have against my poor chef?"

"Oh, you yourself told us he and Gramps were at odds."

"Ah yes, the incident of the plum pudding, but seriously, is it enough of a motive for murder?"

"Maybe, maybe not." He was right, of course. Still, loyalty to Sondra made her blurt out, "But he's definitely a *separatist*. What if our grandfather discovered he was part of an FLQ cell, possible exposure would be a motive, wouldn't it?"

"Do you seriously think so?" Incredulity and something like amused surprise tinged his voice.

Deflated Kit said, "Really, it's my sister that is so convinced of all this."

"So why persist in what must be for you a frustrating enterprise, not to mention a painful reminder of your loss? Why not just move on?"

Torn between profound embarrassment and stubborn loyalty to Sondra, Kit said "Gramps' death was so unexpected, and he was always so careful. It just didn't seem like him to accidentally roll into traffic. It doesn't make sense. Maybe he'd been depressed, maybe—"

"Maybe the brakes did fail or maybe he'd had too much to drink."

"I told you already, he wouldn't have. He hated alcohol; he saw what it had done to my mother. He wouldn't even drink socially."

"Well, that's not what I observed."

"What are you saying, Michel?"

"I don't wish to speak ill of the dead, but, as I mentioned before, he was drinking a lot in the months before he died."

"That's not possible!" Even as she sputtered, indignant at the thought, doubt nipped at her. She remembered Robert Brault's problems with alcohol. Maybe Gramps had joined him. Was that why Robert Brault had acted so afraid? Did he feel responsible for Gramps' death because he'd encouraged him to drink?

"And, why not?" Michel continued. "Old age and disability are not easy things to accept. Sometimes alcohol makes the transition easier. I have seen it more than once with these old fellows. And how would you know? Your visits were rare and your sister's had become infrequent the last couple of months of his life."

His accusation was like a knife in her heart; had her

neglect driven Gramps to drink or to suicide? She bit her lip to keep from leaping to her own defense and Sondra's. Hadn't Sondra admitted that it had been "too long" since her last visit? That damned dream must have come from her guilty conscience; Sondra always had been too sensitive about things.

Michel's voice interrupted her jangled thoughts. "I'm not accusing you, just making an observation."

"Well, his death is hard to accept all the same. And I think we have a perfect right to make inquiries about it. It's only natural!" She did not mention Sondra's preposterous nightmares, because she didn't want Michel thinking Sondra was a lunatic.

"*Naturellement,*" They fell into a silence that lasted the rest of the trip.

Re-entering the city, Kit noticed that there were a number of road blocks and lots of police activity so that they had to take a less direct route back to the café. "I wonder what's going on."

"Could be anything," replied Michel, swerving to miss a pylon.

They were later than Kit had planned as Michel pulled in to park in front of the café.

He turned to Kit and drew her hand to his lips. "I hope you will not let the awkwardness of this day impose itself between us."

Kit had managed to block the afternoon's misadventures from her mind, but now the heat rose to her face at the reminder. "Michel, I'm married . . . I shouldn't be, um, fooling around."

"Until now, I did not see myself as a fool." He reached over and touched her cheek, smiling. "I understand. Still, I come here often after work. I'll be here the day after tomorrow at four p.m. if you want to see me again. I hope you do."

Kit opened the door and stepped out into the overcast

afternoon. How could he understand her so well? His awareness of her felt invasive, accustomed as she was to Paul's obliviousness.

Sondra was pacing the floor in the kitchen when she heard J-P arrive home from work at 4:15 that afternoon. The CBC blared while the kids huddled in the front room, their afternoon snack untouched on the coffee table. He had tried to reassure her, but Sondra would not be comforted. "Go, take the children to the *dépanneur*. I need some whipping cream for Kit's cake." So he and the children had dutifully left her to pace alone.

At 4:30, the sound of a key in the lock brought Sondra to a halt. She dashed out of the kitchen, through the living room and down the stairs in time to accost Kit as she opened the front door.

"Where have you been? I've been so worried! Thank God you are alright . . . " Sondra's voice was a blur of concern and her arms locked around Kit, a mother bear protecting her cub. Sondra began to cry with relief.

"What is the matter with you, Sondra? I am a little late, OK, but I'm fine. I'm an adult, not one of your little kids." Kit struggled out of Sondra's embrace and tried to hold her at arm's length.

Sondra's shoulders were heaving and she found it difficult to get the words out. "Oh God, Kit, I thought I'd lost you too."

"What on earth's the matter, Sonn, are the kids OK? Is J-P alright? What is going on?"

Sondra sat on the first step leading up to the flat and put her head in her lap. Shutting the front door, Kit joined her sister in the cool gloom of the stairwell and put a comforting arm around her shoulders.

"I was so afraid, Kit. When you weren't back by 4:00 I

Evidence of Uncertain Origin

thought you'd been hurt by that bomb."

"What!?"

"Didn't you hear about it on the radio?"

"No."

Sondra looked at her in surprise. "Didn't you notice anything coming back into the city?"

"Well, I did see roadblocks," Kit stammered, "but I thought, we thought, they were for a parade or construction or something. What's this all about?"

"It looks like the FLQ struck again: another letter bomb." Sondra glanced up at Kit with a weak smile and continued. "It was announced on the CBC, around one p.m. or so. A few passersby got taken to hospital. No news on whether they are OK or not, and no names."

She sighed and sat up straight. "So . . . when you didn't show up at four I began to worry . . . you know what I'm like." She threw an apologetic smile at Kit. "I, I guess, I was terrified I'd lose you too."

"I'm sorry I was late, Sonn, we were having such a good time, we lost track and then the traffic and roadblocks."

Sondra could hear the guilt in Kit's voice. "I'm glad you had fun on your birthday, Kit. I'm sorry I freaked out on you. Wow, I almost forgot to tell you about what I found out."

"I'm all ears, Sonn."

"Well, I asked Dad about drugs that could mimic heart attacks and—"

"Sonn, you didn't tell him why you were asking did you? You know he'd want to send you back to the psych ward."

"No, no, give me a little credit, Kit. I was very cagey and led him into the discussion without raising even an eyebrow of suspicion." Sondra leaned back, blew on her fingernails and polished them on her sweater, grinning. "Anyway," she continued, "he said there were a number of possibilities; I copied the names down in my notebook. At least three of them would be pretty easy to get ahold of. Get this, even caffeine in high enough doses could induce a heart attack!"

"That makes one reconsider one's addiction to coffee, doesn't it?"

"And that's not all, Kit, I called the hospital to see how Fred McIntyre was doing..." here she paused for effect.

"And...?"

"Not good, not good at all. He's lapsed into a coma and is uncommunicative. They thought I was his daughter-in-law at first and gave me more information than they meant to. The family will be arriving within the next day or two to decide whether or not to turn off the life support systems."

"Poor old guy."

"Yeah."

Sondra saw Kit's shoulders slump and noted that her earlier liveliness had faded away. A clouded look replaced it. It occurred to Sondra that maybe Gramps' death had impacted Kit more than she'd admitted to. She went on in a gentler tone. "I thought we could try to interview the family."

"Are you sure about this?"

"Absolutely. I wonder; maybe he said something to them before getting sick. I still can't get over how terrified he was when he saw us."

"Yeah, but it's so uncouth, Sonn, we don't know them at all. Think how you'd feel in their place."

"Yes, I get all that, but it's important, it might have bearing on our case."

Kit was biting her lip, a sure sign she was holding back her words. All she ended up saying was, "Maybe so, maybe so."

"Well," Sonn continued, determined to press home her advantage, "I thought we could head back out there tomorrow. Oh, and I found a photo of Annie in Gramps' things. It's a group shot for someone's birthday, I think. Anyway, Annie is in it, so I'd like to take it around Sainte-Anne-de-Bellevue and ask about her. Maybe we can find out where she got to. I'd love to ask her about that briefcase."

Evidence of Uncertain Origin

"You think that, what was her name at the café?" Kit snapped her fingers in the air. "Ah, yeah, Mrs. Grady, was telling us the truth? Wasn't exaggerating about all that?"

"She could've been, I suppose, but why would she want to lead us on?"

"Loneliness, attention-seeking maybe? But you do have a point, Mme. Holmes." Kit smiled at her and ruffled her hair.

Excited voices outside the front door made Sondra leap to her feet. "Yikes! I forgot all about your party—that'll be Jean-Pierre and the kids, they had to make a quick trip to the *dépanneur* for some whipping cream for your birthday cake which very well may be languishing in flames by now!" With that Sondra dashed up the stairs.

Kit enjoyed the birthday party. It took her mind off of Michel, and she was almost relieved that Paul hadn't called. She didn't think she'd have been able to keep the strangeness and betrayal of her afternoon's activities out of her voice.

Sondra had been in her glory, almost back to her gay, normal self. She'd been busy producing tasty treats in the kitchen, while teasing Jean-Pierre mercilessly, threatening him with a whipped cream laden wooden spoon. Jean-Pierre's good humoured surrender was tinged, Kit noted, with cautious relief.

The children vied for the adults' attention, bickering and teasing each other in a way that made Kit nostalgic about her childhood. Content, here in the midst of this domestic chaos, she was enfolded by a sense of belonging, safety and warmth.

Her presents were wonderful: a cable knit sweater from Sondra and Jean-Pierre, a book on the taxonomy of butterflies from the children. Their hand-made cards touched her: Deirdre's had a big butterfly in the middle, replete with as many unnatural colours as she could find in her crayon box, finished off with a near human face, a big smile and a heart encircling it all. Max must have had a lot of fun making his, licking and sticking butterfly pictures all over the front. These he had linked together, like beads on a necklace, with a long winding red line.

Kit saw that her enjoyment of their gifts made her family very pleased with each other. This cheered her so much that even the standard birthday phone call from Emily couldn't ruin the mood.

"Oh. Is that you, Katherine? I tried calling you at home, and you weren't there . . . no one was there. I didn't realize you were in Montréal, but figured I'd try anyway," Her mother's grey voice faltered. "I hope everything is alright . . ."

"Sure, Emily, it's fine. Paul's just really busy right now. So I came up for Thanksgiving."

"Well, that's good, Katherine. Ah, I just wanted to say 'Happy Birthday' to you."

"Thank you, Emily"

"I'm sorry . . . " then the phone clicked. It would've been disconcerting, thought Kit, if her mother didn't always sign off in the same abrupt, sad and hopeless way.

Later that evening after the festivities, J-P volunteered to babysit the children while Sondra and Kit went to the movies. "Take the Money and Run" was playing at the Odeon. They could walk to the Mont Royal Metro station and take the subway downtown. The cinema at Alexis Nihon plaza was right beside the Atwater Metro stop.

"We haven't done this for ages, have we Kit?" Sondra took her sister's arm as they lined up for the movie.

"No, and we used to go to the movies together every Saturday afternoon when we were younger." Kit smiled. "I've missed this, Sonn."

"Me too," Sondra gave Kit's arm a squeeze.

A few minutes later Sondra nudged Kit. "Isn't that the cook, Claude, from Senneville Lodge?" she asked, *sotto voce*, and nodded towards a familiar blond ponytail belonging to the tall bulky man several people ahead of them.

"And look who's with him," Kit whispered.

Sondra put a hand over her mouth and raised her eyebrows in mock dismay. "Claude's roommate André! Sergeant what's his name's nurse from Ste. Anne's."

"Yes, indeed," Kit rejoined, as they watched Claude bend down to say something to his companion, whose paisley jacket and cravat had replaced his hospital whites.

Later, walking back home arm and arm with Sondra and laughing together over Woody Allen's antics, Kit was surprised by a settled happiness. Like a vaguely remembered childhood playmate, she had not recognized it at first.

Nikki Everts

PART VI
Persistent

Felis catus
Domestic Cat

Montréal
Monday, October 20, 1969

*T*he tall man stood staring out over the lake; tendrils of fog blurred the boundary between water and sky, hiding the far shore from sight. He too felt hidden and therefore safe, as invisible now to the prying eyes of the Senneville Lodge inmates in the building across the road and behind him as he hoped his intentions were to them. He smirked, imagining the shock on their faces if they only knew who he really was and what he really was up to.

He would show them all— his family, the Canadian military, those damned shrinks. They would regret labeling him twisted,

Evidence of Uncertain Origin

weak, unworthy. He shook his head as if to change the channel, imagining instead the delicious mayhem and damage his comrade's bomb would deliver to their precious Gare Centrale.

Once we are in control, he thought, I'll throw off my disguise and emerge as the bold, conquering hero. He smiled at the vision of glory playing out in his mind: today's version of his victory scene took place on the steps of City Hall in Montréal, and like de Gaulle, his appearance and speech was accompanied by deafening cheers. In other versions, he was a presiding judge condemning his tormentors to death for crimes against the state. Of course, the crimes were really against him, but in his thoughts he and the coming nationalistic state of a free and sovereign Québec were one and the same.

The muffled sound of a car turning into the Veterans Lodge driveway interrupted his reverie, reminding him that he still had work to do. He relished the challenge. The power he exercised over others through deceit and manipulation thrilled him. He loved the well-played disguise and the adrenalin rush of being close to the edge of discovery yet escaping in the nick of time. His excitement at these times was almost sexual, but what of it? He was sure he wasn't the only one to feel this way.

Some of his past escapes had required the taking of a life. Unfortunate, yes, but necessary to ensure the great gains his success would bring to his country, and, of course, himself. In the grand scheme of things these deaths were not murder, he reasoned, but the actions of a soldier and a patriot.

Though he found no actual pleasure in killing, he was good at it. He wasn't sure when or how it had happened, but somewhere along the way he had acquired a switch with which he could turn off all feeling for others. He wondered how many people shared this gift. His companion did not. Sometimes he worried that the switch would one day stay stuck in the off position.

The tall man watched as the shifting tendrils of fog exposed and then hid the shoreline. What had that English playwright said? "All life is a stage and we are all actors", or some such.

Finally he turned to walk back to his own stage and the role he'd chosen to play on it.

Sunday had disappeared under the domesticity of house cleaning, newspapers, left-overs and television. Monday was foggy, and visibility was poor as they started off toward the west island in Jean-Pierre's red Volvo. Kit was driving more slowly than usual. The CBC news was on: "No arrests have been made in the most recent letter bombing although inquiries continue." Sondra had stopped writing things down in her notebook to listen. She reached over and turned down the volume once the announcer started talking about the weather.

"I wonder what it's going to take for Prime Minister Trudeau to step in and nip the FLQ in the bud." Sondra said. "Québec's Premier Bertrand sure doesn't seem to know what to do with them."

"Why not?" asked Kit.

"Well, the FLQ's nationalism does have support in Premier Bertrand's own political party, the Union Nationale. Not only that, his predecessor, Premier Johnson, was a died-in-the-wool nationalist."

Kit nodded. "I had read that Premier Johnson was soft on the *souverainistes* including the FLQ, but Premier Bertrand isn't so sympathetic."

"Yes, Premier Bertrand is definitely a federalist. He's in a tight spot, no doubt about it. When Premier Johnson died in office last year, Bertrand narrowly defeated the more nationalist candidate to become the Union Nationale party leader. But with such a slim majority I don't think he has the power to do very much. He's been left with a can of worms, that's for sure. I almost feel sorry for him. Still, I wish he'd do something."

Kit nodded. "And things have changed; the FLQ is killing people now. It isn't how it used to be, eh?"

Evidence of Uncertain Origin

"No, it isn't."

"I wonder how persistent they will be, and how far they'll go to shake Québec loose from Canada."

"It's scary. Do you remember the Braydons?"

"We went to school with Patty and Joe."

Sondra nodded. "Well, their parents recently moved to Alberta because of all the oil field jobs and also because of the FLQ. They didn't think Bertrand and Trudeau were strong enough to control them. Did you know that Mr. Braydon was a postman?"

"I bet he's patting himself on the back right now."

When they drove into the hospital parking lot Kit was horrified to see Michel's car in one of the official spots right next to the building's entrance. Panicking, she wracked her brain trying to find a way to avoid meeting him.

Ignoring Sondra's protestations, Kit parked as far away from the entrance as she could. In what she hoped was a casual manner she said, "I've been thinking, Sondra, why don't we split up? We can cover more ground that way. I am really uncomfortable disturbing Private McIntyre's family right now. Don't you think it would be less intrusive if just one of us went?

"Why don't you give me Annie's photo, and I'll start taking it around to the stores in the town. If you give me Serge's address, I can check that out too. I'll take the shuttle bus from here into Saint-Anne-de-Bellevue. You can drive into the village and we'll meet at the tea room in, say, two hours?"

Sondra questioned her with a look, but nodded, opened her booklet and handed Kit a group photo taken at someone's birthday. Gramps was in his wheelchair and Annie was kneeling beside him and smiling. A scarf tied around her neck gave her a jaunty air.

"Good luck, Watson," Sondra said with a wink as she got out of the car and strode towards the main door to the hospital.

Kit breathed a sigh of relief and walked over to wait at the bus stop. A truck drove by her going toward the hospital. It slowed down as it passed and she glanced up. Her eyes met the pale blue eyes of the driver, Serge Schultz. His eyes narrowed—his dislike almost palpable—then he turned and gunned the motor, roaring into the hospital parking lot. A shiver went down Kit's back. Had he been following them?

Get a grip and stop being paranoid she told herself, he's probably the grounds keeper for the hospital too. Still it felt creepy. Kit felt ridiculously relieved when the shuttle bus to Sainte-Anne-de-Bellevue showed up a few minutes later.

Sondra pushed through the hospital doors and stopped to buy some flowers from the gift shop. Pink carnations seemed the most appropriate: respectful without being pretentious or self-important. So armed, Sondra made her way to McIntyre's room only to find the bed empty. She ducked back out before Sergeant Mallory could proposition her and almost bumped into an orderly who was bustling down the hall, pushing a large machine on wheels.

Sondra turned to apologize, only to find that it was André, the orderly they'd met the last time, Chef Claude's "roommate." He was regarding her with narrowed eyes and hands on hips.

"It's you!" André's cheery sing-song had disappeared.

"I'm sorry!" Sondra was disconcerted by his antagonism, so different than the friendliness he'd shown them just a few days before. "You remember me?"

"Of course," Sondra could hear an unspoken "you idiot" in his tone. "You and your sister were visiting Private McIntyre. You're John Flanagan's granddaughter, aren't you? You called my Claude the other day, didn't you?"

His accusation made Sondra step backwards. "Well,

yes..." She couldn't think of anything else to say.

"Well, what do you want, now?" His tone had deescalated from hostile to brusque.

"I'm looking for Private McIntyre."

"He's in Intensive Care, of course." It sounded as though he blamed her for Fred McIntyre's downturn.

"Thank you, where—"

Before Sondra could ask for directions, André had pivoted and was already out of earshot, pushing the wheeled machine down the hallway with undue vigor.

When Sondra finally found the ICU, she saw that Captain Tremblay was just leaving. He looked surprised to see her and paused, as if he might stay, but then nodded to her and left.

When Sondra entered the room she saw that Fred McIntyre occupied one of several beds, the others were empty. Still wired to myriad humming or beeping machines, he looked even smaller than he had just days ago. His eyes were closed and a waxy calm textured the skin of his face. His family members formed a tableau around his bed. The two women and a man were all staring at her with stern and angry expressions.

"I hope I'm not intruding," she blurted out. "I spoke to you on the phone?" Sondra proffered the flowers and waited, wondering if Kit had been right about not coming.

The older woman was the first to speak. "Ah, you must be Sondra, Corporal Flanagan's granddaughter?" Her face softened into a tired smile.

"Yes, I am. I am sorry about all this," Sondra added, relieved. She gestured towards McIntyre's still form, dwarfed by the hospital bed.

"Thank you, please do come in, I'm Celestine McIntyre," said the older woman. "I'm sorry if we weren't very welcoming." She stepped forward, and took the flowers from Sondra, handing them to the younger woman.

"This is my daughter-in-law, Beatrix, and my son, Raymond," she gestured at the man standing beside her who nodded at Sondra. Celestine sat in the chair beside McIntyre's bed, her shoulders drooped as though all the air had been let out of her.

Raymond put a meaty hand on her shoulder. "*Maman*," he said, bending over her, "can I get you something?" Dressed in a worn and ill-fitting brown suit, he was short and stocky, swarthy with greying hair and brown eyes. If he took after his father then McIntyre must be very sick indeed, thought Sondra, glancing at the sick man's thin, comatose face.

"No, no, *merci*, I'll be fine," Celestine replied in a weak voice, smiling up at him and patting his hand. Her scalp was visible through sparse white hair coiled into a neat bun at the nape of her neck.

Sondra shook hands with Raymond and Beatrix. "Your father was one of my grandfather's closest friends, and we so appreciated his coming to Gramps' funeral despite his illness. It was very kind of him." The couple nodded. "I'm so sorry he's had this bad turn," she added.

"Please, excuse us," said Beatrix, her high girlish voice belying her matronly figure, barely confined by a pale blue shirtwaist dress. She tilted her head and added with an apologetic smile, "We thought you were with Captain Tremblay." At the mention of Tremblay, Raymond scowled.

"Oh no," said Sondra, "I'm not with him." She hoped for elaboration.

Raymond needed no encouragement. "Yes," he said, his beefy face ruddy with displeasure. "It is unacceptable, all of this." His face got even redder and Sondra worried he'd rile himself into a heart attack. "They should have told us sooner so we could've said good-bye. It is so hard on *Maman*. They left us no time. We drove night and day from the Gaspé. What do they think? We are not made of money, if we were, do you think we'd have left Papa here?" He swept his arms around to include the hospital, Senneville Veterans Lodge, the whole dismal situation.

His mother had reached out and grabbed hold of McIntyre's limp hand, dabbing at her eyes with a sodden tissue.

Raymond persisted in his tale of woe. "Papa had to be operated on two years ago. They wanted to take out half his bowel, to get rid of the cancer. *Maman* was too frail to take care of him and we didn't have the money for private nurses or a private hospital. This seemed the only option. He had the operation here; then moved to the Veterans Lodge nearby. We've come to see him as often as possible, but, I work and *Maman* can't come on her own. We may not be fat cat rich but that doesn't mean we deserve this disrespect. They should have told us sooner." He was running out of steam; his outrage and guilt seemed to exhaust him. Sondra could understand that all too well.

Celestine added, "We thought he was healthy enough to come home for Christmas. Raymond had already booked time off to drive out and get him."

Beatrix picked up the gauntlet, switching to "franglaise." "Then that *mauvais* Captain Tremblay there, he did not call us *tout suit* when Papa, *il devient plus mal*. Then he comes here and *il feint qu'il se soucie*. I want to spit in his face! We want *la justice!*" Raymond, put his arm around her, clearly pleased by her ire.

"I'm so sorry about your father," said Sondra. "My sister and I went out to the Lodge to pick up our grandfather's things last week. We wanted to thank your father for coming to the funeral. When we heard he was ill, we visited him. He was conscious at the time, but seemed—" Sondra searched for words that wouldn't be too distressing. "—upset when he saw us."

Celestine put her hand on Sondra's arm. "The last time I talked to him on the phone, he sounded well, until he brought up that business about your grandfather's key." Here she looked at Sondra. "Your grandfather had given it to my husband for 'safe keeping,' he said. I could hear the fear in his voice and asked him what was wrong. He said to never mind, but he wanted me to keep it for him."

"Did you receive the key, Madame McIntyre?"

"Oh yes," she said. "I guess it belongs to you, doesn't it? I brought it with me, in case Fred wanted it back. It's in my suitcase at the motel. Shall I mail it to you?"

Later on, sitting in the tea room in Sainte-Anne-de-Bellevue waiting for Sondra, Kit sipped at her tea, and stared at Annie in the group photo lying on the table in front of her. She replayed her afternoon's detective work. How could she present her findings to her sister without encouraging her too much in her delusions? Half of her was kicking herself for even getting involved in this; the other half was starting to get interested in the puzzle posed by Annie's disappearance and Serge's creepiness. Images of Michel persisted in imposing themselves and only with great effort did she push them aside.

All in all she hadn't found out much. Weaving around clutches of giddy Agriculture students, Kit had shown the photo at all of the shops in town, including D'Aoust's, the old general store, and the aging movie theatre next to it. Few people knew Annie Desrocher by name, although some did recognize her. None had seen her in well over a month.

The only intriguing bit of information came from a young, gum-chewing blonde at *Dépanneur Landry*, the corner store beside the quaint Catholic Church. She'd had a summer job working at the *frites* wagon near the locks and said she had seen Annie then.

When Kit asked, "Are you sure?" the young woman

snapped her gum several times, nodded and said she remembered it well because Annie was wearing the exact same print sundress the young woman had seen at D'Aoust's Department Store and was saving up to buy, so annoying. Anyway, she'd noticed Annie and the dress walking arm-in-arm along the canal with a man who had a cane. It was a slow day so she watched them as they approached the converted house trailer to buy a bag of the oily hot fried potatoes she cooked on the spot.

The young blonde claimed that Annie was laughing and seemed happy. Kit had asked for a description of the man, thinking it might be her grandfather who did sometimes abandon his wheelchair for brief forays with a cane. His legs had been weakened from arthritis, diabetes and the shrapnel that had sent him home from World War I.

No, the man was younger, not older. He was handsome and dark. Michel, Kit thought with a start, a pang of jealousy rising unbidden.

I have no right to be jealous, she thought, as she nodded and thanked the young woman with a tight smile.

Kit then went to Serge's home; he lived above one of the stores along the main street, rue Sainte-Anne, not far from the Tea Shop. The entrance to his building was just past the corner on rue Saint-Pierre. She pushed open the outer wooden door; it was old and shedding flakes of white paint. The foyer of the building was dark and stank.

Ah yes, thought Kit, *Felis catus* for sure. She remembered that their urine contained urea which was sticky, and its breakdown products included sulfur compounds as well as uric acid both of which accounted for the pungent odour. It made an excellent territorial marker being both stinky and persistent. Kit figured one of these apartments had to be the domain of at least one domestic cat.

A mailbox at the bottom advertised three flats, marked, A, B and C. Apartments A and B had doors on the first floor.

Nikki Everts

Apartment C's mailbox had a yellowed tag reading "Schultz," and Kit deduced it must be at the top of the worn wooden stairs in front of her. She climbed them, noting as she did that the heady mix of uric acid and thiols along with the undertone of skunk contributed by the mercaptans got stronger the higher she went. Standing before Serge's door on the tiny landing she had wondered what to do next.

Maybe he has a room-mate. She'd dismissed this thought considering his unpleasant personality but decided to knock anyway. She figured she wouldn't encounter Serge since he was busy at the hospital, and, if there was a room-mate, it would be worthwhile to ask a few questions. The only response to her knock was the sound of meowing and some scratching at the door. She waited a bit and imagined the animal on the other side. Cats were more commensal than domesticated, not so different except in size from their wild counterparts. Their natural characteristics of intelligence, social nature, and love of play made them good companions for humans. That Serge had at least one cat made his strangeness more an object of pity than a threat. She descended, convinced that only the cat or cats were at home.

Before Kit could escape, the door of apartment B swung open and a small, stout woman, dressed in a mauve chenille bathrobe, head adorned with curlers, demanded, "What you want?!"

"Um, nothing, really."

"Why you knocking on Serge's door? You da' police or what?" Kit was amazed the woman could speak at all and still keep the cigarette dangling out of her mouth from dropping to the floor.

"No, I just wanted to ask him some questions."

"'Bout what?"

Kit thought a moment. What did she want to find out about him? She decided to go with the obvious. "How long has he lived here?"

"Long time—longer den me."

"What's he like?"

"Poor man, not quite right—" at this she tapped her head, "the war or somet'ing, I figure, but, good to his cats, keeps to himself, no girlfriends." Having summed up Serge's life and character in less than twenty-five words, the woman folded her arms across her ample bosom and gave Kit the once over. "Why you wanna know? You wanna be his girl?"

"No, but thank you." With that, Kit had turned and left; the aroma of old cigarette smoke and cat wafted after her as the outside door slammed shut behind her.

She turned to walk towards the Tea Shop and stopped. Serge Schultz was blocking her way. He stood, his tall figure stooped and foreboding.

"Oh, it's you!" Kit blurted and stepped back, almost tripping over her own feet.

He frowned. "*J'habite ici.* I live here."

His voice was gravelly, probably from disuse, Kit imagined, and nodded. His strangeness frightened her. She gulped, looked around for other people, and saw no one.

"You are too nosy. *Arrêtez.*" He pushed past her, almost shoving her into the road, and went into his building.

Unnerved, Kit walked over to the Tea Shop. Kit wondered if Serge's strangeness would make him more of a suspect or less of one in Sondra's eyes. Either way, he truly was one odd duck or very good at hiding his true identity.

Kit took another sip of tea, thinking that nothing she'd managed to find out so far would dislodge Sondra's fantastical imaginings. More importantly, if Gramps had been infatuated with Annie, and found out about her liaison with Michel, it might've made him distraught enough to end it all, or at least be less careful of himself.

Her musings were interrupted by Sondra, rushing into the shop.

"Kit! Am I ever glad to see you!" Her hair, relishing the

dampness of the day, formed a huge frizzy halo, and the colour in her cheeks seemed more than was warranted by the brisk autumn air alone. She plunked herself down into the chair as Mrs. Grady ambled over to take her order.

"Yes, I'll have your afternoon tea with scones," she said, then, aside to Kit, "I'm absolutely famished!"

"Well, Sonn, you look pretty damned pleased with yourself, tell all, tell all," Kit said with an interest that surprised her.

Sondra shrugged out of her coat and leaned forward, lowering her voice. "Oh Kit, there's something fishy going on, I'm sure of it."

Kit responded with a quizzical look. Encouraged, Sondra related her experiences at the hospital.

The elderly waitress took that moment to hobble over with a tray laden down with tea things. Kit thought it looked precarious and eyed its progress across the uneven floor, ready to leap to the rescue if need be.

When the older woman arrived at their table, Kit exhaled, surprised that she'd been holding her breath.

"Oh, wonderful, tea, just what I needed, thanks." Sondra gushed as Mrs. Grady set out the tea pot covered in a flowered cozy, followed by a porcelain cup and saucer patterned in violets, then a milk jug and sugar bowl bearing a mismatched floral display of roses. The final offering was two warm scones covered by a cloth napkin along with a pat of butter and a dollop of jam.

Righting herself, Mrs. Grady smiled at them winningly and responded, "There now. You're ever so welcome, dearie. Now, I remember you both from the other day, doncha know? Youse were askin' about that young lady." She bent slightly to peer over Kit's shoulder at the photo and pointed at Annie with a gnarled finger. "Well, now, I got to thinkin' about her after youse had left, and I do believe I did see her one more time after that, I did." She nodded her head, as if to agree with herself. "Though I'd not swear on a Bible about it . . . still, I'm almost positive t'was her."

Both Kit and Sondra stared up at her in surprise, waiting for her to continue.

"Well, as I said, I'm almost certain it was her I saw, but, now I might be mistaken. I am older now, doncha know, and the eyes aren't the best. Still, I'm no fool." She waited for their confirmation of this fact. Both younger women nodded.

"So," Sondra asked. "When was this? And what happened?"

"Oh, it was well a'fore Labour Day, 'fore all the students flooded back to the university, doncha know. Lots more work after that for the likes of me. Good business for the Tea Shop they are, bless them! There warn't a whole lot of tea drinkers a'fore then.

"Yes . . . well, then. I did see her. Or someone very like her. I was standing on the stoop, ya know, before locking up at the end of the day and I heard a car beep its horn. Cheeky thing, though I didn't think t'was me they were honking at!" At this she gave a naughty wink and grin. "Well, I turned to look and sure enough saw a car pull up by this here young woman—" she tapped Annie's image in the photo several times, "or someone very like her. Anyway, she stopped. She was carrying a suitcase or something. I thought maybe she was headed for the train or maybe the bus station. I'm nosy like that, I am, it's a terrible fault, I'm sure." Mrs. Grady shrugged and smiled. A twinkle in the older woman's eye belied the sheepish tone in her voice.

"So, this fella in the car opens the door and I figure he's no stranger cuz she's bent over, peeping in at 'im and talking with him for more than a minute or so. Finally, she shakes her head, and starts to be on her way, shuts the door on him. But he follows her in the car like. I watch a bit, to see what'd come next, didn't want anything bad to happen to that there girlie. Thought I might hav'ta call the po-lice. But, after a bit, the fella gave up and drove away. So, I finished locking up and went home."

"Why did you think the person in the car was a man? Did you see him?" Kit asked.

"Well, now you mention it, no, I did not. But, a pretty young thing like that, I was sure it'd be a man after her."

"Do you remember what kind of car it was?" Sondra asked.

"No, it was dusk and I'm not much of one for recognizing cars."

"Hmm," said Kit, nodding and looking away, hoping to dismiss the garrulous old lady so she and Sondra could have some privacy.

"Any little thing I can do to help out I will, doncha know?" Taking Kit's hint, Mrs. Grady ambled back to the curtained area of the shop.

"Well, now, that was interesting!" Sondra intoned between mouthfuls of scone.

"I guess if we can take any of it at face value. It might not have been Annie at all."

"Well, it matches the time of her disappearance. Usually, boyfriends are the culprits in this sort of thing."

"Maybe you've been reading too many detective novels."

"And maybe you don't read enough." Sondra retorted. "So, what makes you think it wasn't her?"

"Well, I'm not sure we can take what a nosy old lady with poor eyesight saw at dusk a block away as gospel truth."

"Granted, it's a little flimsy. Still, it's worth considering," said Sondra. "I think so anyway."

They remained silent while Sondra finished her scones.

"Wow, that hit the spot," said Sondra, wiping the last crumbs from her lips. "So, should I go first or you?"

"Well, I don't have much to tell about Annie, no one's seen her since the summer and no one knew her name or anything, just recognized her. She didn't grow up around here, just worked."

Kit wasn't going to tell Sonn about the man Annie was seen with. Better she keep believing that Gramps was murdered than suspect he'd committed suicide because Annie had broken his heart. Besides, it would probably end up being irrelevant, or so Kit hoped.

"I did check out Mr. Schultz's digs. He's a cat lover and has a very fervent protector in the guise of a cigarette-smoking female gnome." Sondra guffawed, and Kit regaled her with the little she'd been able to discover about him as well as her disconcerting encounter with him on the street.

Mrs. Grady ambled over. "You want I should refill the pot, dearies?" Both nodded.

"And some more scones, please?" asked Kit who had been looking sadly at the few crumbs Sonn had left on the plate.

Once Mrs. Grady was out of earshot, Sondra said, "It doesn't seem like Serge would be able to pre-meditate anything, unless, of course, he's a fantastic actor or someone else put him up to it."

"Like who?"

"Like his buddy, Roger Dufresne."

"What makes you think it was pre-meditated? I thought we were including his friends, as in a fight or something."

"Well, the papers, the key, it all seems connected, like there's something else going on. It didn't feel to me like it was a rash action. In fact, I'm sure it was intentional." Sondra had a far-away look in her eye.

"I suppose," said Kit, "but now we're back to motive."

Mrs. Grady returned with a full pot and scones. She placed the scones on the table and tipped the hot brew into their cups. Kit buttered and began devouring one of the scones, while Sondra sipped her tea and paged through her notebook.

Holding her little book open with one hand and tapping on a page with the other. "Well, I did note down your suggestion that maybe there was an FLQ cell involved."

Kit rolled her eyes. "You're taking that crazy idea of mine seriously?"

Sonn said, "Somehow gardening, plum pudding, political gain, and just plain creepiness don't seem motives enough on their own."

Exactly, thought Kit then said, "Usually it has to do with money or women or both, *cherchez la femme,* eh?"

"Or *cherchez l'homme.*"

"Huh?"

"Oh, well, I'm thinking that André and Claude are more than just good friends." Sondra responded to Kit's puzzled expression. "He was with Claude the cook at the movies the other night, remember? And he and Claude live together."

Kit said, "OK, but what does that prove?"

"Well, I ran into André at the hospital today, and he was really mean to me. He knew I was Gramps' granddaughter and that seemed to make him mad. Claude must've told him about us and Gramps."

"Yeah, but what does that prove?"

"Well, you know, maybe they're, like, together. When we saw them at the movies Claude and André looked like they were on a date, not just two buddies."

"Sondra, how on earth could you tell anything about them? They were what, six or more people between us?"

Sondra shrugged. "But, if they were together, and Gramps got wind of it, he would've taken grave offense."

"Go on."

"Well, Gramps was awfully old-fashioned about sex and all. He didn't take kindly to homosexuals, called them 'deviants' and 'perverts.' Remember?"

Kit had to agree. "Yeah, Gramps wouldn't have hesitated sharing his righteous indignation to Claude's face!"

"If they were separatists, maybe even *felquistes* on top of being homosexuals . . . " Sondra shook her head as though

Evidence of Uncertain Origin

Gramps' indignation would know no bounds.

Kit continued what she knew her sister would be thinking, "And the threat of exposure would give them both a motive." Kit still found it almost impossible to use the "m" word.

"Exactly," said Sondra, "and maybe the papers in the briefcase were some kind of record of their illegal activities and plans."

"But then wouldn't Annie be implicated since Mrs. Grady saw her give Gramps the briefcase?"

"Well, she did disappear—if she were involved, then leaving town with no forwarding address makes perfect sense!"

Kit groaned inwardly, all of this speculation was digging Sondra ever deeper into the murder hole. At least she wasn't haunted by the possibility of suicide. Kit just wished they'd dig up enough facts to convince them both that Gramps' death was accidental.

"And what about the money and papers Serge and Dufresne were looking at in the pub? Maybe they are involved with Claude and André in some FLQ plot together. Maybe Annie was part of it too but changed her mind and decided to give Gramps the evidence he needed to expose them. And, what if the man in the car Mrs. Grady saw was one of them, and had found out about her betrayal. Maybe she was running away out of fear." Sondra bent her head to the task of recording her ideas in the little book.

Kit shifted uncomfortably, what if, she thought, what if Gramps had been murdered? Don't be ridiculous, Kit gave herself a mental shake; don't let Sondra's determination cloud your reason. Sondra was as stubborn as their grandfather had been. Once convinced of something, they were both like dogs worrying a bone and, thought Kit wrinkling her nose, as unpleasant as the mercaptans from Serge's cats' urine. Certainly their convictions could be as caustic to others as that persistent stink.

Kit glanced at Sondra. An almost painful love pierced her as she watched her sister's wild red curls bobbing gently as she wrote in her notebook. Kit knew that regardless of how tiresome it would all doubtless become, she'd stick it out. She sighed, what we won't do for love, my dear sister!

At last Sondra looked up from her writing. "Oh, Kit, I can't wait to get the key Madame McIntyre's going to send me. I think we're getting somewhere. I bet that key will lead us to enough evidence to get the police involved!"

Kit nodded her head, not so sure where it was they were actually getting to, and not convinced she wanted to go.

It was starting to get dark when they climbed into the Volvo. Kit was tired, so Sondra took the wheel, driving through town to the entrance of the 2 & 20 Highway. Accelerating onto the road, Kit thought that they were lucky to be heading into Montréal in the evening against the rush hour traffic.

"Kit, did you notice anything funny about the power steering when you drove in this morning?"

"No, why?" Kit yawned.

"Well, it seems a little unresponsive. I guess I'll ask J-P to take it in to the mechanic."

Kit sat back, and watched as the houses of Ste. Anne scooted by them. Sonn always drove in the slow lane so it would take them hours to get home.

Kit noticed a blue Ford truck preparing to merge into traffic from the Baie-d'Urfé on the ramp ahead. Sondra must've seen it too, because Kit heard the "tick-tick" of the turn signal. Sonn would be pulling into the fast lane to let the truck enter in front of her. But instead of easing into the other lane, the car just kept speeding forward.

Kit sat up, alert. "Sonn! What are you doing! Turn the

Evidence of Uncertain Origin

damned car!!"

"I can't! It won't turn!"

Everything seemed to happen at once. Sondra hit the brakes and Kit was hurled forward, throwing up her hands to brace herself. Kit heard the car horn blaring and saw the truck ahead of them swerve into the fast lane. They avoided a direct impact, but the Volvo scraped along the truck's rear fender. It sounded like giant claws scratching down a blackboard and the contact flung Kit sideways. Her head hit the passenger window. The car stopped moving. She was dazed. Sonn was screaming her name. Kit grabbed Sonn's arm, to reassure her.

Kit looked up. They were now tilted off the shoulder of the road; the blue Ford had come to rest a few metres ahead of them. A man got out of the truck. Traffic zoomed past them.

Someone was trying to open the Volvo's door on the passenger's side, yelling to them in French. Kit couldn't understand what he was saying. Groggy, Kit finally figured out he wanted her to unlock the door, so she did and he helped them both out and onto the verge.

Kit touched her head; it was sticky. She must be bleeding, again, but it all seemed vague and insignificant. All she could do was hang on to Sondra. Kit kept asking Sondra if she was OK. And Sondra kept reassuring her, yes, I'm fine. The steering wheel had kept Sondra from hitting the wind shield or dashboard. The wind had been knocked out of her, but otherwise she insisted she was "fine."

They sat in the dusk on the side of the road until the police arrived. Residents from the houses along the highway brought blankets and tea, which Kit sipped without really tasting. Her head ached. She was nauseous.

Three Sûreté du Québec officers came and were kind. After questioning them, and arranging for a tow truck to move their car, one of the officers drove them home.

Sondra wanted her to go to the hospital, but Kit refused,

remembering her last visit not so many days ago. Her head hurt but the wound was not deep and had already stopped bleeding. Sondra capitulated only if Kit would let her call in their father. This she agreed to as the lesser of two evils.

Shock made her compliant and her father had a gentle touch when it came down to it. He concurred that she did not need a hospital, just rest and a hot cup of tea. He admonished Sondra to wake her up every so often through the night as she might be slightly concussed. He cleaned out her wound and covered it with a Band-Aid. He wouldn't leave until Sondra promised to call him if Kit got any worse.

Kit wanted to make sure she didn't get "any worse" so she took her headache and exhaustion straight to bed. Kit fell asleep lulled by the murmurs of Sondra and J-P in the kitchen discussing the car.

"I'll call the mechanic tomorrow, I'm sure there's a reasonable explanation."

"There better be. That old clunker could've killed us!"

"Thankfully, it did not, *ma chérie.*"

Evidence of Uncertain Origin

Montréal
Tuesday, October 21, 1969

I bet it smells like snow, Kit thought. She was lying in bed looking out the guestroom window at a grey sky. She gently prodded the area just above her right temple where she'd hit the passenger side door. The Band-aid had come off during the night and there was a good sized lump, but no blood. She'd slept fitfully, since Sondra had woken her up several times during the night. At least there was no evidence of concussion— no more nausea, blurred vision or headache— although Kit felt like staying in bed for the rest of the day, no, maybe the rest of her life.

They don't call them comforters for nothing, she thought as she rolled over, snuggled the covers around her and stared at the green and brown leafy patterns on the wallpaper.

Kit wondered what Paul was doing, likely dashing off to classes or having coffee with that cute blonde in his class, what was her name? Rachel, yes that was it. Before she could fall into her familiar despondency Michel came to mind, and she wondered what it would've been like if . . . then chided herself. She wondered whether or not to see him today and if so, how she would angle herself out of Sondra's way.

Her vague musings were interrupted by a firm knock on the door and Sondra's voice, "Hey, are you still alive in there? It's already nine a.m., Jean-Pierre's gone, Deirdre's off to school and Max is watching 'Mr. Dressup'. Come on, we've got some sleuthing to do!"

Kit's groan must have been audible as Sondra laughed and opened the door. "Ha! Caught you napping! *Tempus Fugit* sister, dear!"

"Go away, you torturer of the innocent," Kit mumbled, pulling the covers over her head and engaging Sondra in their old morning routine. Not only were they opposites in colouring, height and body type, Kit was night to Sondra's day.

"Now, now, we'll have none of that," Sondra lapsed into her head nurse tone. "We've got to review our notes."

"Your notes," came Kit's muffled correction.

"Well, I'm glad you're listening to me, Kit. I'm cooking your breakfast and while you eat, I'll review my notes with you. So, come along." With that Sondra pulled back the covers exposing Kit's long frame to the chill of a Montréal fall morning before the heat is turned on.

"Vicious, unkind, cruel, ungrateful, wretched wench," gaining momentum, Kit finished her litany of Sondra's character flaws by hurling her pillow at her sister's head. Anticipating it, Sondra ducked and retreated laughing, closing the door behind her. Kit could hear her say, "Brekkies in fifteen minutes!"

An hour later, fully clothed, Kit finished the last of her eggs, English muffin and orange juice. She sat back, sipping her coffee and listening to Sondra's recitation of the results of their last few days work. Sonn was at the summing up part.

"So, what do we have so far?" A rhetorical question if there ever was one. "One, Annie is AWOL."

"Is that true? Just because we don't know where she is, doesn't mean she is AWOL."

"You do have a point there," Sondra sounded pleased as she jotted something down in her notebook, and looked at Kit. "I've marked it as 'suspicious coincidence' for the time being: leaving her job right after Gramps was murdered. And being seen carrying a suitcase and talking to a man in a car."

"Her disappearance could be unrelated to Gramps' death."

"Or, it could be directly related to it. And if it is, it could mean she had some direct connection to his death, perhaps was even responsible for it. Or thought she was. I mean, if there was an FLQ cell operating at the Lodge and if she'd given Gramps the evidence to expose them, she'd have plenty of reason to leave suddenly if she figured out that he'd been murdered because of the information she'd given him."

At the mention of their grandfather's death, Sondra grew silent and Kit saw the colour drain from her face. As persistent as her convictions were, Sondra's moods had always been mercurial, and Kit, with years of practice, bent her attention to drawing Sondra's interest again. After all, in spite of her own reservations, Sondra's reasoning was valid. "So, what you are saying is, we need to find out what happened to Annie."

Sondra brightened. "Yes, precisely!" She wrote again in her booklet. "That's one of the items on our 'to-do' list."

"There are others?" Kit teased; gentle bantering always bolstered Sonn's spirits.

"Oh yes, we need to keep tabs on Private McIntyre. Also, once we get the key from his wife, we'll have to figure out where it comes from."

"No easy task, I'll warrant." Kit's own mood was beginning to flag; she was tired just thinking about the work ahead of them.

"Why did Private McIntyre's cancer flare up and push him into a coma right now? I'm sure he knows something, especially since Gramps gave him the key. I can't wait to get my hands on it. And why did Private McIntyre react so strangely to our visit? If there was an FLQ cell, Gramps probably told his friends about it, maybe even entrusted his evidence to them. Maybe Private McIntyre was trying to warn us. I mean André was his nurse. What if he knew that André was a *felquiste* and probably involved with Gramps' death? Maybe he was afraid André would see us there and harm us somehow or him."

"Or," Kit countered, "Maybe the key has nothing to do with

Gramps' death. Maybe McIntyre and Gramps had had an argument before Gramps died and he felt badly about it, maybe even guilty. If it was an accident, for argument's sake, maybe McIntyre figured their fight had made Gramps careless. There are a lot of reasons, Sonn, why McIntyre would be upset to see us."

"OK, perhaps, but I still think Brault knew something about Gramps' murderer. Remember his wife saying she'd heard a 'click' on the line after they'd last spoken? I'm sure that whoever killed Gramps somehow killed Brault too. I wish there was a way to figure out if Brault's heart attack was natural or not. After all, a heart attack could be caused by someone injecting caffeine or something, like Dad said."

"Puh-leese!" Kit groaned, "let's not talk about him."

"Come on, Kit. Dad has been really sweet lately."

"'Really Sweet Lately'," Kit bit off each word with as much venom as she could muster. "It can never make up for his being 'Really Awful For Most Of Our Lives'." She glowered at the scarred surface of the old kitchen table, arms folded. Every muscle tensed for a fight while she waited for Sondra's reply.

Sonn sighed. "You're right, Kit, people don't ever change, Dad will be a villain for the rest of his life, no matter what."

Kit glanced up at her. Sondra's look verged on pity. Kit bristled, suspicious. "You don't mean that."

"No, I don't, but that's what you persist in believing." Sonn crossed her arms too and waited. For what, Kit wasn't sure. After all, what more was there? Still, she had promised to try to accept her sister's new take on their father. And she was here to support Sondra, on an errand of mercy, to help with, what? It all seemed to be getting fuzzy. She wasn't sure about anything anymore except the rage that welled up in her whenever her father was mentioned. Keeping that monster in check was exhausting. And this time she wasn't referring to her dad. Her head had started to ache and she didn't have

Evidence of Uncertain Origin

the strength to hold back her words.

"I can't help it, Sonn, I hate him. I just do. Maybe he's changed, but I don't see it. I think he's setting you and Jean-Pierre and the kids up for some big disappointment, like he did to us when we were little. Don't you remember all those days you'd spend sobbing when he didn't show up for your birthday, or Christmas, or Thanksgiving, or Easter, or, any important time for that matter?" Kit enumerated each defaulted holiday on her fingers.

"Nothing Gramps or Grannie Win or I could do or say would comfort you." Kit glared. "I hated him even more for disappointing you than for anything he did to me. I figured I was a big kid, I was older, I could handle it, but not you. You were so soft, so vulnerable, so, so, hopeful, every damn time. It killed me, I wanted to kill him. I still do sometimes." Kit put her hand on her head, the slight pressure helped calm the throbbing.

Kit hated feeling helpless more than anything. In that moment she hated Sondra too for being her one weakness, the one way that their Dad could still hurt her. Tears began to well up in her eyes. "Sonn, I don't need you lecturing me about people changing—even if it is true. I just don't believe it."

"Or, are you afraid to believe it?" Sondra asked in a quiet voice.

"Damn it, don't psycho-analyze me, Sonn!" Kit stood then sat, her head spinning.

Sondra reached across the table and touched Kit's arm. "Kit, I didn't mean any harm by it."

Kit, embarrassed now by her outburst, glanced at her sister, and blew her nose into the paper napkin wadded on the table next to her plate.

Sonn spoke into the silence. "I love you, Kit; you are my big sister and always will be." Kit looked up at her and Sondra smiled. "But sometimes, you are a real pain in the butt!"

"Ha. Well, for your information, Sonn, so are you!"

"I figured as much."

"So, how come you're so smart all of a sudden?"

"Ah, you've finally noticed my brilliance. It took you long enough!" Sondra tossed her head. Her red curls looked as if they had a life of their own.

Kit smiled, thankful for her sister's lightened mood.

"So, here's your assignment, if you dare to take it." Sonn tore off a page from her note book and handed it to Kit with an engaging grin.

Kit put up her hand. "I need a couple of aspirins before I even look at any of your lists."

"Oh, I'm sorry, Kit." Sondra jumped up and rummaged in a kitchen drawer, finding the aspirin bottle and handing it to Kit who popped back two with a last swig of coffee.

Kit glanced at the paper then up at Sondra. "No, fair! You know what I'm doing, but I have no idea what you're up to."

"Ah, my dear Watson, I shall be using the phone to do a little digging about our friend, Roger Dufresne. And today is my big interview with Claude the chef."

"Ah yes, where you must first disappoint his hopes of inheriting Gramps' abundant supply of toilet paper, and then somehow wring a confession out of him. Good luck with that! Ste. Anne's is looking pretty good right now."

"Yeah, I'm nervous about meeting Claude face to face. This will be the first time I confront someone who might've murdered Gramps." Sondra gulped. "And might be involved in an FLQ cell."

Kit's playfulness drained away. This was no game for Sondra, and from Sondra's perspective, she was walking into what could be a very dangerous situation. "Are you frightened, Sonn?"

Sondra nodded. "A little." Kit saw worry lines disturb the smoothness of her sister's brow.

Kit reached across the table and put her hand on Sondra's arm. "You don't have to do this, Sonn. You could wait and I could go with you."

Sondra shook her head. "Nope, not a good idea, we're running out of time, and you need to find out about Annie. I've got to follow through on this, Kit, and really, what could he do to me in broad daylight when you know where I'm going? Whoever is behind this, acts in the dark, secretly. If Claude did murder Gramps, he'll think of some other way to get rid of us and make it look like an accident.

"Besides," Sondra reached for her purse with a mischievous smile. "I have this." She pulled out an aerosol can with a flourish.

"What's that?"

"Mace, Kit, it's meant to disable an attacker." Sondra pointed at an imaginary foe and pretended to spray it into their eyes. "See?"

"Where the hell did you get it?" Kit reached for the can and read the list of ingredients.

"Dad has contacts in the police force and a few years back there was a serial rapist so he got this for me. I've never used it, but I know how to." She gestured for Kit to give it back to her then shoved it into her purse.

"You are still a brave woman, Sonn," Kit stood, stretched then tousled Sondra's hair. "Well, I'll be thinking of you as I reward myself with one of Mrs. Grady's mouth-watering scones."

"You rat! Don't rub it in," Sondra laughed.

Kit smiled to see the colour return to her sister's face. "Will it be OK if I use the loaner car?" asked Kit.

Sondra nodded and handed her the car keys. "Are you OK to drive?"

"If you're OK to confront a possible murderer, I'm fine to go looking for a missing woman." Kit knew, or was almost 100% sure, that there was no murderer to find, but a twinge of anxiety still crept into her tone.

"Good, but let me check your wound. Do you mind?"

"If it'll reassure you, sure, go ahead. The Band-aid fell off overnight, anyway."

"Well, there's a nice scab forming, and a bit of a bruise and bump. How's your other head wound?" Sonn fingered Kit's scalp searching for the other injury. "The older lump is going down. Man, Grannie Win was right, you are hard-headed."

Kit groaned at her grandmother's oft repeated comment on her stubbornness. "I prefer to call it persistence. Besides, I'm not the only one!"

"Okay, Okay" Sonn replied, a smile in her voice. "How's your headache?"

"Now that I'm not ranting about our father, it's almost gone."

"Good."

Kit asked, "By the way, how is the car?"

"There's no real structural damage and the engine's OK, but the driver's side doors are a write off. Thankfully, the insurance will cover the repairs."

"Any idea as to what happened to the steering?"

"J-P told the mechanic that the power steering failed so he'll look into it and fix that too. Are you sure you'll be alright to drive?"

"Yeah, I'll be fine. I'd rather be busy; it'll stop me thinking about things."

"Like Paul? Why don't you call him?"

"No way! What am I supposed to say to him anyway? 'You forgot my birthday—again.' He'll pull the 'Sorry-I-forgot-to-call-I-was-off-learning-to-save-lives' card on me and I'll end up feeling stupid and petty."

Sondra was smiling through gritted teeth at no one in particular as she did battle with the officiousness of

Senneville Lodge's very own "Dragon Lady." She couldn't understand why the "D.L." was stonewalling her today when she'd been forthcoming last week. Unless you were a relative, Pierre Elliot Trudeau, or the Pope himself she would not take a message or leave a message for any of the veterans at the Lodge. Had Captain Tremblay instructed the "D.L." to say nothing and told her to forward all of her, Sondra's, inquiries to him?

Sondra slouched in her chair, feet up on the table and was doodling on the pad next to the phone while she waited for the "D.L." to see if the captain was in and would deign to take her call.

"Yes?"

Taken by surprise, Sondra sat up straight and almost knocked over the cup of coffee she'd been ignoring. "Thanks for taking the time to speak with me, Captain."

"Yes," he repeated. Sondra heard caution in his voice.

"Yes," she echoed. "This is Corporal Flanagan's granddaughter. We've met? And spoken before on the phone?"

"Yes, and we ran into each other at the hospital. You were looking better than the first time we met." He sounded almost amused, to Sondra's chagrin.

"Thanks, yes, well, I am better." Sondra couldn't figure out how to proceed and a few seconds of silence ensued.

"How can I help you?"

"Do you remember what I said about my grandfather's death?"

"That you believed it was not an accident." The Captain's voice was neutral.

"Yes, well, we are," she wanted to say "investigating" but instead said, "following up on some ideas we had."

"I see."

"So, I'm hoping you will tell me if there was anyone who might be upset enough with my grandfather to want to do him harm."

"You do understand that I am not allowed to discuss the personal files of the veterans under my care."

"Oh yes, I do, but I thought if there was anything you could tell me at all, or anyone you think would talk to me about him, I'd be very grateful."

"Well, you have seen for yourself that not everyone loved your grandfather as you did."

"You mean the cook?"

"Corporal Claude Leduc?"

"Yes, that's the one." Sondra put a check mark next to his name on her pad of paper. "Was there anyone else?"

"There was the matter of the poker games."

"I beg your pardon?"

"Your grandfather never spoke to you about this?"

Wow, thought Sondra, was that what was on his mind when he'd called her last summer? "Not in so many words," she said.

"Since there were no formal complaints made, I suppose I could tell you about them. There is probably nothing to it, you understand."

"Of course, please continue."

"Your grandfather approached me a few months before he died. He claimed that there was a gambling problem with the men."

"Did he mention any names?"

"In fact, he accused Roger Dufresne and Serge Schultz of organizing the games."

"Did you believe him?"

"I thought he was exaggerating. The men often play cards and sometimes bet on the games in a friendly sort of way."

Sondra could imagine the shrug that went with the tone of voice. "My grandfather wasn't the kind to overreact to things, Captain."

"Perhaps not, but he had no concrete proof that this was more than a few men playing penny ante. And without that what could I do? I do not have the time or resources to investigate every petty complaint."

"Didn't it occur to you after the fact that maybe it was what got him killed?"

"No, the thought never entered my mind. Now, you will have to excuse me, I have a meeting I must attend."

"One more thing, Captain Tremblay, if you don't mind."

"Alright, what is it."

Sonn swallowed, in for a penny in for a pound, she thought before asking, "Is it possible that an FLQ cell could be operating under cover in the Lodge?" She held her breath.

After a brief pause, she heard an explosive sound that could be laughter on the other end of the phone. "I'm sorry, Mme. Flanagan, I realize this is a serious question for you, but, really, it seems absurd."

"I'll take that as a 'no' then?"

"Why on earth would you imagine such a thing?"

Sondra felt her face get hot; she took a deep breath before responding, "Well, if Gramps found out about it, and threatened exposure, it could be a motive for murder."

"I see." Mirth had been replaced by a thoughtful tone. Then, with a sigh, he said, "Mme. Flanagan, I know your grandfather's death has been a shock. It is always difficult to come to terms with sudden death. I do understand this. However, these suspicions seem, please excuse the term, far-fetched."

Sondra gripped the phone receiver, of course she should've known Captain Tremblay wouldn't believe her. "Please, Captain Tremblay, can you say with complete 100% certainty that none of the veterans or staff at the Lodge are members of the FLQ?"

She heard a sudden exhalation, before the Captain said, "Of course I cannot."

"Thank you for your time, Captain." Sondra hung up. She leaned back in her chair and stared at the ceiling for a few seconds, tapped the end of her pencil on her teeth before she flipped back to the page entitled "Suspects." Roger Dufresne's name was already circled with the word "interview" beside it. She scrawled underneath: "FLQ, money and papers, gambling." Were Dufresne and Serge raising money for the FLQ through their poker games? She'd read articles about the FLQ robbing banks and using the money to fund their activities. Why not poker?

Kit was relieved that there was only one "A. Desrocher" in the phone book she'd just had to rifle through. It was chained to a public and very popular phone booth. Someone pounded on the door while Kit was rummaging through her purse for a dime. Kit shrugged at the bedraggled woman glaring at her through the glass before dropping the dime in the slot and dialing A. Desrocher's number; it was out of service. Kit scrounged the dime out of the coin return, dropped it into the slot again and dialed the phone company. The woman started pounding on the door again. Kit plugged her left ear so she could hear the answer to her inquiry: Annie's phone service had been cut off for nonpayment of her bill. Kit silenced the woman with a scowl long enough to write down Annie's address.

Kit exited the phone booth, and the bedraggled woman pushed by her slamming the phone booth door shut behind her. Kit shivered, from exasperation as well as the damp cold.

Kit found that Annie's address belonged to the upper floor of a duplex on rue Saint-Georges a few blocks away from the MacDonald College campus. A young man answered her knock; his scruffy hair, jeans and grey sweatshirt identified him as a probable student. He had been there since September. When she showed him Annie's photo he shook his head and shrugged his shoulders. "Sorry," he said as he closed the door.

Kit trundled back down the black wrought iron stairs and stood in front of the door to the ground floor flat. A small card taped below the doorbell identified the occupant as "Mme. Gaspar, Concierge/Building Manager." She pressed on the button and waited, wondering why Annie had chosen to leave so precipitately.

Mme. Gaspar was almost as tall as Kit, but older, heavier, better coifed and blue-eyed. She stood in the doorway clutching a broom as if eager to sweep Kit off her front steps at the first opportunity.

Kit gulped, and decided to try out Sondra's lie. "I'm looking for Annie Desrocher. She had been very kind to my grandfather who lived at the Veterans Lodge, and when he died he left her something in his will. Anything you can tell me about Annie's whereabouts would be very helpful."

Thankfully, Mme. Gaspar set aside her broom and invited Kit inside. They stood facing each other in a darkened hallway. Several bulky beaver coats were draped along one wall, large boots lined up below. A mirror hung on the opposite wall above a small table topped with a doily. Despite the astringent scent of bleach assaulting her nose, Kit was relieved to be out of the cold.

Mme. Gaspar answered Kit in clipped sentences: Yes, Annie had left half way through August. There was no explanation or forwarding address. Annie said she'd come back to collect her belongings. But, Annie hadn't come back. Instead, a couple of men with a van had emptied the apartment a week after she'd left. They dropped off Annie's key in Mme. Gaspar's mailbox.

"I don't think they were professional movers," she added.

Kit looked at Mme. Gaspar. How odd, she thought.

"Oh, I don't mean there was anything wrong with them, they just didn't do things properly; that's all."

Kit couldn't keep the dubious tone out of her voice.

"Really?"

Offended, Mme. Gaspar added, "I see plenty of movers in my job, and you can take my word for it, they were not professionals."

"I see, yes, of course," said Kit, hoping to placate her.

The older woman nodded, but raised an eyebrow at Kit.

"Do you mind if I take a look at her rental form?" Kit asked, hoping to find the name of a friend or relative.

Opening a drawer in the small table, Mme. Gaspar pulled out the form and showed it to Kit. She was surprised to see that the only reference name was Michel's. "Wasn't this her employer?"

The landlady glanced at Kit. "Yes, I think he was." The look in those piercing blue eyes intimated there was more to the story. Kit swallowed hard before asking if the employer had visited her at the apartment.

Mme. Gaspar pursed her lips and looked away. "Really, what my tenants do is none of my business."

"I realize that, but anything you can tell me might help me locate her."

"Who did you say you were?" Those piercing eyes again.

Kit stepped back. "Um, my grandfather was her friend? With the will?" Her words trailed off.

"Well," Mme. Gaspar wrinkled up her nose as though she smelled something that needed a good application of bleach. "I'm not so sure about that. If your grandfather was so close to her, you would know already that she didn't have any family: no sisters or brothers, and both parents are dead." Mme. Gaspar reached out and yanked the rental form out of Kit's hands. "I think that's all I have to say to you, Miss . . . "

"Kit, um, Katherine, Katherine Flanagan."

"Yes, well, Miss Flanagan, I have nothing more to say to you." With that, Mme. Gaspar opened the door, and Kit backed out rapidly, almost tripping on the lintel. The door shut in Kit's face.

Evidence of Uncertain Origin

A few snowflakes swirled in the air as Kit turned and walked the two blocks to the replacement car. The heater didn't have time to get going, so she shivered during the five block drive back to the main street. Parking the car she checked her watch: eleven a.m., enough time to walk over to the bus station before lunch.

The "bus station" was more of a bus stop, located along the side of a gas station on rue Sainte-Anne. Kit walked past the single pump, and a bell tinkled as she opened the door into a dingy office. It was stuffy, but Kit didn't care, she was glad of the warmth.

Inside, a young man in greasy overalls lounged in a plastic chair, a car magazine on his lap, while a well-worn woman stood behind a glass partition. Both looked up as she entered.

The woman's mousey brown hair was pulled back in a pony-tail, held so tightly that it made Kit's head hurt to look at it. An insignia pasted on the glass partition indicated this was the part of the office dedicated to the bus company, so Kit walked over to it, and the man went back to leafing through his magazine. Curiosity roused the woman when Kit showed her the photo and asked if Annie had bought a bus ticket a month or two ago.

Mousey Brown picked up the photo; her brow furrowed and she grimaced at it for a few seconds before handing it back to Kit. She shrugged her shoulders and shook her head. "I'm not always on the counter," she replied by way of an excuse. "Come back in an hour, Todd'll be on then. Maybe he'll recognize her. He has an eye for the blondes anyway," she added with a leer that hardened her face. The gas station fumes were starting to make Kit nauseous. Or maybe she was hungry. Kit hoped it was the latter and headed towards the Tea Shop.

Finishing her sandwich, and reviewing the morning's discoveries, Kit could not avoid the uncomfortable thought that she'd have to talk to Michel about Annie. Between the gum-chewing blonde and Mme. Gaspar it looked very much like Annie had had a male "friend" who most likely was Michel. Staring down at the photo, Kit couldn't believe that the perky blonde could be responsible for her grandfather's death, but her abrupt leave-taking, though probably a coincidence, was still suspect, even to Kit. What if Gramps had committed suicide because he found out about Annie and Michel? Had Annie left suddenly out of guilt or worry about scandal and exposure? Or had Gramps discovered that Annie was involved with the FLQ? Kit could kick herself for voicing that ridiculous theory in the first place, but Sondra had latched onto it which meant she'd have to factor it into things too. And, considering the times they were living in, maybe it wasn't so crazy.

Kit sighed, if she were even a little suspicious, Sondra would be chomping at the bit – no matter what, she had to keep even the whisper of suicide away from Sondra's ears. It meant more footwork. She'd have to follow it through to the bitter end to prove to herself as well as Sondra that Gramps' death was a horrible accident and not murder, or worse, suicide.

Kit pushed away from the table and paid for her tea. She smiled at Mrs. Grady who was seated behind the counter and gave Kit a quick nod along with her change. Kit noticed that the normally garrulous old lady wasn't so chatty today, probably because she was engrossed in knitting an amorphous looking garment out of neon-pink yarn with enormous needles.

After purchasing a notebook at D'Aoust's general store across the street, Kit headed back to the bus station and met up with the infamous Todd. He turned out to be a weasel-faced young man in his late twenties, affecting a James Dean look complete with slicked back hair, tight white t-shirt, defiant slouch and a cigarette dangling from his lower lip. He eyed Kit in a methodical way, giving her the distinct impression he was doing it more to keep in character than out of any real sexual interest.

"Marlie said you'd be back," he said, preening himself a little as Kit pushed the photo towards him.

"Yes, I'm hoping you'll be able to tell me whether the girl in the photo bought a ticket from you and if so, where to," Kit tried to smile without giving him any wrong ideas about his powers of attraction.

He stared at the image, giving it his full attention then stared off into space. Kit's patience had almost given out when he said, "I have seen her."

Kit brightened, waiting for more information.

"Around," he added.

"Do you remember if she came in to buy a ticket about two months ago?" Kit tried not to seem too eager.

"I couldn't rightly say, but I don't think so. I did notice her walking about. A cute blonde like that, of course I'd notice, but I don't think she ever took the bus while I was working, and I haven't seen her since the summer." He pushed the photo back and smiled, showing a gap in his teeth. "Sorry, lady," he looked her in the eye and held her gaze a little longer than necessary, beaming a sleepy suggestiveness in her general direction. "Have you tried the train station?"

The train station was next to the 2 & 20 Highway so she stopped by on her drive back to Montréal. It was a quaint brick structure hovering next to the railroad tracks on the outskirts of town. The train attendant, a black man of indeterminate age and nattily dressed in a Canadian National uniform, was helpful. Yes, he had seen Annie; yes he had sold her a ticket. Where to? Well, that he couldn't say with certitude, although it was east.

He pulled off his hat and rubbed his balding head. "I remember her because it was kind of odd. She plunked down some money and asked how far east this would take her. Well, I showed her a couple of train schedules and she picked a place. Let's see, nope, can't remember where to. Anyway, she bought her ticket, one way, and then left. I believe the ticket was for the next day. I didn't notice her getting on the train. It's busy some times, so she might've slipped on without my seeing her."

Kit was discomfited by this news. It looked like Annie had made a run for it; but what did it mean? A guilty conscience couldn't be eliminated, but guilt about what? That her actions had led to Gramps' accident or suicide? That she was afraid of people finding out about her affair with Michel or her involvement with the FLQ or some other as yet unknown reason?

She eased the car onto Highway 2 & 20 for the drive back. Checking the time she saw she could still catch Michel at the café. She flicked on the radio; it was tuned to the CBC, and the news was on.

" . . . no injuries this time although a car parked near the mailbox was damaged . . . " Another bomb, she thought, and wondered where it had been this time. Kit wondered where it would all lead. Despite having almost been killed by a bomb just a few days before, she still felt some bit of sympathy for the separatists, or at least for their desperation and for their devotion to their revolutionary cause. On the other hand, was armed insurrection really going to end well for anyone? The words from the FLQ's pamphlet rolled through her mind "During 1968 we tried to make people understand, in 1969 we will kill those who have not understood." It looked to Kit like they just might mean it.

Kit wished she'd paid more attention to the political upheaval that had been brewing in Montréal over the last years, but since moving to Ontario she'd become cocooned in her own little life's dramas and concerns. She should've paid more attention when she had to read Hugh MacLennan's novel, *Two Solitudes* for her Canadian Lit class. It might've given her more insight into the divide between French and

Evidence of Uncertain Origin

English Canada.

By the time she reached the turn off for boulevard Décarie, Kit had given up trying to figure out what she thought about revolutionaries blowing things up. All she hoped for at the moment was that their activities wouldn't delay her today. How *bourgeois*, she grimaced.

Although Kit wasn't looking forward to bringing up the subject of Annie with Michel, she couldn't figure out a way around it. She had to find out if he knew why Annie had left so soon after Gramps' death. After all, it appeared they had been involved.

The few random snowflakes had stopped falling and the low-hanging afternoon sun glinted recklessly under an overcast sky lighting the almost leafless trees along the road and reflecting brilliantly in the storefront windows. Kit wished for a similar illumination as she drove, but as it stood now she was still very much in the dark. She hadn't even the shadow of an idea about how to broach the subject of Annie with Michel.

Sondra had considered rescheduling her meeting with Claude LeDuc but wasn't sure she'd be able to convince him to see her again if she cancelled. Besides, it wasn't always easy to get babysitting and the girl downstairs had been available this afternoon. So here she was, sitting on a red velvet settee holding an elegant gold-rimmed china tea cup in one hand and poised to select one of the delicate looking sugar cookies being offered to her by Corporal-Chef Claude LeDuc from a matching plate.

"Thank you, Claude, did you bake these?"

"Yes," the big man returned the plate to the ornately carved coffee table and sat in an armchair upholstered in a fabric fraught with a geometric pattern in gold and midnight blue. He crossed his legs and said, "Now, please tell me, what is this about your grandfather's will? I find it puzzling that he would even mention me. We were certainly not friends, you understand."

"I gathered that from your reaction to my sister's and my visit to the Lodge."

Claude flushed. "I take my role very seriously."

"Perhaps too seriously at times, my dear?" suggested André Verdun, who sat draped on the arm of the voluminous chair, his hand resting along the back. His hospital orderly uniform was replaced by fitted brown corduroy slacks and a velveteen smoking jacket in burgundy. A patterned cravat in deep reds, browns and beiges tied the whole ensemble together.

Very nice, thought Sondra as she took a small bite of her cookie. Burgundy would suit J-P; I wonder if I should ask André where he bought his jacket? She discounted this idea. Although André's attitude towards her had warmed since their last encounter, consulting him for fashion advice might be pushing it. Besides, both men were watching her expectantly.

"These cookies are wonderful," she gushed. Then she took a sip of tea, and said, "I do understand that my grandfather could be very opinionated at times. He too was a chef, in the Navy."

"Hrmph, a cook in the navy is not the same as a chef in the army!" huffed Claude.

"There, there, Claude, don't get upset." André patted Claude on his shoulder.

"Yes," Sondra plowed on, "I am sorry that you disagreed with each other about culinary matters. But was that enough to make you dislike him so much?" Sondra held her breath.

André hopped off the chair and sat next to Sondra on the settee. "No, you are right, that was not all."

"André, stop!"

"No, my dear, I must say this for both of us." Facing Sondra, his face stern he said, "Your grandfather was a very nasty little man."

The heat rose in Sondra's cheeks. She balled her fists and wanted to pummel or, barring that, hurl a brutal insult at the man seated next to her. Instead, she took a deep breath and through gritted teeth said, "What do you mean by that?"

"I do not mean to speak badly of the dead, but your grandfather found out about us." André reached over and took Claude's hand, continuing, "Your grandfather held it over Claude's head, threatening to tell the military authorities about us. He made life a hell for Claude. Every day, by looks or sly comments he would mock him. No wonder Claude hated him! I hated him and I never even met him!"

"Is that why you killed him?" Sondra blurted out.

The air seemed to leave the room.

"What?" stammered Claude. "Kill him? No one killed him; he was hit by a car. It was an accident."

The obvious shock on both their faces was rather convincing. Sondra put down her tea cup, preparing herself for a quick exit.

"You have the gall to come into our home and accuse us of murdering your grandfather?" André stood and glowered down at her.

Anger made her bold. "Well, yes that does look like what I've done, doesn't it? But you did hate him, and he is dead."

"And he did not leave anything at all for me in his will, did he?" accused Claude.

"Actually, no, but I needed to talk to you. I needed to ask you, because, you see, I do think he was killed, but maybe not by you."

"That's comforting," Claude said.

"You are a very silly woman." André scolded. "What if we were murderers? Do you think we would let you get away?"

"You don't think I told people where I was coming this afternoon? I am not that silly, and I did not take you for idiots!" Sondra rose. "By the way, just to be thorough, where were you when my grandfather died?"

"Don't answer her, André, it's insulting."

"What harm can it do, Claude? We were on Île d'Orleans. We go there every July for our holidays."

The last Sondra saw of them, they were standing side by side in their foyer watching her walk down the short pathway between manicured bushes to the street. Could Gramps really have been so mean spirited? Well, she thought, no one is perfect, and he was quite old-fashioned in his values.

Sondra stopped and almost turned back. I forgot to ask them about the FLQ, she thought, although it was a moot point now since they were out of town when Gramps was murdered. Unless. She turned to look back at their door, now closed. Unless, she thought, there were other members of the cell who carried out the murder, like Serge and Dufresne and possibly even Annie.

⚜

Kit had decided against stopping in at the flat before heading over to the café, but she did park the car on Hutchison. The walk over was supposed to clear her head and give her a chance to figure out how to approach Michel. Although she was profoundly embarrassed by their last encounter, she also recognized with some discomfort a yearning curiosity. Maybe she was more like her father than she wanted to admit, but she quelled that idea almost before she thought it. The circumstances are totally different, she rationalized.

Sure enough, Kit could see that Michel was already ensconced at the café. Sitting, his back to the window with his long legs stretched out under the table, he was reading a paper and smoking. The picture of suave sophistication, thought Kit. He won't be surprised that I've come, either. His imagined arrogance annoyed her somewhat. She took a deep breath, pushed through the door and walked up to his table where she stood and waited for him to notice her.

Glancing up from his reading, Kit could see Michel start, exclaiming "Katherine!" His obvious surprise at her appearance pleased her. So he wasn't as self-assured as he'd seemed. She relished the sensation of having the upper hand, however brief it may be.

Smiling a little Kit asked, "May I join you?"

"But of course, forgive me, I forget myself, please do sit." He stood gallantly and pulled out the chair for her, although he seemed a bit more unsteady on his feet than she'd remembered. Had he been drinking?

Michel signaled the waitress for a café latte before folding his *La Presse* and setting it down beside his coffee. Kit noticed that it didn't take long for him to recover his *savoir faire*.

Seated now, Kit decided to plunge in while she still had some control of her emotions; subtlety was not her strong suit.

"I didn't want to come, Michel . . . " It was a small lie, she realized, but she had to start somewhere.

" . . . but . . . " Michel said, smiling.

" . . . but, I've got something I have to ask you about."

"And what could that be, *ma belle petite amie?*"

"Well," Kit couldn't help gulping and staring past him, out the window at the shop sign across the street. "Well, I wanted to know about Annie."

Kit caught Michel's startle reflex out of the corner of her eye. It must mean that he and Annie were lovers, she thought with a sinking feeling. His face was backlit so Kit couldn't see his expression, but he shifted as though his chair was uncomfortable. "That is an odd request, *ma petite anglaise.*" His tone was careful.

Nikki Everts

"I guess it is. I mean, I'm not trying to pry, Michel," she was on unsteady ground; should she tell him everything? A part of her wanted to blurt it all out and be done with it, but she had to protect Sondra. Old habits die hard. It was easier to go with half a truth, or was it half a lie? She was jealous of Annie, so she might as well go with that. "It's just that, well, she was pretty and you worked together and I thought, or wondered, if you and she were, um . . . " she trailed off hoping he'd catch her drift.

" . . . were lovers?" Michel said, reaching over to touch her hand and look deep into her eyes.

"Yeah, I guess," Kit turned her face away.

"My little Katherine, she was nothing to me."

"But, you were together for a while?"

"If we were?"

"Well, are you still together?"

"Ah, the married woman asks if there is another woman in the picture, how delicious!" He put her hand to his lips. Michel was teasing her now, and she relaxed a bit.

Kit laughed, embarrassed, and pulled her hand away; after all, she was jealous. Annie was much prettier than she was. "You're right, but I can't help wondering about you and her." She tried her best to look imploring but feared she was exaggerating things. Damn it, she thought, I'm a biologist, not a coquette! She sipped at her *café latte*.

Michel sat back and took a puff on his cigarette, picked a piece of tobacco off his lip with his thumb and third finger, before looking up at her with a crooked smile and saying. "No need to bother yourself about her, Katherine."

Kit leaned towards him and replied, "But, Michel, it does bother me. I don't have a right to ask, but, are you still seeing her?"

"No, Katherine, I am not still seeing her."

"Well, were you in love with her?"

Michel heaved a sigh, sat up, stubbing out his cigarette as

he said, "The short answer is 'no,' but I see that I cannot escape your interrogations, so here is the small story of Michel and Annie.

"We started working at Senneville Lodge around the same time. We often worked late together. We were both lonely. She was an attractive woman." Michel finished by shrugging his shoulders, raising his eyebrows and sending her a look that implied their affair was an inevitable outcome of the circumstances.

"So why did you stop seeing her since it was so bloody convenient?" Kit asked.

Michel smiled sadly. "You understand how these things go, Katherine; she began to want more. She was upset when I told her I did not. That was the last time I saw her. She told me then that she could not continue working with me. She did not show up for work the next day. I called, but she wouldn't answer and the next thing I knew she'd left town. That was that."

"Did the residents find out about your affair?"

"*Mais non!*"

"Why not?"

"Come now, you cannot be that naïve? After all, have you told your sister about our meetings?" He sent her a penetrating look.

Kit's face felt hot. "Well, no, I have not."

"Yes, exactly, some things are private. Besides, Annie was popular with the men. It might have made things difficult."

"And how did Annie feel towards them? Did she ever talk about them with you? Complain about them? Have favourites?"

"She was good with the men and liked them. In any case, she never complained to me about any of them. She didn't have any favourites. She kept it professional."

A surge of indignation on her grandfather's behalf made Kit rummage through her purse for the photo of Annie and her grandfather at the party. Finding it, she plunked it down in front of Michel. The snapshot showed Annie's hand on her grandfather's shoulder. He was seated in his wheelchair looking up at her while she smiled down at him. Poking at it, she demanded, "How 'professional' does that look to you?" Kit's vehemence surprised them both.

Michel glanced at the photo, then he picked it up for a closer look, leaving Kit for the moment to ponder the possibility that maybe Annie had liked her grandfather; maybe she had encouraged him, even innocently. Maybe her dour, no nonsense grandfather had fallen in love with Annie. Stranger things had happened.

Compassion for her grandfather welled up in her: such a sentimental and romantic malady. All those jokes about rich old men marrying young beautiful blondes had to come from somewhere.

Michel returned the photo which she tucked into her purse. He leaned back and asked, "So, why is this so important to you, Katherine?"

His blunt question startled Kit into blurting out, "It worries me because if Gramps was in love with her and found out about you both, it might have made him careless, depressed. It might have contributed to his death."

"Ah-h, yes, I see."

Kit had no one else with whom to share her concerns that Gramps might've been suicidal. Michel sat waiting, as if he could see that there was more she wanted to get off her chest. It was such a relief to speak, to unburden herself so she continued.

"Before, you said that Gramps thought someone was stealing from *him*. Maybe it wasn't from *him*; maybe he was trying to find out if you knew anything was missing. You see, Annie gave him something, papers. And she was scared when she did it. Could he have helped her steal these papers from someone? He might've agreed to help her out of chivalry and love, but if it got him involved in anything illegal, he'd never forgive himself. Coming to you might've been an attempt to find some workable resolution. Failing that—"

"Failing that you think he'd want to end it all?"

"Well, what if he then discovered that you two were having an affair?"

Michel deftly lit another cigarette, inhaled and blew a smoke ring into the air. Kit sat exhausted and watched the shape dissipate into nothingness.

"It is not impossible," Michel remarked.

"Oh God," moaned Kit.

Michel put his hand on her arm. "But, it is certainly not proven and without evidence—isn't it better to just let it go?"

"I wish I could, and I would if it weren't for Sondra. She is bound and determined to get to the bottom of this, and I am bound and determined to help her. That's why it is so important to find Annie. Do you have any idea about where she could've gone?"

"No, we did not spend our time together talking about friends or families or histories."

Kit rested her elbows on the table and held her head. Random possibilities swirled through her mind. She looked up. Michel was watching her, his eyes reflecting a dispassionate interest. "Honestly, Michel, I feel so confused."

He nodded and smiled. "Go on."

"We've even wondered, as crazy as it sounds, if Annie might've been involved in some separatist plot which Gramps found out about."

Michel leaned back in his chair and laughed out loud. "Are you asking me if Annie was a member of the FLQ?" He could barely get the words out he was laughing so hard. He finally sat up straight, wiped his eyes with the napkin, looked at Kit, eyes still glinting with amusement and said, "I highly doubt it."

"I gathered as much," Kit said; she found his merriment at

her expense humiliating.

Michel put his hand on her arm, placating. "I meant no harm by my laughter. I just found your question surprising."

"That's obvious," Kit replied, partially mollified. She smiled at him.

With that, he stood. "I am sorry to have to leave but I am expected elsewhere," he announced. He bent over her to kiss her hand then he kissed her on the mouth.

Kit responded in spite of herself.

"I see we have some unfinished business, *ma chérie*," he whispered into her ear. He pulled back, looked into her eyes. "Join me tomorrow at the chalet."

"I can't," Kit stammered.

"Oh?"

"I'm going to visit my grandparents tomorrow."

"Haven't they both passed on?"

"The cemetery, I promised myself I'd go to the cemetery tomorrow. I haven't been since, since—" Kit couldn't finish the thought.

"The funeral?"

"Yes."

"Well, I see my charms cannot compete with the dead," he said before turning, grasping his cane and walking towards the door.

Her heart pounding, Kit watched him as he left, his movements feline despite the limp.

Thankfully, there were no mailboxes along Sondra's route back from "Meet the Teacher" night at Dierdre's school. Sondra was humming "Blowing in the Wind" as she walked, while snow began to fall in earnest. J-P had had to work so she'd gone on her own. What else is new, she thought. The school was just a few blocks away, and Sondra had enjoyed being with the other parents, eating cookies and looking through the school work in Dierdre's little desk. The relaxed, welcoming atmosphere had been just what she needed: no verbal sparring, or watching what she said, or girding her loins to confront potential murderers. The teacher was young and pretty, although she didn't have a lot to say about Dierdre. Sondra wasn't surprised; she knew her daughter tended to fly under the radar at school.

Kit had offered to babysit; Sondra was thankful and surprised. Kit had almost pushed her out the door. Maybe Kit needed a break too; she had seemed edgy that evening and uncommunicative.

The flat was quiet as Sondra hung up her coat. The light was still on in the kitchen, so Sondra headed across the living room, hoping to review the day's events with Kit.

The telephone rang as she passed by; it sat on an end table beside the sofa, so Sondra plunked down and picked it up.

"Hello?" Sondra said. Kit appeared and stood in the doorway to the kitchen watching her.

"Sondra? Sondra Flanagan?" A man asked. "It's Raymond McIntyre."

"Oh yes, how is your father?" Sondra feared the answer.

"That's why I am calling. He died a few hours ago."

"I am so sorry. He was a good friend to our grandfather." Sondra glanced at Kit, whose eyebrows were furrowed in a question. Sondra nodded and Kit turned back into the kitchen. "Please accept our condolences."

"Yes, well, thank you."

"How is your mother doing?"

"It's hitting her pretty hard, you know."

"I can imagine. Thank you so much for the call. Please let us know when his funeral will be."

"There is one more thing . . ."

Later, Sondra was sitting across from Kit at the kitchen

table. Kit had fixed their traditional comfort drink, hot Ovaltine; their occasional slurps punctuated the quiet burbling of the aquarium in the living room. Sondra watched Kit who was tracing a crack in the table with her finger.

"I don't get it," Sondra finally said.

Kit shifted in her chair. "Yeah, it is strange, but people in comas often do 'wake up' just before the end. Paul says that the terminally ill sometimes rally hours before they die: last words and all that."

"I know, I know, but, Kit, why would his last words be directed at us? Why not say something about how much he loves his family, or say good bye to them, or . . . "

"Maybe he was delusional, that's always been a possibility."

"I don't think so, Kit. I think he sensed I was in the room and needed to tell me something. Why else would he wake up right after I left and say, very distinctly, 'Tell her about the toilet paper.'?"

Sondra glared at Kit, who had put her hand over her mouth, trying to stifle a guffaw.

"I'm sorry, Sonn, I can't help it."

Sondra relented. "OK, I guess it is a little bit funny, but just a very, very little bit."

"What is it with this toilet paper thing, anyway?"

Sondra pursed her mouth, she'd been thinking about this. "Well, McIntyre must've known about Gramps squirrelling away all that toilet paper in his trunk. And it must be important."

"Do you think we should go through the trunk again and look more carefully at the toilet paper?" Kit's question was almost serious.

"Maybe," said Sondra. She stood and stretched. "We still haven't reviewed the day's findings together, Kit. And I think we need to add this new information into your category of 'evidence of unknown origin'."

Kit groaned. "Un-*certain* origin, Sonn, uncertain origin.

And, technically, we do know where it originated from."

"Yeah, but we don't know what it means." Sondra smiled. She pulled her notebook and a pencil out of the pocket of the apron she always left hanging on a hook by the stove.

Describing the results of her investigation that day, Sondra was gratified by Kit's reaction to her conversation with Captain Tremblay and her interview with Claude. Wide-eyed and attentive, Kit kept her comments until the end, and even then all she said was, "Wow."

Kit started to fidget when it was her turn to talk.

"What's the matter, Kit?" Sondra asked. Sondra could tell something was bothering her. Was Gramps' death impacting her, or was it her birthday? She looked into Kit's hazel eyes, and Kit immediately bent her head to avoid Sondra's gaze and stood.

"Oh, I just miss my smokes, I guess," Kit said and started to pace while she related her discoveries. Sondra wrote as she listened. Something wasn't sitting right with what Kit was saying, but Sondra couldn't put her finger on it. Something about Annie, she figured. The flow of Kit's speech became choppy when she got to the part about Annie leaving town. It sounded to Sondra like Annie was running away from something, or someone. Sondra suspected her motive was fear, but of what?

Kit finished and sat down.

Sondra said, "I'm sure that Annie is somehow involved in Gramps' death. Perhaps she witnessed it or did it herself. Maybe they met and went for a walk, maybe she had wanted the briefcase back and Gramps didn't want to give it to her; maybe they argued. Maybe she was part of an FLQ cell and Gramps found out and threatened to expose her. In any case, the timing of Gramps death and her disappearance are so close they must be connected."

"Well," said Kit in her most annoyingly older-sister tone of voice, "I highly doubt that Annie would've been strong enough to break Gramps' neck. Or even know the first thing about how to go about it."

"I hate to admit it but you do have a point," said Sondra and recorded Kit's observation in her note book. When she looked up Kit was staring at her. "What?" she asked.

"When did you find out that Gramps' neck had been broken?"

"You mean, besides the dream?"

"Yes."

Sondra sighed. She shouldn't be surprised that Kit would think that the details of her vision originated from some human agency. "The same day you did, when we went to the police station."

"Are you sure Dad didn't tell you about it?"

"Yes, I'm sure."

"Hmm," replied Kit.

"Honestly, Kit, no one told me. We didn't discuss the details of his death. It was all too awful." Kit's disbelief deflated her.

"Sorry, Sonn, I just had to ask."

"That's OK." She got up. "Now, I'm exhausted," Sondra returned notebook and pen to her apron, gave Kit a hug. "I'll see you in the morning, Kit."

Kit watched Sondra's back disappear through the kitchen doorway, relieved that she'd managed to avoid telling Sonn anything about Michel and Annie. Dangerous information that could lead Sonn to suspect suicide, which would certainly destroy the peace these last few days had seemed to bring her sister.

Then there was that damned dream. She could see how upset Sondra was that she still doubted its veracity. She shivered as she thought about the details. It was so uncanny.

Evidence of Uncertain Origin

Had Sondra's subconscious mind received subliminal information from someone about the killing blow and then regurgitated it in her dream? This was the likeliest explanation, Kit thought. She recoiled at Sondra's invocation of a supernatural explanation to account for the dream's accurate description of the cause of death.

Despite Sondra's protestations, Kit wondered if someone else might've hinted at the cause of death in her presence. Had Jean-Pierre known about it and let something slip?

Kit tapped on J-P's study, peeking around the door to ask him her question. She wasn't pleased with his response; he'd heard about Gramps' broken neck when Sondra told him after their visit to the police station. Before then J-P hadn't really thought about the details of how Gramps had died; it had just seemed obvious that getting hit by a car would kill an elderly, frail man.

Kit needed to find out how Sondra had learned of Gramps' broken neck. Inwardly, she was teetering on the edge of a dark and terrifying void. Due north on her moral compass was already slipping, and without a rational explanation for this damned dream of Sondra's Kit feared she would fall right in.

That left their father. For sure he had read the coroner's report. Kit gritted her teeth; she would have to contact him. He must've been the one to let the information slip out. She'd call him tomorrow, before visiting her grandparents' graves.

PART VII
Protective

Pinus strobus
White Pine

Montréal
Wednesday, October 22, 1969

*T*hey'd finished their early breakfast at an all-night diner near boulevard Pie-IX and boulevard Rosemont. Exiting the restaurant, they walked towards the Botanical Gardens. Snow made the sidewalks slippery and amplified the chill of pre-dawn. They crossed the street to walk along boulevard Rosemont beside the Garden's grounds. Weather and the early hour ensured the privacy of their conversation. Even so the shorter man leaned towards his companion before speaking in a low voice.

"They're getting too close for comfort."

"Yes."

"Your magnificent plan isn't working." He kicked at a sodden piece of litter. *"If you don't do something soon..."*

The tall man quickened his pace, silent. His companion recognized this unusual reticence as anger. The shorter man halted and grabbed the other's arm to stop him. Pulling him around so they were face to face, he said, *"Too much is at stake, not just your cover but our whole operation needs to be protected."*

"You think I don't know this," hissed the taller man and yanked his arm away. His shoulders slumped.

The shorter man drew out a rumpled pack of cigarettes and shook out two. He knew and trusted his friend's intelligence. They'd been through a lot together and he had supported the tall man through his difficulties, vouched for him with the other felquistes, stood with him in their commitment to Québec's freedom. Tabernak, he'd even accepted the other man's leadership. But he also knew his comrade's weaknesses and these worried him.

The tall man shook his head as though clearing it of cobwebs and accepted the peace offering, inhaling deeply. After some minutes he smiled and said, "Don't worry my friend, I will do what is necessary."

His voice had returned to its usual cool confidence, and the shorter man, now reassured, nodded. They turned and walked back towards boulevard Pie-IX, the conversation over.

The day was cloudy and cold; a powdering of snow sequined trees, but was melting away on the streets and sidewalks by the time Kit left the house. She took the bus along chemin de la Côte-des-Neiges and disembarked just before Remembrance Way. The street wound up and over Mount Royal, delineating the Mount Royal Park on the east and the Notre-Dame-des-Neiges cemetery on the west. She walked from the bus stop past the Armoury then turned right onto Remembrance Way. If she kept walking it would take her about an hour to get over the mountain and arrive at avenue du Parc, not far from Sondra's. To her right she could see the path that veered into the park and up the hill to Beaver Lake. For four springs and summers during her university years she and Sondra had made the trek every Thursday evening to join the folk dancers at the chalet on Beaver Lake. Those had been happy times; Grannie Win was still alive and Gramps' war injuries hadn't yet crippled him.

Kit needed someone besides Michel to confide in. She couldn't be open with Sondra. The merest whisper that Gramps might've committed suicide by proxy would certainly reanimate Sondra's conviction that she was the cause of his death and push her back into a deep depression. Kit couldn't risk it.

Kit was walking on a tightrope, trying to keep her balance as well as Sondra's. Weariness and confusion dogged her steps, threatening to tip her over and send her crashing. How long could she maintain her role in the charade of Sondra's "investigations?" Or hide her liaison with Michel? How could she explain any of it to herself? And where was Paul in all of this? And what about Sondra's shifting allegiances? Including their detestable father in Sondra's family life shook Kit up in ways she didn't understand. The growing suspicion that Gramps might've chosen to die fed her own guilty conscience. Could she have prevented it by being more attentive? Worst of all, even her conviction that Sondra's dream was just a dream was weakening.

Maybe the dead don't live on after death, maybe they do. In either case they are good at keeping secrets. Although on second thought, maybe not, considering Sondra's dream. Kit shook her head and grimaced. What is wrong with me, that I'd even jokingly give that dream credence?

She walked further up Remembrance Way, crossed the street and turned into the cemetery through a wrought iron gate. Kit looked around, trying to remember where her

Evidence of Uncertain Origin

grandparents were buried. A path leading down the hill seemed most familiar, so she took it. Maple trees escorted her as she walked along. It looked so different now, with the snow covering the graves and the trees almost bare of their bright leaves. Gramps' interment had been during a heat wave: the trees shading the gravesite, the priest sweating in his surplice, the clods of dirt thudding on the coffin.

She paused as she came to an intersection, looking around for some familiar landmark. Rows upon rows of tombstones filled the hillside in front of her, like seats in a theatre: everyone hushed, anticipatory, waiting for the curtain to rise. Beyond them, like the helmeted head of some portly opera singer, she could see the dome of St. Joseph's Oratory peeking through the tree branches.

Finally, Kit recognized the set of three concrete steps stuck into the side of the hill. She walked over and mounted them; once at the top she saw the two large maple trees that had shaded them during the interment.

A single grey marble tombstone marked both her grandparents' graves. It was solid with little adornment, simple and straightforward, like her grandparents. A cross on its side, curling leaves chiseled in for a border. Their names and the dates of their births and deaths were incised in the centre. When Grannie Win died, her father had tried to persuade Gramps to include something more decorative, but Gramps had put an arm around him and said, "She's dead, son. She didn't care in life about such things, you can be damned sure she doesn't care about them now! She'd rather you spent it on the living, you can count on it."

Kit stood behind the tombstone and looked down at the two snow covered graves: one still slightly mounded, the other flush with the rest of the grounds. The dissonance of death assailed her. She still could not believe that her grandparents were here, under this cold and quiet earth.

Kit closed her eyes and bowed her head. The solemnity of

the place seemed to require it, but she was not praying. Long ago Kit had foresworn her grandmother's faith, coming to believe her religious notions were as full of superstition and bigotry as the Spanish Inquisition despite the oft repeated claim that God loved her. A claim that seemed ridiculous in light of all the awfulness of the world, and, even if God did love her, what good did it do her? If anything, in this day and age, even if God existed, He, She, or It was irrelevant.

Kit turned and leaned back against the headstone; in the utter stillness of the place, her thoughts drained out of her, leaving in their stead a deep sadness that was not altogether unpleasant.

"Gramps, I'm sorry I didn't visit you more often. Now that you're gone, I have no one to talk to. I have no idea why I'm leaning on this gravestone talking to the air. Maybe I'm crazy. Anyway, I'm confused. I thought I knew what I wanted. I wanted Paul. Now I have him, I wonder if he is who I thought he was. Well, I guess, to be fair, I'm probably not who I thought I was either. I thought I was more like you than I am."

Heat flooded her face. "I was almost unfaithful to Paul. No, wait, in a way, I was, in my heart anyway." She twisted to look down at her grandmother's grave. "Well, you'd understand that, Grannie. You always told me that God judges the intentions of the heart. So, I guess I'm guilty on that count." She resisted saying Michel's name aloud here, as though neither grandparent could endure hearing it from her lips. She decided to change the subject.

"So, what is this you are doing, Gramps, plaguing poor Sondra with dreams of murder and mayhem? You shouldn't have played such tricks on her. She might've been hurt. You might've driven her to a nervous breakdown or something. Think of the kids!

"If you wanted to be so mischievous you could've sent me the dreams." An unexpected pang of jealousy struck. "Yeah, and why didn't you send me a dream too, for that matter? I loved you too. I did, I did . . . " Tears began to flow down her cheeks. She wiped them away.

"No, I'm mad at you Gramps, really, really mad. You should've known better—and you shouldn't have gone and died on us! You should've been more careful."

She paused in her tirade as the awful possibility that he might actually have killed himself hit her full force. She cried out, turned and fell to her knees. Grasping hold of her grandparents' tombstone she pressed her head against the cold granite of it. "Oh God, Gramps, please, please, please tell me you didn't kill yourself."

The silence of the place swallowed up her words, even as she spoke them. The cold air began to freeze the tears on her face. She brushed them away with her sleeve. Kit needed to blow her nose. Why, oh why did she never remember to bring tissues? Rummaging through her pockets, she finally found an old paper napkin.

"Katherine!" The voice startled her and she looked around, guilty, as though she were a trespasser. It took her a moment to locate the source. A lone figure was standing at the top of the concrete steps she'd so recently ascended, a lone figure who was wearing an expensive camel hair coat with suede cuffs, matching leather gloves and a fur hat. What on earth was her father doing here! She scrambled to her feet, heart pounding.

Trapped, she watched him stride toward her. Though small for a man, he carried himself with such confidence that people were surprised to find he was only five-eight.

He walked around the graves to stand before her, took her hands in his and pulled her close enough to kiss her on both cheeks, his trim goatee grazing her skin. She submitted to his affection. Releasing her, he looked intently at her, but she avoided the piercing gaze of his deep-set, hazel eyes, so unnervingly like hers.

"So, Katherine, your sister told me I could find you here."

Dratted blabbermouth, Kit thought. "Oh?" she said and hazarded a glance at him, curiosity getting the best of her discomfort at being alone with him. She saw crows' feet had gathered around his eyes. His skin, always tanned and well shaven, had begun to lose its tautness and his wavy brown hair, so well-coiffed, had started to turn white at his temples. He's getting old; the thought startled her.

"Well, my receptionist said you had phoned me this morning and when I called Sondra's, she said you were up here, so . . . " He shrugged and smiled, letting her fill in the blanks. She looked down to hide her annoyance and stomped her feet to warm them up a bit. She sighed and thought, I might as well get it over with.

"I did have a question for you, about Gramps' death."

He tilted his head, taken aback, and frowned. "Whatever for?"

Did he think she wanted to confide in him about something more personal? What an idiot!

She cleared her throat to remove the contempt from her voice before she spoke. You catch more flies with honey than with vinegar, or so her grandmother had claimed. We'll see, thought Kit, and brushed off the bit of snow from her knees.

"Well, Gramps' death was so sudden. I've had a hard time adjusting to it. So has Sondra. In fact, I've been worried about her; it seems that she has been sort of obsessing about how he died."

Her father nodded in agreement then took out a cigarette. Kit stared as he tamped it on his gold cigarette case; she could almost taste that first puff. She shook her head to banish the temptation to join him. Before igniting it with a matching lighter he said, "You've stopped smoking, haven't you? Do you mind if I do?"

She did, but shook her head again. "No, go right ahead."

"So where do I fit in? Why did you want to talk to me?"

Evidence of Uncertain Origin

Always the egoist, Kit thought. It always has to come back to him. "Well, I wanted to talk to you about how to handle her interest in his death. She's been quite upset about him. Anyway, I'd wondered when you'd told her about the fact that Gramps' neck had been broken."

He inhaled and after a pause said, "I didn't discuss the manner of my father's death with your sister at all. With her, um, medical history . . . " He stopped and glanced at her to make sure she understood what he was alluding to.

As a physician he shouldn't be so prissy about his own daughter's bout with mental illness, thought Kit, irritated, but she nodded that she understood.

He went on, "I'd thought it wouldn't be a good idea and had made a point to avoid the topic altogether. I didn't even discuss it with Jean-Pierre."

"Do you think Marie-Claire might've said anything to her?"

"Hardly. I didn't discuss it with her either. I never talk shop with Marie-Claire." He looked at her. "Sondra does know about how he died by now. She took your visit to the police station quite well, I understand. So, what's this all about, Katherine?"

"Nothing, I guess, really," Kit wanted to drop the topic now that she had the information she'd needed from him, as distressing as it was, but clearly he expected more. "Well, she and I are awfully close," she soldiered on, "and I've been terribly worried about her, I mean, that's why I came down and all." She tried to look guileless.

It must've worked because her father smiled in what Kit could see he hoped was a paternal manner. Stubbing out his cigarette butt on the bottom of his shoe he flicked it toward the maple trees behind her then said, "Well, Katherine, she's worried about you, too."

Her father might as well have punched her in the solar plexus. Sondra had been talking to him about her. How dare she? Something shifted deep inside of her, throwing her off balance. It had always been the two of them, together against all comers, which really meant their father. Now, with everything else, that too had changed. Kit's façade of casual tolerance melted away as anger surged through her, shocked betrayal fueling her fury.

"Why was she blabbing to you about me?" Kit hissed.

"Are you OK?" He seemed shocked by her hostility and stepped toward her. It looked for one awful moment like he might try to touch her. Before he had a chance to, Kit pushed him away and he tripped over his own feet landing on the ground. He looked ridiculous and confused by her apparent change of mood.

"Ha! It serves you right!" Kit wanted to kick him now that he was down and took a step closer to him.

He looked up at her, his face wearing an expression of stunned surprise. How could he not see how much I hate him? Kit thought, contempt vying with rage.

"What, what are you talking about, Katherine?" He remained seated, legs splayed out in front of him. His left pant leg had climbed up his ankle exposing a patch of bare hairy skin above his black sock.

"How can you be so utterly dense and stupid?"

"I, I, don't know what you mean."

"Yes. You. Do." Kit spat each word out.

"Does this have to do with your mother?"

"No, you idiot, it has to do with you."

"Katherine! I will not have you speaking to me in that way. I may not have been the best father, but I am your father and deserve at least a modicum of respect!" He struggled to his feet, pulling his pant leg down before pulling himself to his full height in front of her.

Kit wanted to push him back down and pummel him. Well, the cat is out of the bag, I'm not going to hold back on him now, she thought.

"How dare you play the 'father' card on me? It is far too

late for that one, Dad." The sarcasm was cathartic. She tossed her head, crossed her arms, planted her feet wide apart and glared full force at him.

Her father deflated in front of her eyes. Gone was the confident air, the sophisticated superior demeanour. Like a fist to his gut, her words had left him breathless and pale.

"Well, what do you have to say for yourself, Dad?" The word held a little less sarcasm this time. "And don't for a minute pretend ignorance. You are too damned smart for that."

"I, I, don't know what to say." He stood helpless before her rage.

"You could try saying you're sorry."

"For what?" He was beginning to rally. "For divorcing your mother? That was the best thing I could've done for you and Sondra. She was a danger to you both. Do you think I didn't love her?" He turned away then getting hold of himself went on. "Do you think I didn't try? Do you think I didn't blame myself for her drinking? God, Katherine, I look at you now and I see her, before the bad days, and I remember how beautiful she was, how brilliant and witty she was. And I feel like shooting myself all over again." He put his head in his hands.

"What do you mean, 'shooting yourself'?"

"Never mind about that, I shouldn't have said anything."

"What did you mean, 'shooting yourself'? Dad, tell me."

"You don't need to know about that."

"Yes, I do. You owe it to me."

He looked at her and for the first time she saw confusion and pain in his eyes, and, yes, defeat. "I'm sure you can guess."

"You tried to kill yourself?"

"I was a doctor. If I'd wanted to kill myself I'd have been able to." His voice had a tortured quality to it Kit had never heard before. He wiped his hand across his forehead. "I did try. I've never been good with guns. It was your grandfather's service revolver, from the war. It misfired, the bullet grazed my scalp. Lots of blood. Scared me sensible, as Mother would say." He had a wry, sad smile.

"Why?"

"Why did I try to kill myself?"

Kit nodded.

"I didn't think I could live without your mother. I didn't think I wanted to."

"What about us? Sondra and me? Didn't you care about us? Didn't you want to see us grow up or anything?"

"I wasn't any good for you girls. You had my mother and father who adored you," his voice was hoarse, weary. He stopped speaking, staring at the maples past her left shoulder. Kit sensed there was more, said nothing and waited, almost breathless.

A breeze blew past them strong enough to elicit a soft sigh from the trees behind her. Kit pulled her coat around her and shifted her feet. Her father shivered, shoved his gloved hands in his pockets and continued.

"The truth of it is I'm a coward. It hurt too much to see you both, but, especially you, Katherine. So much like your mother," he reached out and touched her hair. He sounded sad, wistful. "And, I believed I had destroyed her; I was afraid of hurting you too. I thought you were better off without me." He shrugged and bent down his head as though he were ashamed.

She almost felt sorry for him, but then she remembered the years she had spent aching for his attention, crying on her bed when he missed her birthday and comforting Sondra when he'd stood her up. She stiffened. It was too soon for forgiveness, much too soon. "And so you went off and lived happily ever after with all your fancy ladies. How did you think that affected us, Dad?"

Though the words held much less venom than her prior

assaults, she might as well have slapped him. Still, he reached out to her. She brushed his hand away and pushed past him.

"Katherine!" She heard him call after her, but it only made her run towards the steps and down them as quickly as she could. She turned and headed up the path away from him. In no way did she want him to see her tears.

Late morning found Sondra standing in the cafeteria doorway of Senneville Lodge watching Roger Dufresne play cribbage. Really, she reflected, it could've gone either way. The "Dragon Lady" had been disinclined to believe her reason for wanting to visit, and was in the middle of lecturing her when Captain Tremblay opened his office door. He waited until the "D.L." came up for air, after she'd finished informing Sondra that she could not, would not and should not be given a day pass, no matter what.

"What's this all about?" he'd asked pulling on his overcoat.

Sondra jumped in before the "D.L." got her breath. "I wanted to return Monsieur Dufresne's book," Sondra waved her own tattered copy of Dickens' "A Tale of Two Cities" for emphasis, hoping they wouldn't notice its title. "I found it in my grandfather's belongings," she lied.

Tremblay had leaned on the "D.L."'s desk, touched her shoulder and said in that mellifluous voice, "I think, out of respect for her grandfather, we can make an exception in Miss Flanagan's case," then he smiled and winked at Sondra before picking his cane out of the umbrella stand and limping out of the room.

The "D.L." had bent down her head to fill in the required form and was blushing an unbecoming shade of hot pink. She shoved the visitor's card at Sondra without a word or a glance. Sondra wondered whether the "D.L."'s embarrassment came from being gainsaid by her boss or because of his touch. Either way, Sondra had murmured her thanks and hastened out of the office before the "D.L." regained her composure.

She stopped in the foyer and glanced out through one of the windows bordering the front door. Sondra watched the captain get into his car and drive off. Then she headed down a corridor toward the cafeteria.

Waiting for Dufresne to finish his game, Sondra checked her watch; it was eleven thirty. She had three and a half hours before she'd have to pick up Max and be home for Deirdre's return from school. She was starting to get cold feet.

What am I doing here? He could be a murderer; he could be a murderer and a *felquiste*. Am I putting myself in danger, again? Well, she reasoned, he can hardly kill me in broad daylight. Besides, Kit knows I'm here, J-P knows I'm here, and even Captain Tremblay and the "D.L." would be upset if I were knocked off under their noses.

Dufresne's opponent stood, signaling the end of the game. Oh well, in for a penny, in for a pound, Sondra thought, then squared her shoulders and walked into the room.

Ten minutes later she was sitting with Roger Dufresne looking out at the lake, the surface still as molten lead. Flakes of snow blurred the vista of distant hills and drifted down to disappear into the icy waters. Sondra made sure that she was in plain view of the Veterans Lodge Administrative buildings. They were sharing a bench across the street in the small plot of park owned by the Lodge and bordering the lakeshore.

Roger leaned over and stubbed out his cigarette on the underside of the park bench. He was a small man, well groomed, clean shaven, and his hair, still dark, bristled with military correctness. He looked at Sondra, coughed, then said, "I cannot say I miss your grandfather; he was the proverbial 'thorn in my side.' We were competitors and perhaps too alike to ever be friends. Still, it was an unpleasant way to die, hit by a car." He shook his head.

Sondra thought he was not very big and she could probably escape if he tried anything. The walk down to the little park had left him breathless which meant she likely could out run him. He did not appear to have a weapon at hand and she was well out of his reach, sitting scrunched up at the far end of the bench.

Watching him, she asked, "What if I told you that it wasn't an accident, that my grandfather had been murdered."

"*Tabernak*," His eyebrows raised and he looked at her. "You're serious, aren't you?"

Sondra held his gaze and nodded. She shivered a bit, and shoved her mittened hands into the pockets of her car coat.

Roger Dufresne pulled another cigarette out, coughing as he did so then lit it, before continuing in a matter of fact tone, "And you suspect that I killed him."

"Yes, I did wonder about that. You seemed to hate him, to have something special against him, the way you treated us when we came to get the trunk. And I heard things..."

"What kind of things?" Dufresne straightened, turned his head towards her. His eyes narrowed with hostility.

Sondra stumbled to her feet, fearful; maybe she'd better not mention the FLQ just now. "Well, that's why I wanted to talk to you, to find out." She eyed the distance to the gate, her escape route. Sondra moved to stand behind the park bench, clutching the back of it. The bench between them gave her some small margin of safety.

Dufresne began to laugh. "Sit, sit, I won't hurt you. What a joke." His laughter had set off a coughing spell, and it took him a few moments to recover. He spat into a clean white handkerchief, folded it and returned it to his pants pocket before gesturing to her to sit down.

"It's no joke, I assure you." Sondra remained standing. "Why do you say that?"

"Well, for starters, I was in communications, not the

infantry, never was much good with guns, so the idea that I'd kill someone is ridiculous!"

"What about your friend, Serge, there? Maybe you put him up to it?"

This was greeted with a shake of the head. "I highly doubt that. Besides, why would I want to go to the trouble of killing your grandfather? It doesn't make sense."

"Wasn't he collecting evidence that you and Serge were running an illegal poker game on the Lodge grounds?"

"Who told you that?" His tone hardened.

"Well, were you?"

"Your *grandpère* was a snoop, a spy, a turncoat!" Roger stood and threw his cigarette butt towards the lake. It arced and fell short, melting into the snow that had started to accumulate along the shore.

Sondra wondered at his choice of words, could Gramps have spied on them and discovered they were FLQ? She went on, "Were you?"

He huffed and turned to face her. "Yes, but we did it for the men. It was entertainment for them; they needed something to look forward to each week."

"You mean besides cribbage, golf, the gym, and movies?"

"How is any of that exciting?"

An idea struck Sondra. "And you got a percentage as 'the house,' didn't you?" Sondra remembered the pile of money on the table in the pub. "You were counting it up when we saw you at the pub."

Dufresne shrugged then coughed before saying, "Serge and I took the risks, brought in the booze, found the location, set things up, organized it. We deserved to be paid for our troubles. We were providing a service."

Yes, and maybe much more than that, thought Sondra, and maybe you spent it on bombs. She watched Dufresne closely and alarm tightened her voice as she said, "I've heard the FLQ funds their bombs by just that kind of illegal means."

Evidence of Uncertain Origin

Dufresne gave a little start and shifted so he could look straight at her. He had deep set piercing blue eyes under heavy eyebrows. "You're serious, aren't you?"

Sondra nodded, wondering if she should just turn around and leave now.

"So, let me get this straight," he was waving a finger at her. "You think Serge and I are handing over our house take to a bunch of FLQ bullies?" He frowned at her. "Why on earth would we do that?" He took a deep breath, and a moment later said, "Unless you think Serge and I are running an FLQ cell out of the Lodge." He looked directly at her.

Sondra shifted, uncomfortable under his gaze.

"Ha! That's exactly what you are thinking." At this, the small dapper man burst into laughter which triggered another coughing fit, followed by a few minutes of recovery. "That's rare," he proclaimed, wiping his eyes, "I haven't heard anything so ridiculously stupid in a very long time."

"Well, you do wear the *fleurs-de-lis* pin. Doesn't that mean you're a *separatist*?" Sondra tried to keep from sounding defensive.

"But of course! Yes, I voted for the Parti Québécois but that doesn't mean I'm a *felquiste*, you bloody little fool!"

"Sorry," was all Sondra could think of to say. She stared out at the lake, gathering her thoughts. "So, did you know my grandfather had found out about your poker game?"

"Of course, the idiot came to us himself. He said he was 'honour bound' to take me aside and lecture me about the damage I was doing. He told me he'd have to report it to Captain Tremblay if Serge and I didn't shut things down immediately."

"What did he mean by 'damage'? How could a friendly game of poker hurt anyone?"

"It didn't, not really."

Sondra waited, staring at him as he fidgeted. Ah, thought Sondra, he's feeling guilty about something.

"OK, OK, so one of the men got in over his head a little, didn't know when to stop, a right fool when it came down to it. Whose fault is that? We were all adults."

The penny dropped and Sondra said, "It was one of my grandfather's friends, wasn't it?"

Dufresne nodded. "Private McIntyre, to be precise."

"So, how much did he owe you?" Well, that would explain Gramps' intent pursuit of Dufresne. He was loyal to a fault when it came to friends and family. She relaxed a little.

"Three hundred dollars give or take."

"More than he could pay back on his pension, right?"

"Yes, and more than we could afford to cover, Serge and I. But we had to swallow that loss. Your grandfather was insistent. He threatened to make the administrator shut us down."

Sondra figured Captain Tremblay had turned a blind eye to Dufresne and his poker games. After all it had been his veiled hints that had led her to Dufresne. "Why would the administrator kowtow to my grandfather?"

"I asked your grandfather the same question, of course. He said he planned to tell Tremblay he'd go to the local press if Tremblay didn't put a stop to the games!" His ears reddened and he spat on the ground. "It was blackmail, no doubt about it, but I did not kill him!"

Kit was out of breath by the time she got to the bus stop across from the Remembrance Gate. She'd arrived in time to see the bus trundle up the hill and cursed at missing it. It had started snowing again and there was no bus shelter on Remembrance Way. Her tears had dried, her body was limp, and the heat she'd built up running was dissipating.

Kit had begun to shiver uncomfortably when a familiar car pulled up to the bus stop. She saw it was Michel. He opened the passenger door. Grateful, she got in and shut the door behind her.

"Ah, *ma petite*, your good uncle Michel has rescued you from the cold."

Kit looked at him, and wondered why he seemed so pleased with himself. Her query evaporated in the warm embrace of leather seats and relief at having escaped from her father's distressing presence and the cold.

"Thanks, Michel."

"So the visit with the grandparents did not go well?"

"Why do you say that?" Kit did not want to mention her father, did not want to think about him, or about Sondra.

"You look glum . . ."

"I don't want to talk about it, Michel." She tried not to be snappish, but Michel's cheery probing bothered her.

"*Certainement, ma petite*," he replied and fell into silence as he drove on.

Kit had closed her eyes and held herself until the shivering stopped, unwilling to show her extreme emotional state to Michel. By the time she'd relaxed and had enough control over her feelings to be confident she could talk coherently she opened her eyes and sat up.

"Where are we going?" she asked, surprised that they were no longer in the city.

"Ah, the day is still young and I thought you might benefit from a ride in the country. Perhaps you'll let me cook you a meal at my chalet?"

Still angry and miserable, Kit thought, what the hell, I've had it with everything and everyone. "OK," she said and felt her face go red. "Um, will Jean-Marc be there?"

Michel chuckled. "Don't worry about him, *ma petite*, he has his own work to do; relax and enjoy the ride." And she did, stifling the qualms that tried to rise up regarding her last visit to the chalet.

Michel brought out his cigarettes and must've noticed her

watching him as he lit up. "Do you want one?" he asked, shaking the pack so that one slid out toward her.

The hell with it, Kit thought, taking the cigarette and inhaling when Michel one-handedly struck a match and lit it for her.

"Were you following me, Michel?" She asked between puffs, the familiar sense of peace and focus calming her. God, she'd missed this.

"What do you think?" Michel's mischievous tone told her that he had.

"Why?"

"We have some, unfinished business, I think, *non?*"

Kit turned her head to look out the window. She did not answer him. She did not want him to see the effect his words had on her and picked at the first topic that came to mind to switch attention away from her. "So, Michel, what do you think about all these bombings?"

She felt him tense. "Why do you ask?"

"I just wanted to know what you thought. I mean, we've talked a bit before about separatism and the FLQ. And, you work for the government, and you're French Canadian . . ." she shrugged, letting her words trail off.

"And so you thought you'd ask your *oncle Michel* his considered and supposedly informed opinion about such things."

Kit smiled. "Well, yes." Thankful her ruse had worked.

"Well, strategically, I think it's a brilliant move."

"You can't mean that, Michel." Kit was alarmed.

Michel laughed. "I'm speaking from a military point of view." He looked at her. "Of course."

"Of course," she echoed, reassured. "How so?"

"Well, if I were part of the FLQ, I'd want to force my enemy to react. I'd want to force them to overplay their hand."

"You mean, by bringing in repressive measures? Or

bringing in the army?"

"Exactly," Michel seemed pleased that she understood. "That's the best chance a revolutionary movement has of rousing the population to an armed overthrow of the, the..." Michel seemed to be having a hard time finding the right word.

"Government?"

"I suppose."

"But wouldn't that make things worse?"

"Worse than what? You've seen the way the English Canadian industrialists treat the French Canadian workers in this province. I'm surprised they haven't risen up before this."

"Well, it isn't just French Canadian workers that suffer. I grew up Irish, Catholic and working class, so I know what it feels like too."

"Well, maybe you're actually a secret member of the FLQ." Michel teased.

"No matter how poor I was, I'd never want to bomb or hurt innocent people," Kit protested, indignant.

"So you say," Michel continued, "but maybe you protest too much."

Kit rolled her eyes.

"Maybe I need to worry that you are going to kidnap me, a federal government employee, and hold me for ransom. I did not think to check you for weapons before you got into my car."

"Ha!" Kit played along. "Well, you need to be more careful, Michel. I could be a very dangerous woman."

"Yes, indeed, I am sure you are."

Kit started a fire in the large fireplace while Michel cooked. The fragrance of onions reminded Kit how hungry she was. Standing in front of the roaring blaze she gazed out onto the lake. Ice was beginning to form along the far shore;

dark, choppy waves in the middle swallowed up the snowflakes wafting down. The sun, now well past its zenith, stained the clouds a lighter shade of grey. We must be facing south west, Kit reasoned.

Michel brought out their simple meal of onions, potatoes and sausages in a single bowl with two forks, along with a bottle of red wine tucked under his arm. They sat together on one of the sofas, eating and watching the water.

"When do you actually work?" asked Kit.

"Why do you ask?"

"Well, it seems odd that you have so much free time to gallivant around the countryside."

Waving his fork like a sceptre, Michel replied, "We executives can set our own hours." He winked at her.

Kit looked shocked.

"Oh, I make up the time, I assure you." He turned to face her. "Do not worry, there's no need to feel like an evil woman luring me away from my duties with your seductive beauty." He smiled while Kit's face flooded with heat.

"Come here, *ma petite*." Michel, took her fork from her and placed it on the coffee table, drew both her hands to his lips and kissed them. His hands were cold, his lips warm, feverish even.

Thrilled and horrified, Kit melted at his touch. Her heart raced and her thinking blurred as he pulled her closer to him. Arms around her he kissed her on the mouth. In this place so far away from all she had once known of herself and of her life, wavering between vertigo and desire, she yielded.

She had climaxed, a rarity, and had begun to weep. Michel took this all in stride, as though he expected it, kissed her tears and held her until she calmed. Embarrassed by her own passion, she could not look at him. He laughed at her, sitting up and rummaging around for his cigarettes in the clothing piled beside them on the floor and offered her one. They smoked together in silence.

Kit pulled the quilt around her and watched him. Something snapped inside her and she sat up. Pushing the hair off her forehead, as though that would help her think more clearly, she said, "What am I doing?"

"Enjoying your life, *ma petite*, is it such a crime? Life is way too short to worry about such things, *n'est-ce-pas?*"

"Maybe," she stared confused out at the lake. The dampened sun was starting to disappear behind the hills. "Oh, my God, what time is it?"

"Oh, three, maybe four."

Kit, anxious now, stood to put on her pants and shirt. Sitting beside Michel she hurriedly pulled on socks and boots then stood again.

"And where do you think you are going, *ma petite?*"

"I've got to go back home."

"I don't think so."

"What do you mean?" She turned to face him, hands on her hips.

Michel ignored her and began putting on his own clothes.

Kit watched him. "Michel," annoyed now, "what do you mean?"

Slowly, methodically, he turned to her, speaking clearly and coldly. "I mean that you will not leave here." His eyes, now cold as the lake, regarded her without emotion, without menace, without warmth.

She stepped back, afraid.

"Oh, no you don't." Michel, lightning fast, grabbed her wrist and drew her back to sit beside him on the sofa. His grip was hard, strong, angry. She stared down at the hands that had so recently caressed her; the long, tapered fingers encircled her wrist. She froze in horror.

Unbidden Sondra's words rushed into her mind: "Two hands with long tapered fingers."

Don't be silly, Kit told herself, but a chill had settled on her and all she wanted to do was leave this place. Instead, heart pounding, she sat, compliant, and tried to smile, as though it all were a joke, as though Michel were teasing her. But a sidelong glance at him did nothing to allay her fears.

He sat beside her, implacable as the Buddha. His grip relaxed on her wrist, but before Kit could pull away, it tightened again at the sound of footsteps outside. The door behind them burst open. Both Michel and Kit swung their heads around to see Jean-Marc stomp his heavy booted feet before entering, laden with packages.

Kit caught Jean-Marc's shrewd glance at her and paled. This has all been planned, she thought, and her heart sank.

Jean-Marc and Michel spoke together rapidly. Kit could only pick up a few of the words: dangerous; now; sister; finish; grandfather. Jean-Marc knew about Sondra, and somehow this all had to do with her grandfather. None of it made sense to her. Thoughts and images kaleidoscoped through her brain: Sondra's conviction that Gramps had been murdered, Michel's hands, the fear in Private McIntyre's eyes, their near accident on the 2 & 20, Sondra and Max's near miss, Annie's disappearance, the photograph of Annie with the yellow scarf. Kit glanced at the stairs to the loft and saw in her mind's eye the stained scarf hidden in the bureau drawer above her. Then it dawned on her: the stains were dried blood. Her panicked mind tried to remember if the scarf itself was yellow, but she couldn't. Kit was caught in a Kafkaesque nightmare. She shrank back within herself.

Michel seemed to sense her fear and confusion. He looked over at her; a faint smile flickered across his lips before he returned to his conversation with Jean-Marc.

He's enjoying my distress, so sure he's got the upper hand, she thought. This made her angry and the heat of it cleared her mind a little, enough that she determined to get away. Enough to make her devious so she hung her head to hide her face from Michel while she thought about what to do

Evidence of Uncertain Origin

next.

Kit heard paper rustling: Jean-Marc unwrapping the parcels he'd brought while still carrying on his conversation with Michel. A few minutes passed before she heard him open the door and with a gruff farewell, slam it behind him.

"Where is he going?" Kit asked in a small voice, looking around for something to grab onto, something to use for defense.

"*Notre ami* has his work to do downstairs. There is a workshop under the balcony," Michel replied evenly, "and I have mine, here." She shrunk away from him.

Kit eyed the almost empty wine bottle on the table. Michel shifted his position to face her and Kit took his momentary imbalance to wrench her hand away and jump up from the couch. He looked startled as she grasped the neck of the corked wine bottle and brandished it in what she hoped was a threatening fashion.

Michel laughed; it was a hollow, humourless sound. Kit stood, panting, in front of the fireplace, waiting, unnerved, but with all her animal instincts on high alert. Michel regarded her, almost pleased.

"I knew you would be a challenge, *ma petite lionesse.*" As though reasoning with a small child or a lunatic, Michel continued speaking in a calm voice, reaching for his cane and rising as he did so. "But where will you go once you finish me off? Do you think Jean-Marc will ignore my demise?"

Michel had been moving slowly, hypnotically, until he was standing. Kit watched in helpless fascination. His next movements were lightning quick; the cane swung up and using it like a sword he lunged at her with it. Too late to dodge away, Michel's cane thrust her back into the fireplace just as she threw the bottle at him. She landed with a thud as the bottle hit Michel a glancing blow on the side of his head before smashing on the coffee table splattering the floor with shards of glass and wine. The blow was enough to daze him for a few seconds while Kit, clothes starting to smolder already, scrambled up out of the ashes, scattering some of the glowing embers from the fire onto the wooden floor. She touched her hair, fearful that it might be alight, but it was not.

Kit paused long enough to see Michel shake his head and put his hand to his temple, glancing amazed at the blood on his fingers. Then, she bolted across the room, through the kitchen and, pushing open the door, she stumbled out into the darkening day.

Sondra had arrived home by two p.m. and was delighted to find a small neatly taped package lying on the floor behind her front door. She grabbed it and charged up the stairs, flung her coat at the coat tree where it failed to find a hold and slumped to the floor. Ignoring it for the moment, Sondra collapsed onto the living room couch, tore open the package and read the note from Celestine McIntyre. Then she unfolded the tissue paper that enclosed the key.

It was ordinary and worn, a short brass key. The business end was a small cylinder with an oblong piece of grooved metal attached. A series of numbers were engraved into the flattened top of the key.

It looked to Sondra like the key to a locker and she knew of only two public places in Montréal that had lockers: the train and the bus stations.

Sondra got up off the couch with a sigh, dropped the key and note into her jeans pocket then trudged towards the kitchen. Dinner was the last thing on her mind, but the family had to be fed. All she could think about while chopping the onions, green peppers and mushrooms for chicken cacciatore was how to extricate Kit and herself that evening so they could go looking for the locker.

J-P would be useless; he always brought home work.

Evidence of Uncertain Origin

Maybe, despite Kit's protestations, their father or Marie-Claire would be available to babysit while they sleuthed. Sondra threw the chicken pieces that had been defrosting into a pot, smothered them with the vegetables, seasoning and a can of tomatoes, covered it and slid it into the oven.

She washed her hands and picked up the phone to call her father and was thankful to find that they both would come to babysit.

Kit had not arrived by dinner time, and Sondra had been unable to eat; worry had stolen her appetite. At least there hadn't been any bombings that day, thought Sondra, trying to stay calm. Despite her best efforts to hide her anxiety from them, the children must've known something was wrong. They were subdued and hardly spoke throughout the meal.

They cheered up though when their grandfather arrived with Marie-Claire after dinner. Marie-Claire immediately settled down with the children who were tussling on the living room rug.

Sondra's father looked around uneasily, eyebrows furrowed. "Is Katherine home?" he asked, without taking off his overcoat.

"Not yet, Dad. I haven't heard from her since she left this morning, and, honestly, you look as worried as I feel. What's happened to her?"

"Nothing, I hope." He gave her a peck on the cheek then turned around as if to go back down the stairs.

"You just got here."

"I am sorry, but I've got something I have to attend to, Sondra. Please tell Marie-Claire I'll call for her later on."

"Does this have to do with Kit?"

His concerned look gave her the answer.

"What happened, Dad? Did you see her today?"

"Yes. After speaking with you, I went straight over to the cemetery and found her there." He did not continue, his shoulders slumped and he looked down at the floor.

Sondra put her hand on his arm. "And it did not go well, did it?" she said.

"No, it did not." He looked at her with gratitude; she saw that he did not want to go into detail. She could imagine what their encounter had been like all too well.

"When was that?"

"Around noon." He told her about running to catch up with Kit, but failing to. Sondra sensed that there was more to the story but that he'd told her as much as he was willing.

He squared his shoulders and touched her face. "Don't worry Sondra, I'm sure Kit is OK. I'm going out to look for her." Sondra stood at the top of the stairs, watching him descend. She wasn't convinced and couldn't bear waiting around all evening for news of Kit.

"Wait a minute, Dad, I'm coming out too." Sondra gave Marie-Claire a quick low-down on the kids' bedtime routine, kissed them both and peeked into J-P's office to say goodbye. Then she hurried off to join her father who was headed out to avenue du Parc to hail a cab.

Half an hour later her father dropped Sondra off at the Bonaventure train station. Gramps had always loved trains, so it had been natural to try here first. She had found a bank of lockers and it had only taken a few minutes for her to find one that shared the same number as the key she held up before it. She was shaky and her hand was perspiring, and worse, she was uncertain about everything. Even her dream seemed faded and unconvincing; maybe she was crazy after all.

"Well, Gramps, here we are," she said, taking a deep breath as she inserted the key and turned it. She had to yank at the door to open it. She peered into the dark interior and, sure enough, there was an old, beat up brown leather brief case pushed to the back.

She hauled it out and set it down on a nearby bench and stared at it for a few moments before unsnapping the clasp to

Evidence of Uncertain Origin

open it.

"The papers!" she gasped, pulling out a sheaf of them in amazement. She couldn't believe that they were actually where she'd thought they'd be. They were covered with numbers and appeared to be photocopies of purchase orders, invoices and receipts from a number of different companies. She saw that one of them was Proctor and Gamble, producers of toilet paper.

Sondra shivered, remembering all the toilet paper crammed into Gramps' trunk. It made no sense now, but she hoped it would sooner rather than later. Sondra looked around; the few travellers sitting on the adjoining benches were attending to their own business, oblivious to the Pandora's Box she had opened. She shoved the papers back into the case, closed it and hurried out into the early evening.

Kit clambered up the railroad tie steps as fast as she could. Her feet were leaden and panic made her limbs seem to move through molasses like in a bad dream. She crested the top of the hill as she heard Michel calling her, as though nothing were wrong, as though she was some foolish six-year-old. A part of her believed she was over reacting, jumping to insane conclusions, and she almost turned back. But the memory of those cold eyes and long fingers clasped like iron handcuffs around her wrists drove her on.

Kit started to run along the road; without thinking she headed back toward the small village on the other side of the lake. She had rounded a bend and was out of sight of the car when she heard the engine turn over. He's coming after me, she thought.

Turning to her left she plunged into the woods, hoping that he wouldn't notice her footprints in the snow. Once under cover, she ducked down and listened. The car's tires crunched against the gravel road as Michel drove on by, the engine sound swallowed up by the surrounding forest. She let out her breath, stood and wondered what to do next.

Kit looked around and noticed she was standing in a white pine forest: *Pinus strobus*. She took a deep breath and was comforted by the trees which were making a comeback. Once plentiful, the English had stripped Québec of white pines for their ship building during the Napoleonic wars. The white pines of Québec had helped to defeat the French. How ironic, she thought.

The sound of a car coming back, wheels slowly crunching the gravel along the road, mobilized her. She ran further into the woods where the snow was deeper and bushes tugged at her legs. She heard the engine stop and then a car door opened and shut. Kit froze like some hunted animal and looked around, desperate for a hiding place.

Pinus strobus; if birds could find protection under its canopy and strong branches, so could she. She'd have to climb into one of the tall pines surrounding her. Yet, looking at the ground, her tracks through the snow were clear. She'd have to throw Michel off somehow. So, she stomped forward a few metres, veered to the right and down a slight incline to where a creek burbled, ice stretching its chill fingers from the bank. Kit broke the ice along the edge, hoping Michel would think she'd plunged into the creek. Then she back tracked, clambering up the bank, trying to step backwards and only in her footprints.

"Katherine, oh, Katherine," Michel's voice was cajoling and friendly, as if they'd lost track of each other by accident. She could tell that he was still at the roadside. Standing in her footprints beside a cluster of three white pines, she bent back some branches and stepped into the space between the trees. Under the boughs pine needles were still free of snow and they muffled her movements. She hoped the slight impressions her footsteps had made under the trees would

Evidence of Uncertain Origin

not be noticed. The branches were low enough to the ground on the tree furthest from the road to make the start of her climb easy enough. Fear drove her on. She hoped the rustling of her hasty ascent wouldn't give her away.

"Katherine, *ma belle petite amie*, do not make me have to find you. It is getting dark. You will get very, very cold out here all by yourself."

His voice was moving. She stopped climbing and listened. He must have stepped into the woods, and she figured he'd be following her trail. Kit straddled the nearest branch and grasped the trunk with arms and legs. Pine pitch, not yet frozen, was sticky on her skin as she pressed her face against the cool rough bark, pleading with the tree to hide her.

"You do realize that I am not a bad tracker. It hasn't been that long since I've hunted. I shot a deer back here last year. A lovely young doe, she was; tender and delicious."

Kit's heart pounded and she was panting. Michel was getting closer and closer. She took a deep breath and thought, If I panic I'm done for.

"Come, come, Katherine. Did you really think I could hurt you? You ran off for no reason. I wasn't serious, I was joking, seeing how you would handle yourself. Quite well, I might say. Yes, you were quick and quick witted. You've made your *oncle Michel* very proud of you.

"But this, this is going too far, *ma petite*. This little game of hide and seek you are playing." His tone was conversational, slightly scolding, slightly amused.

Kit felt foolish. She wanted more than anything to believe him, to call out to him, laughing, and return with him to the warmth of the house, but a deep primordial fear kept her still and pressed against the tree.

Michel stopped beside her hiding place. She was terrified; had her ruse failed? She heard him strike a match, smelled the phosphorus ascend in the cold sharp air and heard the intake of breath as he inhaled. She held her breath but began to shiver.

Like a small hunted animal, Kit was immobilized by dread. Stillness was her cloak of invisibility; that and the dusk which was starting to overtake them both.

He waited, silent now, and Kit knew he was listening for her. As long as he was not sure that she was here, she might have a chance. She tried very hard to silence her breathing, to time it with his slight movements. A desperate desire to live arose, transcending her rational mind. It sought for help from any and all of the unseen forces that humans have called out to from the beginning.

Her grandfather's words, "There are no atheists in foxholes", exploded in her memory, and her thoughts cried out, "Oh God, help me!"

As if he'd heard her, Michel's voice wafted up. "Katherine, Katherine, Katherine, there is no help for you, no white knight to come and rescue you. You are entirely at my mercy." This was followed by a soft, merciless chuckle. "No, wait, I should rephrase that, at my disposal.

"I know you can hear me, Katherine. I will find you. And I won't be happy that you have caused me this trouble." He sounded reasonable, but annoyed. Like a concerned parent with a recalcitrant child. She heard snow crunching and supposed Michel had begun to walk again, she hoped he was angling toward the creek.

Kit took a ragged breath and tried to calm her racing thoughts. Should she try to make a get-away now, while she could hear Michel's uneven gait getting fainter? How soon would he figure out that she had tricked him? Did he have a gun? Did he know she was up here all along, his steps away a trick to flush her out?

There were only two absolutes she could think of: one, she would die of hypothermia if she stayed up in the tree, and two, there was no other action she could take that was guaranteed to gain her safety. Her survival depended on too many variables, too many shaky "ifs": if Michel followed her false trail, if her ruse gave her enough time to climb down and run back to the car ahead of him, if he'd left his keys in the ignition, if he didn't have a gun, if the dim light would be enough cover to protect her in case he did have a gun. If, if, if. None of it was certain, all of it risky, and Kit was no gambler.

She had seconds to decide and in the end the deepening chill of evening forced her hand. Kit scrambled down the tree as fast and silently as she could.

Sondra was home; the children were snug in bed and Marie-Claire off in a cab. Sondra and J-P had spent the last hour, heads together over the kitchen table, trying to organize the huge volume of papers from Gramps' briefcase that now littered the kitchen table. Focusing on the puzzle of the papers was helping to keep the worry at bay, at least a little bit.

Sondra leaned back and stretched, then looked at J-P with a question in her eyes. "Well? What do you make of it all?"

J-P rubbed the bald spot crowning his head. "It's a little soon to say..."

"This isn't a courtroom! Give me your opinion, you big galloot!"

Sondra glared at J-P's amused smile, his typical response to her half-teasing insults.

"Patience, *ma petite choux*, I will give you my opinion, as long as you do not quote me on it." He winked at her.

"Jean-Pierre, this is serious, my grandfather is dead, my sister is missing, and these papers may be the key to why this is all happening and how we can find Kit."

"Of course," J-P's hand on her arm was soothing.

"So, what do you make of it?"

"Someone has been cooking the books, to use the

technical term."

"Yeah, I noticed there seemed to be two versions of most of the invoices."

"Precisely, the only differences between them are that one version lists a price lower than the other, and, although the dates and amounts of inventoried items are the same, the letterheads are from two different companies."

Sondra picked up two invoices and pointed to the company headings. "Yes, this company sells a higher end product than this other one."

"And the record of receipts from the Ministry of Veterans Affairs shows that only one of the similar invoices was paid."

Sondra picked up two papers and squinted at them. "The costlier one, in this case."

"As I said, it looks like someone was embezzling the government: buying cheap product, but putting through purchase orders for the more expensive items, and we can assume, pocketing the difference."

Still hesitant to share her convictions with J-P, Sondra thought that at last she'd stumbled upon the most likely motive for Gramps' murder—money.

Waving a handful of invoices, J-P said, "How bizarre, Sondra, most of the invoices seem to be for . . . "

" . . . toilet paper." Sondra smiled at J-P's raised eyebrows. It wasn't often she was able to surprise her phlegmatic husband.

As soon as her feet touched ground Kit shoved the pine branches away from her face, intent on making a run for it back towards the road. Instead she found Michel waiting for her. He was leaning against the trunk of a small aspen some three metres away and he held a gun in his right hand. A smug smile twisted his long face.

"Katherine, Katherine, Katherine," he exclaimed, shaking his head in mock disappointment, "I told you I was a good hunter." He pushed himself off the tree and, motioning with the gun, indicated where he wanted her to move.

Kit's heart sank as she turned and began to trudge back towards the road. She walked as slowly as she could manage, hoping to delay the inevitable while Michel's voice followed.

"I had such high hopes for you, Katherine. I even thought you might join us. We are not monsters, not at all like they write about us in the press. We are doing all this for a cause, a noble and just cause. Not for ourselves but for the future of a *Québec Libre*."

Revelation overtaking fear, Kit stopped in her tracks and whirled around to face him. "You. Jean-Marc. You belong to the FLQ!"

"Ah, clever Katherine," His sarcasm stung her. Michel waved the gun at her and made a little bow. "But of course!"

They stood for a moment, regarding each other. Kit searched his face for some smattering of warmth, something to give her hope. All she saw was the icy dark blue of his eyes.

His eyes narrowed and he waved his gun. "Enough, keep going." Michel's tone was gruff. Did she hear a note of regret? She turned away from him and started walking, slowly. The barrel of Michel's gun prodded her to pick up the pace.

"Yes, there is a definite connection between us, Katherine. I felt it that first day you came into my office with your silly little sister: she, so earnest and curious, you, so protective and disbelieving. What were you hoping to discover, you two? Do you think I did not realize that you were up to something? Rather, not you, your sister.

"You are much too logical, too rational to indulge such farfetched and imaginative ideas. Yet, odd, isn't it, how these things work out. Try to look on the bright side: I'll be sparing you from the embarrassment of having to admit to your younger sister that she was right and you were wrong." They had reached the road and the car. A faint smell of smoke hung in the air, a homey smell, dissonant in the circumstances.

It seemed like Kit was watching all of this through the wrong end of a telescope. She thought in a detached way about Paul and wondered how long he would grieve her loss, wondered when and where Michel would kill her.

She clambered up the verge and stood on the road, turning to face him. Desperation made her blurt out, "My sister will figure out what happened to me."

"Ah, yes, she will suspect. And perhaps even suspect me, but you have told her nothing about us, have you? I was counting on your Anglo shame to keep your mouth shut." He gloated, and she hated him in that one moment more than she had hated anyone else in the world, even her father. It emboldened her to speak again.

"She will figure it out. Besides, how can you kill me here, out in the open, anyone could drive by. How will you move my body? How will you explain my body on this road?"

"Ah, Kit, my logical queen, yes, these are things that I have been pondering. Perhaps you will disappear. The lake is deep. Perhaps you will run off with a paramour. I think your sister may suspect that such a one exists, *non?*" He shrugged, tilted his head and smiled at her with cold eyes. "She just does not realize it is me."

Kit stood shivering. The sun had set and the light was leaving the sky, a rosy glow was all that was left edging the dark rim of trees above them. The snow had stopped falling; the first few stars were dimly shining. The night would be clear and cold.

"Open the door to the car and get in, on the driver's side, *s'il te plais.*"

Michel kept his gun pointed at her while Kit walked around the car and slipped into the driver's seat. She left the car door open. Michel had to turn away from her to angle himself into the passenger's seat. In that brief moment, Kit slid out of the car and rolled onto the ground. A shot rang out, the bullet whizzing through the open door behind her. She rose to a crouching position and hunkered down beside the back rear wheel looking for a way of escape.

"*Merde*," Michel muttered as Kit heard him bump his head getting out of the car. She took the opportunity to run for the opposite side of the road, hoping the twilight would compromise his aim. It did not. The second shot hit her in the left shoulder with a shocking force. It spun her around so that she fell down into the ditch at the side of the road. Gravel and snow broke her fall, and she lay there stunned on her back, the white pines impassive above her.

She heard the crunching of Michel's boots as he rounded the car and began to cross the road. Shock numbed Kit to what she knew must come next. The breeze off the lake was freezing something wet rolling down her cheeks. They must be tears. "Oh God, Oh Jesus, Oh God," she moaned, half in pain, half in despair.

Just as the top of Michel's head appeared above her, Kit saw a fire ball erupt behind him followed almost immediately by a thunderous blast. The eerie silence that followed was pierced by a dreadful howl, more animal than human, and the sound of gravel scattering. Michel had turned and was rushing back toward the chalet. Kit was left alone, temporarily forgotten.

The chalet, Kit thought, the blast had come from that direction. She remembered the coals that had scattered from the fireplace when she ran away. There must have been explosives in the chalet, and in an instant she understood: Jean-Marc. No one could survive that explosion.

Kit willed herself to move. Pain engulfed her left shoulder and arm, and she groaned as she rolled over and stood. She held her upper arm steady to reduce the fire in her shoulder and touched something slippery; it must be her own blood.

Stumbling, she made her way over to Michel's car and sat in the driver's seat, a profound lethargy pulling her down.

The keys were in the ignition, so Kit swung her legs into the car. She let go of her arm and reached around her body to pull the door shut, moaning as pain radiated into her chest and down her left arm. She sat back to gather her strength before attempting to start the car. All Kit could think of was to drive away, far, far away.

The relative safety and warmth of the car released a wave of exhaustion that threatened to make her pass out. Kit leaned her head forward on the steering wheel to rest, for just a second, she thought.

Before she could slip into the welcoming darkness, uneven footsteps on the gravel road made her snap her head upright to peer through the windshield. In the dimness, silhouetted by the glow from the burning chalet, Kit could see Michel as he limped toward her, gun hanging from his right hand as he maneuvered the uneven terrain without his cane.

Panic cleared her mind at once. All senses on high alert, Kit realized that Michel had not seen her yet. Was, in fact, stalking towards the spot where she had fallen. This gave her a few extra moments; she hoped they'd be enough. Still, be very still, she told herself, and squeezed her eyes shut, afraid he would sense her watching him through the gloom and find her.

He passed within metres of her; she tried hard to remember how many steps back and away from the car she had fallen: one, two, three. Now, while he was facing away from the car, Kit, turned the key in the ignition, pulled the gear shift into drive and shot forward toward the burning chalet, grasping the steering wheel with her right hand.

Above the din of the revved motor she heard shots, but she dared not look back. It took all of her strength to keep the car from fish tailing into the ditch as it lurched forward. She had little strength left and every movement of her upper body sent sharp daggers of pain into her shoulder.

Before she could get around the curve and out of his range, she heard more shots. The steering wheel yanked itself out of her grip.

"Shit! The tire!" Kit grabbed at the wheel again, but could not control it. The car careened to the right, went off the road and hit a tree.

The impact stunned Kit for a moment, but the sharp pain in her shoulder brought her back with a groan. She looked up and could see in the driver's-side mirror that Michel was approaching the car.

Slowly, methodically, he walked toward her, his face, illumined by the fiery glow, a mask of rage and anguish. His eyes never left her. She tried to get out the passenger's door, but the car was tipped and the door was jammed shut. She turned to grasp the driver's side door handle with her right hand and almost blacked out from the pain as her left shoulder compressed against the seat. By then it was too late. Michel wrenched open the driver's side door, took a firm grasp of her hair and pulled her out of the car. She screamed.

"I should kill you right now," he said, his voice hard and cold and as sharp as a knife. "Jean-Marc is gone. You murdered my best friend, and," he spat out the words, "you will pay for it." He gave her hair a savage yank. She stumbled against him and cried out. "But, I cannot carry you to the lake so you will have to oblige me by walking there yourself." He let go of her hair and prodded her in the ribs with his gun.

Kit began to cry, and Michel slapped her across the face. "And to think I once thought you beautiful enough to fuck! Look at you now, *putain,* whore." He spat on the ground beside her. "*En avant!*"

Kit turned and stumbled forward back along the road, her desolation complete. Head bowed, grasping her injured shoulder, she sobbed to herself, sad at last to lose the life she had so little valued of late. Kit looked up. The moon had risen—a fingernail moon. Clean and sharp it sat above the trees, smiling crookedly as she staggered along in the darkness. It was unbearably lovely.

"*Ici*, turn in here."

Kit saw a slight opening in the underbrush, a trail towards the lake? If she started down that path there would be no return. She collapsed in a heap on the road.

"Get up!" Michel kicked at her with his game leg. She groaned and sat up.

"I'm too weak, Michel," she whimpered.

"I don't care. Get up!"

Desperate now to prolong her life any way she could, grasping at straws, Kit said, "Not until you tell me why."

"Why what?" Michel leaned over her, menacing. Silhouetted by the faint glow of the chalet's burning, he was haloed in orange and red.

"Why you killed my grandfather."

"He was like you and your nosy sister, too smart for his own good. Now get up." Michel waved his revolver for emphasis.

"That isn't a reason."

"No, perhaps not," Michel leaned over to poke her with the gun. He laughed, mirthless and cold, when she cringed away from it. "He found out about my little trick. *Mon petit truc*."

"Which was what?"

"If you can ask so many questions you are well enough to move, get up." Michel kicked at her again, his boot connecting with her rib cage.

Kit screamed.

"Shut the fuck up and get moving."

Bent over in pain, Kit said through gritted teeth, "No, tell me." She lifted her head and added, "I have a right to know."

"Ho—Ho! You think you have rights now," Michel bent over and prodded her in the chest with his pistol.

Kit cried out; she hurt all over, but desperation made her

bold. "If you want me to get up and walk you are going to have to tell me, or shoot me right here and drag me to wherever you want me to be."

"You do have a point, *putain*," Michel replied.

Kit heard a slight change in his tone. My God, she thought, he wants to gloat, to brag, to tell me how he outwitted us all, to rub it in before he kills me.

His right hand keeping the revolver pointed at her, Michel reached into his jacket pocket with the other. She watched, fascinated, like a bird watching a snake or a cat. He pulled out a pack of cigarettes and shook one out, grabbing it with his lips. Returning the pack to his pocket, he withdrew a book of matches, bent one and with a swift sure movement struck it, lighting the cigarette and sucking in the smoke. He shifted his weight, slightly.

How steady is he without his cane? A glimmer of hope made her wonder if she could trip him.

Gesturing to the skies with his gun, Michel began, "I skimped on the small things, toilet paper, toothpaste, soap. I invoiced the government for large quantities of high quality items, but I actually purchased the cheapest ones. Ha! Trudeau paid for the bombs that blew up his precious mailboxes. Ironic, *non*?" Michel gave a derisive snort, pleased with his own cleverness.

Too weak to do more, Kit hugged her knees with her uninjured arm, slim warmth against the night's chill.

Waving the gun, Michel went on, "So, all was going well until your grandfather got elected to head up the Residents' Committee. It was intended to be a welcoming committee for new residents, but your grandfather decided it gave him the right to interfere with the running of the Lodge. He kept requesting the higher quality toilet paper. 'The lads deserve the best,' he'd tell me."

"And you'd smile and agree with him," Kit replied.

"Yes, now you are beginning to understand. He found out

what was actually invoiced and figured it out."

"Annie." She couldn't keep the weakness and despair out of her voice.

"Ah, yes, my clever one, she betrayed me to your grandfather, but don't worry, she got what she deserved in the end. Such disloyalty is unforgiveable, you understand. We could not allow her to go unpunished. *C'est la guerre,*" Michel shrugged.

Kit began to shiver. "What then?"

"Oh, so you want all the details, why not." Here he paused and his gaze burned into her. "He thought I was doing it to get rich off the backs of the veterans, for my own benefit. What an insult! I was doing it all for the greater good, but he would never have understood.

"In fact, he came to me, 'man-to-man,' he said." Contempt dripped from his voice. "He should never have put his nose in it. He should have left it alone." Was that regret?

Kit started to cry, how like her grandfather, she thought.

"He wanted to give me a chance to own up to it myself, to make good, or he would turn me in." Michel's voice was incredulous. "I suggested we meet at the top of the driveway; I told him I'd pay him back what I owed and give him an explanation. Well, I did both, but not in the way he expected." His laugh was shallow, dry, empty.

"His death was an unpleasant necessity, for the cause, you understand." Michel made it sound as though Gramps had forced him to do something unsavory, as though he, Michel was Gramps' victim.

Pain, cold and despair made Kit's voice dull and hoarse. "So, you broke his neck and pushed him into the road. He was dead before the car hit him."

"Of course, you fool." Michel stubbed out his cigarette and kicked at her. "OK, story time is over, get up!"

Kit groaned and stood. She was dizzy and shaking uncontrollably.

Evidence of Uncertain Origin

"Now, get moving!"

Head down, Kit turned towards the denser darkness between the trees that indicated the path to the lake. As Kit turned she thought she heard the sound of a car engine.

Michel poked her in the back with his gun. "Hurry up, damn you!"

The force of his push made her trip and, weakened, she fell forward, tumbling down the slight embankment and landing in the ditch on her shoulder. The impact shot pain through her whole body and she shrieked. Michel scrambled down after her, grabbing her good arm and yanking her to her feet. He pushed her from behind towards the path.

Before they could turn to disappear into the woods, bright lights rounded the bend, coming from the town and blinding her.

With her last bit of energy, Kit lunged back up the embankment waving and falling in her attempt to regain the road. She heard a shot, but felt no pain, no impact. Michel had missed her, he must've been blinded momentarily too. She saw a fire truck lumber past her, followed by a police car. As Kit struggled to stand the car lights caught her and it stopped, spraying gravel.

Kit could hear Michel curse then heard his uneven footsteps. He's trying to hide in the underbrush, she thought.

Two policemen exploded from the car. Firearms drawn, they dashed off; after Michel Kit hoped. Kit watched as the back door opened and, in disbelief, saw her father step out. He now stood, and, one hand shielding his eyes from the bright headlights, peered down at her. "Katherine?" he asked.

She started to laugh hysterically, it was all so preposterous. Then she fainted.

PART VIII
Awake

Papaver somniferum
Opium Poppy

Montréal
October 22 - 30, 1969

"How did you find me?" Kit addressed her father who was sitting on one side of her bed at the Royal Victoria Hospital. Paul was standing behind him, his grey eyes watching her every move. The red roses he'd brought sat in a vase on the window sill, bright against an overcast sky.

It was late afternoon, and Kit had finished her first real meal since the ordeal. She felt awkward and not just socially. Her left shoulder was swathed in bandages; her right side ached whenever she reached for a spoonful of Jello and her

Evidence of Uncertain Origin

face hurt, which made opening her mouth a challenge. Not to mention the fact that her mobility was limited due to the needle that attached her right hand to the bag of fluids hanging from a pole beside her bed.

Sondra sat on the other side of her bed, holding her left hand. The nurse had just left after injecting Kit with a painkiller. Derived, no doubt, thought Kit, from *Papaver somniferum*, the opium poppy. As her aches and pains began to seep away, gratitude welled up for the ancient plant, used medicinally since 4,000 BC and displayed on the coat of arms of the Royal College of Anesthetists.

Kit settled back, enjoying the pleasant fogginess as it enveloped her, glad that she was not lying dead by the side of the road. They don't call it the "sleep-bringing poppy" for nothing, she thought. Kit felt an uncommon magnanimity and beamed at the room, even though it included her father and Paul.

"I followed you after you ran off in the cemetery," he explained. "You got into a car and it worried me, Katherine, because you were so upset, so I took down the license plate number. I have some contacts in the police force and they were able, after a few hours, to give me the name and address on the registration. Honestly, Katherine, I didn't intend to interfere in your life."

Instead of taking offense, all Kit could manage was a slight smile. She noticed Paul's quizzical look, and a vague unease flitted through her mind then disappeared, swallowed up, no doubt, by the poppy.

Her father continued, "But when I found out from Sondra that you hadn't gotten home for dinner, I went directly to the Sûrété."

"He was going to kill me," murmured Kit. "Where is he?" she wondered, had she said it aloud?

"Dead," Her father replied.

From a great distance Kit heard herself ask, "What

happened?"

"The two policemen who came with me chased him through the woods. They heard a yell then a splash. He must've stumbled over a cliff into the water. It took them ten minutes to find him, and by then he was dead. The autopsy results aren't in, but I suspect he broke his neck, drowned, or some combination of the two."

Through the blissful fog of poppy juice Kit noticed a uniformed man sitting at her door. How long had he been there? She pointed at him, saying to no one in particular, "There's a policeman..."

"Katherine, he's there to protect you. The police are unsure who Tremblay and his accomplice were. Mafia? Hells Angels? FLQ? You could be in danger and you might have information they want." He looked at her and added in a whisper, "They think you might be part of their gang."

As though in a dream, Kit replied, "The FLQ, that's a laugh." She tried to laugh, but the puffiness around her left cheek made it difficult.

Kit looked at Sondra. "He killed Annie." Sondra nodded. "And Gramps," Kit added.

"I thought so," Sondra's words were the last Kit heard before drifting off to sleep.

Kit woke with a start; it was pitch-black outside. Her heart was pounding, and sweat soaked her body. A deep sense of shame flooded her as scene after scene of her interactions with Michel passed before her, unbidden and unstoppable. She, who had so judged her father for his sexual infidelities, had herself done the same thing. Kit began to weep.

The guard, disturbed, stood and asked, "*Mademoiselle?*"

Embarrassed, Kit muttered, "Nightmare, *cauchemar.*"

"Ah," he replied, sitting again.

Kit's heart knotted into a small painful fist as she imagined telling Paul, but the thought of not telling him made her nauseous. She tossed and turned until the night nurse made the rounds and, finding her fretful, gave her a shot of blissful forgetfulness.

Two detectives arrived the next morning. One was younger and slimmer, the other fatter and balding. Neither was in uniform. If being out of uniform is meant to put me at ease, thought Kit, it's not working. She ached all over, but all the nurse would give her was a couple of aspirins. No more "sleep-bringing poppy" for her.

"I'm Chief Inspector Clancy from the Service de Police de la Ville Montréal," began the older man, "and this is Inspector Labelle, from the Sûrété du Québec. May we ask you a few questions?"

"Do I have a choice?"

"Not really," said the younger man, smiling and withdrawing a pencil and small notebook from his suit jacket pocket.

Kit shrugged and nodded.

"It looks as though you have single-handedly destroyed a dangerous gang," said Inspector Labelle, "so, of course, we are curious about who they were and how this has happened."

"It was all an accident," Kit blurted out.

"Really," intoned Chief Inspector Clancy, and rubbed his chin. They looked at each other and waited for her to continue.

Kit leaned back, closed her eyes, and, speaking in a monotone, told them what Michel had told her, there in the dark woods.

"I'm tired now," she said when finished. "Do you mind?"

Pocketing notebook and pencil, they left, promising to return the next day.

Sondra and Paul were with Kit during visiting hours that evening and Sondra had finished telling Paul her dream. Sitting in the other chair, Paul's brow was furrowed and his mouth pursed. Sondra figured he was processing this new information.

Sondra felt light and free for the first time since Gramps' death; it was wonderful. She turned to Kit whose face still looked like hell; her hair could sure do with a wash, but overall, Sondra thought she seemed more herself today.

"So, Kit, my so-called 'evidence of uncertain origin' turned out to be pretty certain after all," teased Sondra.

"Yeah, so it seems, although I doubt they'll include dream interpretation as a course at the police academy."

"We could start our own school, 'The S & K School of Paradoxical Investigative Techniques'."

Kit nodded. "It does have a ring to it, but shouldn't it be 'K & S' instead? After all I am the older and wiser sister."

"Have you seen yourself recently, Kit? Older for sure, but man, I'm not convinced that wisdom is your strong suit!"

Sondra saw the sadness in Kit's eyes despite her smile and attempt at gaiety. Paul, too, looked haggard. He had not taken his eyes off Kit since they'd arrived. Her father had made them both promise to hold off on "the Spanish Inquisition" as he'd termed it. Sondra was willing to wait to ask Kit her questions, but she could see it was killing Paul.

"Sonn, tell me about the papers and the key," Kit asked.

Sondra complied, ending with, "J-P says there's enough evidence to have convicted the Captain of embezzlement because his signature was on all of the paperwork. It's been going on long enough that J-P figures thousands of dollars were siphoned off by his little scheme. It's incredible that toilet paper, soap, napkins, cleaning products, all that kind of stuff could net so much filthy lucre."

"Just think 'Amway'," said Paul. Kit smiled at that one and

Evidence of Uncertain Origin

Paul looked a little less unhappy. Then he asked, "What happened to all that money?"

"It went toward FLQ bombs," said Kit.

"So, how did your grandfather get involved?"

"He told me..." Kit began.

Sondra answered Paul's quizzical expression in a stage whisper, "She means Captain Tremblay."

Sondra saw Kit blanch at the mention of his name.

Kit shifted, cleared her throat, and continued, corroborating what Sondra and J-P had deduced from the papers in the briefcase.

"Sounds like the kind of fight-for-the-underdog your grandfather would relish," Paul commented, "but how did he get hold of those papers?"

Sondra told him about Annie and Mrs. Grady.

"You both could've been killed too," said Paul, shaking his head.

"Several times as it turns out," volunteered Sondra. "Guess what, Kit; J-P's mechanic said our power steering was sabotaged. Fluid leaked out through a hole poked in the line. That Captain Tremblay could easily have done it while I was visiting the McIntyres at the hospital. And, I bet the second car at the chalet is the one that almost ran over..."

"Visiting hour is finished, my dears," the nurse interrupted. Starched and bristling, she ushered them out, allowing only cursory goodbyes.

To Kit's chagrin, Clancy and Labelle continued their persistent prodding. Based on her information, they dredged the lake before it froze solid and found the remains of a woman's body. Dental records confirmed the body was Annie Desrocher's.

Inspector Labelle told her that Jean-Marc Lachance had

been a radical during college and the police had kept tabs on him as potential FLQ. His diploma was in chemical engineering, part of which included the use of explosives, for mining and demolition work. They confirmed that the body found in the burned down chalet was his.

"I haven't read about any of this." The newspapers J-P had brought her were in her lap. Kit rustled them for emphasis.

"It's police policy to keep these things quiet," said Labelle.

Chief Inspector Clancy must've noticed Kit's shocked expression. "Otherwise the *felquistes* will get the jump on us."

"But what about the explosion and fire?"

"An unfortunate accident, nothing sinister about that, hundreds of house fires happen every fall and winter, and so many rural homes use propane for heating and cooking that the odd explosion is not considered unusual—local news only."

"And the bodies in the lake?"

Labelle smiled and shrugged. "People fall into lakes and drown all the time up north. The locals write them off as careless tourists and don't publicize these unfortunate events—bad for business."

They pointed out that the news black-out also kept Kit and her family safe from reprisals. Kit hadn't thought about that.

Labelle explained, "The FLQ cells work independently, communicating via code names. That way, if one cell is discovered, they cannot give away information to us about the others."

Both men looked at her. "Mrs. Benton," said Inspector Labelle, "you must tell us about your involvement with Michel Tremblay."

Chief Inspector Clancy added, "Unless you give us some reason to do so, we cannot strike you from our list of possible FLQ terrorists."

So, in the end, it wasn't a priest or Paul or even Sondra

who heard her confession, but two stone-faced policemen who ended up believing her—shame weighted her words with gravitas.

Like it or not, her father checked in on her every day so that, gradually, Kit acclimated to his presence. To her surprise she even looked forward to his visits. It's amazing what boredom will do, she thought.

One afternoon he brought chilling news. The bodies of both Fred McIntyre and Robert Brault had been exhumed and autopsied. The pathology report found high levels of caffeine in the femoral blood so the coroner ruled that the manner of death was murder and the cause of death was caffeine intoxication. Since the two men were elderly, the resulting heart failure had seemed due to natural causes.

Kit was stunned.

"Captain Tremblay had the opportunity to administer the caffeine, and his friend, Lachance, must've been the one who extracted and concentrated it from coffee, but of course with both dead, there's not going to be an inquest."

"I guess they were killed because they knew or suspected things," she said. "Poor old guys, I'm sure Gramps didn't realize that his high minded meddling would end up with all three of them dead, and Annie, too."

"No, I'm sure he didn't. Nor did he imagine his actions would precipitate the destruction of an FLQ cell and by his granddaughters no less!"

Nikki Everts

Montréal
October 31 – November 2, 1969

Paul came alone during visiting hours the night before his train left. Palpable awkwardness followed him into the hospital room. It's now or never, thought Kit, a familiar knot closing around her chest.

Paul leaned over to kiss her; his grey eyes mirrored her own anxiety. "Something's bothering you, Kit. I don't think it's just your injuries, but, maybe I'm wrong, maybe I'm imagining things."

"No, Paul, there is something—wrong." Kit gulped.

"OK," he took her hand.

They sat there together in silence until Kit took a deep breath and began. "I've been unfaithful to you, Paul." His hand tightened on hers and she heard his sudden intake of breath.

"His name was Michel. He was the man who tried to kill me, who killed Gramps, and Annie. He even tried to kill Sondra and Maxie."

Once started, everything rushed out in a torrent. Finishing, she said, "I can't believe I was such a fool, Paul." Kit stared at the metal end of her bed, unable to meet his gaze.

"Are you done yet?" Paul's voice was hard and his grip had become bone-crushing.

"You are hurting me, Paul." Kit pulled her hand away. Anger at his roughness gave her the impetus to go on.

"I've been asking myself how I could've betrayed you and not only you, myself. Paul, I've done something I've spent years hating my father for doing." Kit hazarded a glance at him.

His face was pale; the vein in his temple throbbing. Through clenched teeth he asked, "So, how could you do this to me, to us?"

Kit's face reddened, and she blurted out, "Maybe you should ask yourself that question."

"Me? What do you mean?"

"I have played second fiddle, no tenth fiddle, to your ambitions, your life, your schooling, your career."

Paul said, "But, I was doing all this for us, Kit."

"Really, Paul, really? Once you decided you wanted to be a doctor there was no discussion. I was just along for the ride. No, I was along to pay for the ride." Kit waited for him to respond; when he didn't she continued, "Don't you realize how wretched I've been? I was alone every night, living in a city where I had no friends, working at a mind-numbing job to support you, your aspirations, your career."

"I, I thought you were OK with all of it."

"You were too damn busy to notice." Kit couldn't keep the bitterness out of her voice.

"I wish you'd said something, Kit," his voice deflated.

"Would it have made a difference?" Kit shifted to look directly at him. "And don't tell me you haven't been attracted to the other students, like that Rachel you talk so highly of."

"But I never . . . " he sputtered. Paul turned his head away from her but not before Kit saw the colour rise in his face.

"Well, obviously you thought about it." Kit replied, her voice hard.

"But I didn't act on it." Paul was silent for quite a while. Then he said, "So, now it's my fault you slept with another man?"

"I wasn't looking for a lover, Paul, but I was easy game for Michel. I felt so dead inside, so disconnected from you—damn it all, Paul, you'd even forgotten I was going to Montréal! Michel made me feel alive. I wasn't faultless, Paul, but I didn't set out to hurt you."

"But you did," Paul said.

Kit winced and glanced at him; Paul's shoulders were slumped, and his hands fisted beside him. Overwhelming sadness welled up in her and she began to cry. "God, Paul, I'm so sorry."

"Me too, Kit, me too." Paul reached for her hand.

A bell rang signaling the end of visiting hour. They looked at each other.

"What now?" Paul asked.

Sondra sat there, trying to digest Kit's confession. Her sister had not looked at her the whole time, staring instead at her hands, which were clasped so tightly the knuckles looked white.

"Say something, Sonn, please." Kit broke the silence.

"Well, if you think I'm going to scold you, forget it."

"I almost wish you would."

"I suppose." Kit finally looked up. Her poor bruised face seemed frozen in despair.

"Oh Kit," Sondra put her arms around her sister who started to cry. After a while Kit's sobs subsided so Sondra sat back down and handed her a box of tissue.

Watching Kit blow her nose, Sondra said, "I wondered what was going on with you, Kit. I'm surprised, but not surprised. I'm just glad you got out of it alive."

Sondra smiled at Kit's shocked expression. "Don't look so flabbergasted, Kit, I'm not the Spanish Inquisition. And don't worry; you can stay with us as long as you need to."

By Monday, Kit had managed to sleep through the night without pills and was ready to leave, though the ribs on her right side hurt if she shifted suddenly, and she still couldn't use her left hand without twinges of pain radiating from her shoulder. Her separation from Paul was an ache of a different sort.

Labelle and Clancy drove her back to Sondra's. The world had changed since she'd last been in it: the trees, shed of their remaining leaves, stood stark against the glittering light of the first real snow fall of the season. Brilliant sunshine reflected off the snow covered street, imbuing the houses, lampposts, street signs with a cleanliness verging on purity. She took a deep breath of the chill air, and felt awake and truly glad to be alive for the first time in years.

Kit thanked the two officers, and started towards the stairs. Nudged by Sondra, J-P galumphed down to relieve Detective Labelle of her bag.

Kit grabbed the railing and looked up at her family, ranged at the top of the stairs: Sonn, the kids, her father, Marie-Claire. I must be grinning like a maniac, Kit thought, because my face hurts like hell. But she couldn't stop herself and did not want to.

Weakness made Kit pause and lean on J-P's arm several times before making it to the top of the wrought iron stairs. She turned to wave good bye to Labelle and Clancy as though they were old friends. Both men had watched her ascent from the street below. They shook their heads, smiling, and waved back before getting into the car to drive away.

Her father held the door open, waiting for her to walk through it. She touched his arm and surprised both of them by whispering, "I'm glad you're here, Dad," as she entered the vestibule.

Kit could see nothing inside the flat, her eyes not yet adjusted to the dimness. What an apt metaphor for the life ahead of me, she thought. Kit was walking into uncertainty and, oddly, it didn't bother her. Instead she felt exhilarated. Something alive and as yet unnamed was growing within her.

She paused in the dark for a moment then, smiling, Kit grasped the bannister and started her slow climb up the stairs.

Postscript

A year after the events providing the setting for this work of fiction the FLQ pushed their agenda of a free and sovereign Québec to the breaking point. Pierre Laporte, the Deputy Premier and Minister of Defense for the province of Québec, and James Cross, a British Diplomat, were both kidnapped by separate FLQ cells. Prime Minister Pierre Elliot Trudeau sent in the Canadian Military to search for the two missing men throughout Montréal and environs. Check points were set up on the highways that crossed the border with Ontario.

There is still debate around the necessity for what some called a heavy-handed approach by Trudeau. When a CBC journalist questioned him about the military presence and asked, combatively, how far the Prime Minister would go, the elder Trudeau's famous reply was, "Just watch me!"

Trudeau invoked the "War Measures Act" for the first and so far only time in Canadian history. This act suspended *habeas corpus*. As a result, 497 people were arrested; many of these were separatist sympathizers. They were kept in prison without being accused of any crime until the "October Crisis", as it came to be called, had been resolved.

In the end, James Cross was released unharmed; his kidnappers were caught and granted safe passage to Cuba with Castro's approval. Pierre Laporte was killed by the

FLQ's "Chenier Cell" whose members were apprehended, tried and convicted for kidnapping and murder.

The kidnapping and murder of Pierre Laporte resulted in the loss of most of the support the FLQ had enjoyed from the general population. It wasn't long before their activities tailed off and the FLQ became a part of history rather than an active movement.

Many former FLQ members and sympathizers aligned themselves with the Parti Québécois (PQ), some of whose members were elected to Québec's provincial parliament. The PQ's mandate was both broadly socialist and separatist. The Bloc Québécois was formed as a federal political party in 1991 after the failed attempt by Prime Minister Brian Mulroney to grant the provinces more political power. The Bloc had a *souverainiste* platform similar to the Parti Québécois and for a time had broad support in Québec, becoming, ironically, Her Majesty's Loyal Opposition in the Canadian Parliament from 1993 to 1997.

Representatives from both *souverainiste* parties continue to be elected by Québec citizens. Currently, 41% of Québec's federal members of parliament belong to the Bloc, while the Parti Québécois holds only 8% of the seats in Québec's National Assembly. There's a new political party in Québec, led by former PQ cabinet minister, Francois Legault. The Coalition Avenir Québec now leads Québec's National Assembly. A populist party, it strongly supports Québec autonomy, rather than separation, and represents a shift to the right politically.

A referendum was held in Québec in the 80s asking the question whether or not Québec should separate from the rest of the Canadian Confederation. It was rejected by 60% of voters. A second referendum almost twenty five years ago also lost, but by a slim margin, slightly more than 50% voted against it. Recently, Québec's Premier Legault has promised never to hold another referendum on leaving Canada.

Although the yearning for a separate and sovereign

Québec has diminished in the almost fifty years since the "October Crisis" of 1970, it whispers through today's strong undercurrent of Québec nationalism.

         Ontario, Canada – August 2020

Acknowledgements

You cannot raise a child without a village—the same can be said for writing a book, especially one that took more than twenty years to complete. This story owes so much to so many that I am doomed to forget a few—my apologies beforehand.

Without Gord Jones' positive critique of my writing I would not have had the courage to pursue and complete this story. Mavis Fenn and Brian Lindsay are my novel's god parents: through years and years and years of monthly meetings they saw my story grow to "adulthood," giving valuable advice regarding my characters' behaviours along the way; their wise encouragement and direction got me through many a challenging plot twist. Lou Allin, now sadly deceased, was a mystery writer and Crime Writers of Canada mentor who read my very first draft, let me know it was a tale worth telling and showed me how to do it better. A promise to Kevin Rush led me to include a second *felquiste*. Jane Pelton inspired me to change the shape of my narrative by including a second point of view. Rianne Lovett and her band of merry bibliophiles read one of my many drafts and suggested I flesh out the villain. Terrence Thomas asked for more red herrings to throw the reader off the scent. Marilyn Kleiber, of Sundragon Press, insisted I get rid of adverbs and qualifiers and made me murder the passive voice. Suzanne Côté made every effort to ensure my French usage was correct; any remaining *faux pas* were committed after her careful perusal. Jane Lindsay meticulously proof read my manuscript and wrangled the commas into tidy consistency. Katie Thorpe read my final draft and ensured my timelines and other era-related details made sense. M.M. Penniston used her skills as a retired Legislative Assistant to mop up residual inconsistencies as well as the insidious punctuation and English and French language errors for the third edition. Anthony O'Brian designed the fabulous cover. Marian Thorpe worked with great patience and enthusiasm to guide me through the publication process under her imprint, Arboretum Press. Jeremy Luke Hill, the Vocamus Writers' Community and the good folks at Guelph's Bookshelf made room for me to write. Thank you to all who have given me feedback and encouragement along the way.

I am deeply grateful to my family: to my sister Dana, who is the artist in the family and who has consistently encouraged and championed my writing; to my sister Stephanie, who is the most well-read person I know and who has stood by me through thick and thin; to my children Jesse, Sarah, Gabriel and James and my grandchildren Fenris, Sierra, River, Emily, Aurora, Amelia, Quinn and Rayna Bloom: your love helps me to get up in the mornings—the first step to writing. I hope that this book is worthy of you.

About the Author

After graduating in 1969 from the University of California, Berkeley, Nikki travelled for several months, arriving in Montréal in April, 1970 where she lived until 1992. Nikki came of age in California during the sixties and held a sympathetic view of the *Front de libération du Québec* until the October Crisis. The events leading up to the FLQ's kidnapping and murder of Pierre Laporte, the beauty of Montréal and the complexity of Québec politics inspired the setting and backdrop of *Evidence of Uncertain Origin*, Nikki's first mystery novel.

Nikki lives and writes in Guelph, Ontario. She has self-published a book of poetry, *connect dis connect* with the help of Vocamus Press and developed writing workshops under the auspices of her small business, Scripted Images.

p. 4, 10, 52, 57, 85-86, 87-88, 90-99,

Made in the USA
Middletown, DE
01 May 2021